My memories are the treasure of my life

Ellen Gilman 2018

The Best Doggone Bakery

Ellen Gilman

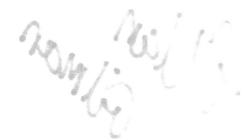

ISBN: 978-1-54396-946-7

This book is a work of fiction. Places, events, and situations in this book are purely fictional and any resemblance to actual persons, living or dead, is coincidental.

To Steven: Thanks for all your love and support, without which none of this would be possible.

To Charlie, Johnny, Giovanna, Katie, Nicholas, Alexis, Bridget, Spencer, and Colin: Hugs and kisses. You are everything to me.

PART ONE

CHAPTER ONE

For Sale

Tires screeched. *Bam!*

Millie jerked her head up while retying Annie's kerchief to see two cars collide in the street right in front of her. At the same time, Luke barked and wrenched his leash out of her hand, tucking his tail between his legs and taking off in a full-out run.

Oh no!

Millie knew the combination of loud noises and Luke was a recipe for disaster. *Why didn't I have a better grip on his leash?* She bit her lip and took off chasing him while tugging Annie behind her. She thought she should be able to grab him; he couldn't go fast dragging his leash. Besides, any other scenario was unimaginable.

"Luke, stop! Come back here!" Millie screamed. With her heart pounding, she flew after him, praying he'd be okay. What if she couldn't catch him?

She ran on, gripping Annie's leash as tightly as she could in her sweaty hands, her laser-like focus on Luke making her clumsy. She tripped headfirst, managing somehow to hold onto Annie's leash when her hands hit the rough cobblestones. *Crap—of all the days to be wearing wedges.* Getting up hastily and not taking any time to even check herself for scrapes, she whirled around and realized she couldn't see Luke anywhere. She couldn't believe it.

Outside the front door of Frannie's Flowers were two humongous clay pots filled with tall boxwoods totally blocking Millie's line of sight. Did Luke whiz past there and past the next store, Julie's Jewels? What if he tried to cross the street? The park sometimes had squirrels chasing each other up and down the trees. He loved to try to catch them.

Suddenly, Millie saw a flash of his tail, and off she went in hot pursuit, trying desperately not to trip or fall again.

Several pedestrians were in Luke's path. "Help! Stop my dog—please!" she yelled.

One older man lunged for Luke's leash, almost falling in the process, and he would have if the person walking beside him hadn't held out his hand to steady him. Luke zigzagged around them and kept on going.

Quite unexpectedly, a thought popped into her head: *Is it possible Luke is heading in a familiar direction?* Praying she was correct, she chased him as he headed down the narrow brick path to the old farmhouse where Christopher's Ice Cream and Cookie Shoppe was located. She almost laughed. Here she was, frightened to death he might get killed, and he seemed to be thinking about one of his favorite foods—yogurt.

The old white clapboard house, now the ice cream shop, was finally in sight. Sure enough, Luke was sitting on the walkway leading up to the old, faded red front door. Millie slid to an abrupt standstill. He was a glorious sight, sitting there with his sable fur glistening in the sun. Most importantly, he was in one piece. *Thank goodness for that.*

Rushing up to him, she plopped down and flung her arms around him, at the same time making sure to hold onto Annie's leash. She buried her head in his soft, sweet-smelling, downy fur and erupted into deep, gut-wrenching sobs while every part of her shook.

She adored this dog, a sheltie she and her husband had rescued.

"I don't know what I would have done if something had happened to you," she managed to choke out between breaths, her cheeks wet with tears.

Luke nudged her with his nose and then proceeded to lick the tears off her face. She sighed and hugged him tighter—probably too tight, as he tried to give himself some wiggle room. Just then she heard the wail of a siren in the distance. In her rush to catch Luke, she had forgotten about the accident. Hopefully, everyone was okay.

After a long, drawn-out minute of holding, squishing, and squeezing Luke for the pure joy of it, Millie glanced around.

She shook her head. It was strange. Usually, there would be lots of people milling around. It was then that she saw a small sign hanging on the doorknob. She thought about getting up to read it, but there was no way she was letting go of Luke's leash or Annie's. Thankfully, they were sitting still from their run though the Commons. It didn't hurt for her to sit still either while she caught her breath, allowing her heart to stop thumping.

Eventually, she did wander up just far enough to read the sign.

**Thanks for ten wonderful years of patronage.
We're closing permanently. We will miss you.**

"Sheesh! Christopher's is no longer. Sorry to tell you, but you guys won't be getting your yogurt here today. Not that you deserve it, Luke, frightening me the way you did."

Millie traipsed over to one of the small windows, pressed her face against the glass, and peered inside. She could see only a tiny bit of the inside. None of the high-top wrought iron tables or black and pink polka-dot chairs were visible. She had fond memories of sitting with her parents and three brothers squeezed in next to her. They had been known to tease each other mercilessly about who had more ice cream on their faces and clothes than in their mouths. Those had been fun times when her parents were still alive.

Christopher's shop was a fixture on this street in Houndsville and a place where visitors to the Eastern Shore of Maryland came to eat ice cream. Less than a block away was a new shopping district, Houndsville Commons, that had new storefronts with unique items and quirky names like Frannie's Flowers, Julie's Jewels, and Bridget's Bookstop to entice those same tourists.

Christopher's closing left Millie thinking wistfully about the past. She remembered the day four years ago, not long after she married Carl, when this old, well-known ice cream spot had come on the market. The rumor was that Christopher was planning to move to another town. She thought it would be a great spot for a dog bakery, and she suggested to Carl that they buy the property.

The day before they planned to sign the contract, Carl sat with Millie, took her hands in his, and told her they needed to talk. She'd remembered being frightened and holding her breath, not knowing what to expect. He told her he had a cost overrun on his newest building project and couldn't buy the farmhouse. Of course, that was disappointing, but it wasn't anything she couldn't handle. It made Millie think about Carl's father. He had started gambling, landed in bankruptcy court, and eventually lost his business. Carl was ashamed of his dad for disappointing his family and vowed it wouldn't happen to him. That's why this revelation came as a shock. Usually Carl was so conservative in choosing his projects. Of course, this meant the bakery was going to be put on hold.

As it turned out, Christopher's own plans had changed, and he had ended up staying. Millie wondered what his story was this time. Was he just shutting down the shop, or was he closing and selling the farmhouse? And if he was selling, would he go through with a sale this time? She didn't want to be let down again if she was lucky enough to persuade Carl to buy the old place. It was then that she noticed a sign stuck in the grass on the right side of a huge oak tree. She walked over to it. It was a For Sale sign. She touched it with her hand and ran her fingers over the words.

Millie's imagination ran wild. She turned to look back at the farmhouse. She could totally envision her two beloved shelties, Luke and Annie, sitting side by side with their heads hanging off the edge of a huge leather sofa. Around them were golden retrievers with kerchiefs around their necks, beagles, and even collies begging for delicious-looking treats while humans watched and sipped coffee. How fun it could be.

Could her dream come true? She couldn't imagine anything more perfectly suited for her. She loved dogs, sometimes even more than people. Her heart started thumping again, her stomach fluttering as though a million butterflies were inside. She took deep breaths to try to stay calm.

Millie chewed her lip thinking about what she should do right now. *Oops, that hurt.* Her lip was sore from biting down on it when Luke had run off.

An old high school acquaintance, Annabel Larson, owned and operated Miss Annabel's Tea and Coffee Emporium. It was nearby in the Houndsville Commons. Annabel, the local busybody, most likely would know why Christopher was selling. Millie thought that maybe she should go there right now and tell Annabel what she was thinking. She started to walk in that direction but paused and stopped herself. It would be better to talk to Carl first.

She wished he was here with her. His smile and one of his special squishy hugs always gave her confidence. Lately he had been extremely busy running his now very successful construction business, leaving her feeling somewhat lonely. Hopefully, helping her open the bakery would ignite his interest, and he'd spend more time with her.

Millie pulled Luke and Annie toward her for one last cuddle. She shuddered to think she might not have been able to do that if events had taken a different path. She took a deep, satisfying breath. "Come on, let's head home."

She raced to her car, getting tangled up in leashes and slipping on the cracked pavement. *These darn wedges causing trouble again— you'd think I'd go more slowly, having already tripped once.* After struggling to open the door with sweaty hands, she eventually got herself and her dogs inside and tried to calm her beating heart.

* * *

Millie snuck up on Carl and wrapped her arms around him as he stood in his closet fingering his shirts. "Hi."

He turned to face her. "I was wondering where you were."

She smiled.

"Uh-oh! I know that lopsided grin. Something's on your mind."

Millie nodded. "Yup! I was walking to Bridget's Bookstop today, until I had a detour." She held up her hands. "Don't ask. I'll give you a clue. There's a For Sale sign outside of Christopher's."

"Really? The building is for sale again?" Carl frowned, looking puzzled, and peered into her eyes. "Oh, I understand. You're worried that you won't be able to find salted caramel pretzel ice cream that's as good as his." He grinned at his own joke.

Millie studied Carl's face carefully, looking for a signal that would let her know he'd figured out what she was thinking. His face lit up like a light bulb, and he smiled. "Ah, I know where you're going with this now."

"You keep urging me to find something to do that I'm passionate about." She stood up on her toes, held onto his shoulders, and lightly brushed her lips against his.

Now she had his attention. He took her chin in his hand and tipped her head up. "So, tell me more," he said, showing off his crinkly smile. *Jeez, I love that smile.*

"Okay. After my parents' accident, you know it was my responsibility to find work, and I enjoyed working at the plumbing supply company. Now, thanks to you, I'm lucky enough to have a choice of what I want to do, and I know exactly what that is. I'd like nothing better than to open a dog bakery. Now seems like a good time. You're really busy, and Christopher is selling. Hopefully, this time he'll stick to whatever his plans are." Millie had spoken so fast that she had to stop to catch her breath. "Well?"

"Sounds like you already have a plan." She watched Carl run his hand through his hair from his widow's peak to the back, over and over, a sign that he was considering her words carefully.

"Yes, it feels like I've wanted to do this forever. I figured we could discuss it over dinner at the inn."

"Good call." Carl reached out to tousle Millie's blonde pixie mop. She in turn reached out and mussed up his already disheveled hair. He then playfully tickled her, captivating her with his wavy dark hair, easy sexy smile, and hazel eyes.

Twirling around, Millie strolled into her closet and picked through her clothes until she settled on her favorite black dress. It just needed some jewelry to spruce it up, and tonight her choice was a newly bought sparkly sheltie pin and a matching ring on her middle finger. Rings, necklaces, and bracelets—any piece of jewelry gave her a happy feeling, like eating a piece of chocolate did. She could never have too much.

"Are you almost ready?" Carl called.

"Just about. I want to take Luke and Annie outside before we leave."

Luke, hearing his name, ran over to her, tapped her legs several times, and looked up at her.

Millie laughed. "So, cutie, you want to go out? Okay, let's find Annie."

Spinning and barking, Luke took off down the hallway, his toenails clicking on the hardwood floor. Annie was in the den. She wagged her tail and nuzzled Luke.

"Come on, you two," Millie said after watching them wander around outside for a few minutes. "It's time to go in. It's cookie time."

She left Luke and Annie in the kitchen gobbling up their treats. As she walked down the hallway to the bedroom, she saw that Carl's office light was on, and she hollered, "I'll just grab my handbag, and I'm ready to go!"

It was a short drive through the winding streets of Houndsville to their favorite restaurant in the Buckshead Inn. Located a few blocks past downtown Houndsville, the eighteenth-century inn sat on an inlet. White twinkling lights nestled in the boxwoods surrounding the entrance made Millie think of Christmas, her favorite holiday.

She graciously smiled at the valet as he opened the car door for her. Carl grabbed her hand, and they walked up the steps leading to the massive, carved wood front door together.

After the maître d' led them through the small foyer to the once magnificent Crystal Room, Millie noted that the room looked shabbier than usual. The ornate chandelier, for which the room was named, didn't glow or shine as brightly as she remembered, and the dimmed wall sconces needed new toppers. The ones there now were yellowed from age.

When they were seated at a small table in a corner that overlooked the bluestone patio, Carl lifted his arm so Millie could tuck in next to him and they could face the twinkling lights on the small ornamental trees outside.

Almost immediately the waiter stopped by the table. Millie ordered a glass of wine, and Carl ordered his usual Johnnie Walker Black.

"Jeez, this place is starting to look really run down," Millie said softly as she placed her fingers on Carl's forearm. "Did you notice how threadbare the chairs are? And the room is half-empty."

Carl shrugged, "Maybe Brenda is too old to run it."

"That's sad. I love it here. I remember coming here with my parents."

"I know. You always want to come here." Carl pulled Millie in tight next to him and turned to face her, his eyes twinkling. "Forget about this place. I'm anxious to hear our plan for the bakery."

She loved that he had said "our plan," but she wanted to give him a good answer, and his sexy smile was diverting her attention from the bakery to what they might do at home later. "I've got a bunch of ideas, but for now I have one major question." She sat up straight, twisting her ring. "Do you think I'd be good at having my own business?" she asked tentatively.

Carl stared into Millie's eyes. "Sure. I'd bet on you. You're optimistic, and when you take up a challenge, you do your best to do a great job." He grasped her hands in his larger ones. "I know how much you've always wanted to do this, but there's a lot for us to think about. This is a big undertaking, and you'll need lots of help. How about waiting until the retail spaces at my new project on the inlet are done? I'll have some great storefronts, and you'd get a good deal." He laughed and tickled her.

"Oh, Carl, that would be really nice," Millie said as she held his hands in hers, "but honestly my heart is set on the farmhouse. It has an old, unique charm about it, and I know exactly what I'd like to do with it."

"In that case, I've got to figure out if I can come up with the money to invest in it. A lot of money is tied up in my inlet project," Carl said, pulling his hands from hers and tapping his fingers on the table.

Millie bit her lip. She really wanted to do this, but only if it was a joint decision. She didn't want Carl to do it if it put too much pressure on their finances. She held her breath and, letting it out slowly, said, "I know you're familiar with the property. Could we just go check it out and then talk about it?"

Carl nodded. "That sounds reasonable. I'll call the broker I use and talk to them, but you need to understand buying this building could be a major headache. It's probably a hundred years old." He shook his head. "Bringing it up to code could be a big problem."

Millie couldn't help herself, but she blurted out, "I know I'm jumping ahead here, but the last time I thought I'd be doing this, I gave it a name. Do you want to hear it?"

"Why not? You're going to tell me anyway." Carl gave her one of his lopsided smiles.

Millie stared into Carl's eyes and, with a slightly unsure voice, said, "It shall be named The Best Doggone Bakery, and we will serve yummy pastries to our discerning furry customers."

Carl burst out laughing. "Cute. But seriously, Millie, slow down. I know how much you want to do this, and I'm willing to help you, but we are not talking about me buying you a piece of jewelry or rescuing another dog. This could affect our relationship and our plans for having a family. Even if the building looks good to me, there's such a thing as due diligence. That means checking the structure, location surveys, zoning, and more."

The waiter interrupted them. "Excuse me," he said as he placed their drinks on the table. "Would you like to order your entrees now?"

"Sure," Millie said. "I'd like the chicken Parmesan."

Carl ordered the strip steak. The waiter asked for his preference on how he'd like it prepared, and after jotting down their orders and telling them he'd be back with the breadbasket, he left.

Millie sighed. This interruption was a good thing. It would give Carl time to think. He always liked to look at a problem from different angles before he made a decision. She took a sip of her wine, enjoying the view out the window while waiting for Carl to continue.

"Okay, we'll go look at Christopher's. But even for you, my love, I won't buy the building unless the deal is a solid one. Remember, any investor would do the same. Besides, you wouldn't want to open your business only to find some problems with the building. That'd be a disaster, and you'd be devastated."

"I know you're right, but I bet it'll all work out, and then I promise I'll find the best people to help me. Actually, I even have someone in mind." Millie winked and tapped his chest.

Carl's eyes twinkled. "Clever!"

Giggling, she smiled as she thought, *So far, so good.* They'd go look at the building and then decide whether to go forward with her plan.

The rest of the dinner was a blur. Millie knew from looking at her empty plate that she had eaten her chicken Parmesan, but she was too excited thinking about the bakery to enjoy it. However, even though she was keyed up, she did remember the delicious piece of the chocolate cheesecake she and Carl shared for dessert.

On the ride home, Millie stared out the window, taking time to peek over at Carl, until he finally said, "Millie, what is going on in that mind of yours?"

She reached over and squeezed his leg. "That someday soon I could be opening The Best Doggone Bakery."

Back home the dogs followed Millie into the bedroom. Carl was already there with the TV on. After putting on an oversized T-shirt covered with multicolored paw prints and brushing her teeth, she climbed into bed.

Annie settled into the dog bed by the window, but Luke sat on his haunches, tapping the bed with his paw and staring up at her—his personal signal that he wanted something from Millie.

"Does this mean you want to get up on the bed, Luke?" she chuckled. She lifted him, placing him between her and Carl.

What Luke did next was a surprise. He crawled on top of Carl with his nose touching Carl's face, placed one paw on each side of his head, and slobbered him with kisses.

Millie and Carl exchanged a glance, and she burst out laughing. Carl tried to talk, but he couldn't get the words out. "I guess you missed me," he finally managed to say.

Eventually, Luke settled himself in a spot between them. Carl plumped up his pillow and in minutes was sound asleep, smiling.

Millie reached for the remote, flipping channels to possibly find an oldie-but-goodie movie.

She looked over at Luke, the events of the day bringing back that time about two years ago when she and Carl had first brought him home.

Millie and Carl had decided they wanted another sheltie, a second one to be company for Annie. For the first few weeks in their house, Luke seemed so unhappy. He didn't care to be petted, and he stayed by himself. It made them wonder if they would ever be the right family for him. After a gut-wrenching conversation, they came to a decision. Carl called Charlotte at the rescue organization to tell her they were bringing Luke back to her.

Even now, the memory of that day made Millie cringe. She could put herself back in the car with Luke sitting motionless on her lap, his head on his paws. She peeked at him, and for one quick second, he ever so slightly raised his head and stared at her, his huge brown eyes appearing miserable and forlorn.

She shut her eyes, remembering a life-changing moment years before when she had seen a similar look on another dog's face.

That time it had been Laci, an incredible sheltie and her first rescue. Poor, sad, abused Laci had needed lots of time to adjust to a new home. Could it be that Luke was the same, that he was sad and just needed more time and lots of love?

"I can't do this," she said to Carl.

Carl glanced at her. "So, I guess you want me to turn around?"

She could barely get the words out. "Yes, please. Let's go home."

Leave it up to her wonderful, compassionate husband, who needed no further encouragement to do exactly as she requested. As Carl turned the car around, Luke looked up at her. She swore she saw a glimmer of something indefinable in Luke's deep brown, expressive eyes that was seared in her memory forever. At that moment, she knew without a doubt they had made the perfect decision.

Millie now wiped a tear from her cheek and clicked off the TV. What memories! Sometimes, one seemingly small moment could have such a profound effect on one's life. If she could just turn her vision of a dog bakery into reality; Luke could spend all day, every day with her. It would be his heaven on earth. He could be with her and Annie and, at the same time, have access to lots of good treats. And that would be heaven on earth for her, too!

Millie reached over to touch Luke. She smiled through her tears. Somehow, she'd figure out how to use her bakery to help save other dogs and help them find happiness and wonderful "furever" homes. That would be her life's mission!

CHAPTER TWO

The Process

A paw slid up and down Millie's arm, making her giggle. Then a cold nose tickled her nose. "Luke, you cutie. You think it's time to get up?"

Millie rolled out of bed and headed toward the kitchen with Luke and Annie beside her. Luke barked and wagged his tail as Carl stopped to kiss Millie before he left for work with a promise to contact his real estate agent.

In the kitchen, the aroma of coffee made her grab a mug and fill it to the brim. Sipping it, she walked over to the small, round kitchen table and sat looking outside at the colorful fall leaves, her thoughts on the bakery. Momentarily, Luke joined her, sitting on her feet while Annie slid into a spot near them.

"Guess what, you two? I'm going to open a dog bakery." Some people might have considered it strange that Millie loved to talk to her dogs, but she didn't care. She giggled. "And do you know what that means?" Luke tilted his head and placed his paw on her lap, as if he were paying close attention. "You'll get cookies, lots of them. And maybe, if you're good, I'll name one after you."

Millie wished she could call and share her plans with a friend, but Joy and her family had moved to Colorado and were in a different time zone. Her other good friend, Carolyn, was most likely still sleeping. She tapped her fingers on the table and sighed. It was premature to share, but she certainly could consider who she'd like to have work with her. Thinking about it, she decided Carolyn would be a great choice. They had been partners on the high school tennis team and worked well together—after all, they had won the state's doubles championship. But what had sealed the deal on their friendship was the day they found a scraggly-looking dog on one of the school's tennis courts. They named him Howard, and Carolyn took him home. When no one claimed him, Howard stayed with Carolyn for the rest of his life. Now they both had rescue animals.

Millie remembered struggling to be a good student, but she excelled at tennis. When it was time to apply to college, her parents were unable to come up with tuition; her best chance was to get a scholarship. She had just been granted a full scholarship to a college in Florida when her parents tragically died in a terrible car accident. That one fateful day had changed her life forever.

At that time, her older brother, Bradley, was finishing his junior year of college. When he and Millie discussed their new circumstances, Millie was adamant that he stay in school and graduate. But for him to do that meant making the gut-wrenching decision for her to stay home. She had two younger brothers—the twins, Nicholas and Grant—who needed her to stick around at least until they finished high school. Her parents would have expected that of her. It really wasn't a difficult decision; family came first.

During that traumatic time, when Millie and her younger brothers lived with their aunt, Carolyn and her parents provided a good support system for a young person trying to work and at the same time be a parent to her younger siblings. Carolyn made herself available for Millie, who was overwhelmed by her fate and as a result withdrew into herself. Working wasn't easy when her friends were in college, but then it all changed for the better when she met Carl through her job. He had come into the plumbing supply company where she was working to order some supplies for one of his projects. He immediately caught her attention with his easygoing manner and the air of maturity that surrounded him. The fact that he had twinkling hazel eyes and a killer smile added to his allure.

They started dating, and he told her that he had opened his own construction firm when he had graduated from college, using money from a trust fund his grandfather had set up for him. Even though he was building his business, he found time to spend with her. He was twenty-six. She was twenty.

After Carl found out about Millie's situation, he lavished her with fancy dinners and some wonderful weekend getaways. Not since her parents' death had anyone really focused on her needs. Her life was filled with worrying about bills and trying to be a parent to her younger brothers. She even had to make sure they did their homework. She never had money for manicures or anything remotely special. His thoughtfulness was something she would never take for granted. He made her laugh, and he constantly tickled and hugged her, something she missed a lot after her dad died.

Millie fell in love with Carl over the next year. Two years later, in the same month her twin brothers graduated from high school, she married the love of her life.

She was in a good place now, and really, what harm was there to call and share? She chewed her lip, she ran her fingers through her hair, she played with the phone, but then she couldn't stop herself and punched in Carolyn's number.

When Carolyn picked up, she sounded out of breath. Millie laughed, imagining her short, curvy friend dressed in her baby pink sweats and matching pink sneakers, with her curly red hair in a crooked topknot, racing for the phone. "Sounds like I caught you at a bad time? You sound busy."

"No, just frustrated. I'm trying to stop Oodles from stealing Levi's dog food. My crazy cat prefers his food to her own."

Millie giggled. Carolyn loved her rescued animals as much as she did. She had rescued Levi, a West Highland white terrier, when he was four, and a year after Levi was rescued, she found Oodles, an all-black cat except for a white tip on her tail, wandering outside her house. When no one claimed Oodles, she was welcomed into the household. Carolyn's love of animals was great; especially since Millie thought whoever ended up working at the bakery should be a dog owner. "Well, I'm glad you answered."

Carolyn hesitated. "What's up? Are you okay? You sound so serious."

"I'm fine. It's just that . . ." Millie held her breath and then in a swoosh blurted out, "What would you think if I told you I'm hoping to open a dog bakery?"

"Ah, the dream resurfaces, and now you couldn't wait to tell me." Carolyn's throaty, infectious laugh made Millie smile.

"Yes. Only this time, let's hope it works out."

"Well, hang on. This calls for a cup of coffee and a doughnut."

Millie waited. Her friend's sweet tooth was her weak spot.

"Okay, I'm back. Got my doughnut, and it's yummy. Fill me in. Why now?"

"Christopher is selling the farmhouse. You remember when I almost got to buy it before. I've always thought it'd be the perfect spot for my dog bakery."

"Well, it's been something you've wanted to do forever, and it's a sure thing no one loves dogs more than you."

"True, but it will take a lot more than that to do a good job, and there's so much I don't know." Millie hoped this was a subtle suggestion that Carolyn could help her.

"Seriously, Mil, go for it! You've wanted to do this for years. You'll figure it all out. Get yourself to the library, look on the Internet, or better yet, go to Bridget's and buy a book. You're not stupid. I bet there's one of those Dummies books about starting a business. Seriously, you're a quick learner. Just find some good people to help you."

Millie smiled. Carolyn's answer was a perfect setup for her big reveal. "I think I have." Taking a deep breath, she asked, "Will you do this with me?"

The silence was palpable.

Then Carolyn gasped. "No way! Hold up! You're kidding, right?"

"Nope. Right now, I'm totally serious. You just said I should find good people to help me. Who better than you?"

"Okay. Slow down. A second doughnut is called for here. By the way, that new grocery store near me has the best frosted chocolate ones around."

Millie shook her head. If Carolyn kept this up, she'd eat a half dozen before they hung up.

"Yum, this doughnut is amazing." Millie could swear she heard Carolyn smack her lips. Was Carolyn wasting time trying to find a way to say no diplomatically? *Darn.*

"Mil, you're the best friend ever, but you have to know this conversation is not at all what I expected when I answered the phone. I figured you'd want to meet for lunch or hit the stores for some shopping." Millie could hear Carolyn's loud sigh through the phone. "I'm being serious now, and what you're asking is huge. It'd be a major commitment."

"Agreed. Maybe we could meet and talk about it?"

"I don't know. You know me; I'm a real homebody."

"Oh, come on. We can meet at Miss Annabel's. Have a cup of coffee and one of her delicious scones." Millie bit her nail. Another of Carolyn's favorite munchies was Annabel's homemade scones, so this was a calculated request.

She could barely hear Carolyn breathing. Millie wondered what her friend was thinking.

"Oh, come on. We haven't been to see Annabel for a while. We can find out the latest gossip on Christopher's. And one last thing: I'll respect whatever decision you make. We've been friends forever, and I don't want that to ever change. You could always help me by listening to my plans."

"All right, I'll meet you Friday, but I'm not at all sure about doing this bakery thing. Don't plan on me saying yes."

"Got it. See you Friday."

* * *

Later that evening, while Carl worked in his office, Millie sat on her bed reading. She read the same page for the third time. She sighed and shut the book, tapping her fingers on the cover. So what if she called another person about the bakery?

She couldn't open a bakery without a baker, and MaryEllen would be the perfect person for the job. Not only did she love to bake, but her parents also owned a bakery, and she always talked about helping them out. Now that MaryEllen had permanently moved to Houndsville and was living with Millie's older brother, Bradley, she wasn't working. Taking a deep breath, she picked up the phone.

MaryEllen answered. "Hello?"

"Hi," Millie said. "Are you busy? Can we talk?"

"Oh no. Are you okay?" MaryEllen asked hesitantly.

"Sure," Millie chuckled. "But you're the second person to say that to me today. I guess I must sound unusually serious, but it's actually because I have something to ask you."

"Okay," MaryEllen replied, drawing out the word.

Millie crossed her fingers. "I'm going to open a dog bakery. I need a baker. I'd like you to do it."

"Hold up!" MaryEllen said. "Did you just say you wanted to open a dog bakery and you want me to be the baker?"

"Yup. Here's the scoop. Christopher is selling the farmhouse. I'm betting that Houndsville dog people will love a place to sit and relax with their dogs. Their dogs can have a treat and they can get a cup of coffee."

MaryEllen's belly laugh was a welcoming sound to Millie's ears. "My kind, sweet sister-in-law-to-be, I can so imagine you doing this. Wait until I tell Bradley. For now, tell me more."

Boy, "sister-in-law" and "kind and sweet" in the same sentence sounded really good to Millie. "Carl is scheduling an appointment for us to go see the building. He'll help me with contracts and all sorts of things I know nothing about. I'm trying to get ahead of the game by making sure I have great people helping me, like you." Millie held her breath.

"Oh, so he knows you want me to be the baker, and he thought I could do it?"

"Of course. Why not?" Millie hadn't really said anything to Carl, but she knew he liked whatever MaryEllen baked, especially her six-layer chocolate cake.

Millie could hear MaryEllen clearing her throat. "I never told you this, but I always thought I might like to have my own specialty bakery someday. I like the idea of baking for a small niche market, like weddings. I love to decorate cakes, and of course I love to eat the frosting."

"Who doesn't love frosting? That's the icing on the cake!" Millie giggled at her own pun. "Wow, so this should be perfect for you!"

"I don't know about that. I don't think baking for dogs is anything like what I've done before. Besides, who will help me? This sounds a little overwhelming."

"Oh, I have a few people in mind to help us. Since you like to bake cakes, just think: We could have birthday parties for dogs. Not exactly like a wedding, but it still involves a cake." Millie laughed. "But you know, I have an even better idea." She paused, thinking it was time to use her ace in the hole. "Why don't you talk to Bradley, see what he thinks."

"Okay, that sounds good."

Millie smiled to herself. If MaryEllen showed any interest in the project, she knew Bradley would encourage her. He wanted his sister and his prospective wife to be good friends, and he already thought Millie was a dog nut, so he'd probably think the bakery was a good idea.

"One last thing," Millie pleaded. "When you talk to Bradley, please tell him to keep this to himself. No calling his twin brothers."

"Oh, I get that completely," MaryEllen said. "If they decide to tease you, the three of them together can be merciless."

Millie chuckled and drummed her fingers on the book she'd been reading. "That's okay. If I get to open this bakery, I'll be too excited to care."

Right now, Millie certainly would have been happier if MaryEllen had said yes, but she had lots of time to seal the deal. After all, she hadn't seen the place with Carl yet, and MaryEllen hadn't said no. "Okay, I'll wait to hear from you."

Carl walked into the bedroom as Millie hung up. "Who was on the phone?"

"MaryEllen. I wanted to know if she'd be interested in helping at the bakery. I do need a baker, and she'd be perfect."

"Aren't you jumping ahead a bit here? We haven't even decided we're buying the building yet."

"But if we do, I want to be ready," Millie said cheerfully.

"You realize now that Bradley is involved, he'll want to tell the twins," Carl warned her.

"I thought about that, but I couldn't stop myself. Hopefully, Bradley won't tell."

"Good luck with that. Your brothers are as thick as thieves."

Carl walked over to his side of the bed and tickled Luke, who still had his head on Carl's pillow. "Luke, you are going to have to share that pillow with me."

Millie just sat and watched to see what would happen. Carl probably hoped his tickling would encourage Luke to move to the foot of the bed. She didn't believe that would make a difference, and it wasn't until Carl climbed into bed fifteen minutes later that Luke moved—only his move involved lying with his head on Carl's leg, using it as a pillow.

Carl raised his eyebrow. "He's pillowing me."

Millie laughed so hard that her stomach hurt and she could barely talk. "Well, he needs a pillow, and yours is already taken."

CHAPTER THREE

Gathering Leaves

Tap, tap. Millie rolled over. Luke licked her face. She giggled. "Okay, you can stop. I'll get up."

Millie threw back the covers and hugged him before climbing out of bed. Peeking out the draperies on her patio door, she could see it was sunny. *Good.* She would be able to spend some time outside. She threw on her grungy old sweats.

"Okay, Luke, and you too, Annie. Let's get the newspapers."

The three of them walked outside. It was cool and crisp, a perfect fall day. As they walked down the driveway to get the newspapers, the sun warmed her face while she noticed a mixture of red, yellow, and orange leaves covering the grass. Many remained in the trees, making a kaleidoscope of colors. It was a perfect day for raking leaves, especially with the slight breeze. She sniffed the air. That fall smell of wet leaves surrounded her. She liked that.

Millie found a rake in the garage and figured she'd start on the front lawn, where the sun was bathing a part of the grass in a golden hue. While Luke and Annie pounced in her piles, making her leaf-raking exercise futile, she wondered when she and Carl would get to see Christopher's, hoping it would be soon.

She knew she was being stubborn by wanting to open the bakery only in that spot. The space was perfect for her vision of decorating it like an old manor house, a comfortable and chic place with overstuffed chairs and sofas.

Her dogs would sit by her side, and her staff would look super cute with bib aprons and baseball caps with a Best Doggone Bakery logo. Humans would relax with homemade coffee drinks while their dogs sat at their feet.

Millie's attention was drawn from her vision when Annie taunted Luke to play. It was something she rarely did, and Luke took up the challenge.

They sprinted off, herding each other like typical shelties. Flying through the leaves, they ran back and forth, making a mess of Millie's piles. She wondered why she had even bothered to rake the leaves in the first place.

Finally, tongues hanging out, Luke and Annie landed in front of her. She could have sworn they were smiling.

"Okay, you guys, we're done here. Time to go in."

Walking up the steps to the kitchen, Millie heard the ringtone of her phone and sprinted to answer it. The caller ID read "MaryEllen." She pressed the talk button. "Hi. Do you have news?" Millie grasped the phone tight and chewed on her lower lip.

"Well, I'll start by telling you that when I told Bradley what you were up to, he laughed so hard he had to sit to catch his breath. Then he said something like, 'It figures my sister wants to spend her days with dogs,' but when he finally could talk, he agreed that it'd probably work out great. He said no one loves dogs more that you do, so why shouldn't you open a dog bakery? He actually thought it made good sense—not to mention, of course, he loves my baking. The end result was that I should do it if that was what I wanted."

Millie pumped her fist in the air. "Yes! I knew my sweet older brother would understand. Your timing is perfect. I'm going to meet Carolyn tomorrow morning; I'm betting I can convince her to do it now that you're our baker."

"You mentioned you had other people in mind to help. Who's that?" MaryEllen asked.

"Todd."

"You mean Bradley's old high school friend?"

"Well, we were both friendly with him, but yes, that is who I meant. The week our parents died was exam week for Bradley. Of course, he came home, but he had to head back to school for makeup exams. Bradley asked Todd to stand in for him. I used to call him my second older brother. He was the one who checked out my dates and made sure I was always home safe, besides tutoring me with my least favorite subject, math."

"Yeah, Bradley is always telling me that he felt bad that he got to finish college and you had to work. He'll always be your biggest fan," MaryEllen said.

Millie smiled. "You know, it all worked out great. I met Carl because I was here. So, here's the scoop about Todd. He recently told me he hates his job, and I'd love to have him on our team. In high school I kept trying to get him to hook up with Carolyn. They finally got me to sit with them so they could tell me that they just wanted to be friends, and to quit my matchmaking, but even now they keep in touch, so having both of them working with us would be perfect."

"I bet Bradley will be happy to hear that. I don't think he's seen Todd in a while. Oh, by the way, when I told him you hoped to buy Christopher's, he thought that spot was perfect."

"I think so, too. It's right near the center of town and not far from the park. I'm always seeing people with their dogs when I go to the Commons to shop," Millie added.

"So, what's your next step? MaryEllen asked.

"The meeting with Carolyn Friday."

"Well, call me after you meet with her."

"For sure."

"Oh, one last thing," MaryEllen said. "Bradley was curious to know when you're going to tell Nicholas and Grant."

"It's way too soon. Tell him that the three of them will still have plenty of time to tease me."

"You know he has trouble keeping a secret, so don't wait too long."

Millie laughed. "Some things never change."

Only Luke was there to see her huge grin when she put down the phone.

CHAPTER FOUR

Miss Annabel's

It was nine o'clock on Friday morning, and Annabel's was mobbed with the breakfast crowd. It was easy for Millie to spot Carolyn, who was wearing a hot pink turtleneck. She was seated at a small, round, high-top table on the left side of the main dining room.

Millie walked over and threw her jacket on the seat across from Carolyn's. "Hi. I see you already got coffee and your favorite chocolate chip scone. Give me a minute to get a latte."

The line moved quickly, and she returned to the table in no time.

"I didn't see Annabel. Did you?" Millie asked as she sat across from Carolyn. "I want to tell her my plans. I bet she'll be happy for me."

Carolyn frowned. "Maybe you should wait to tell her. What if it doesn't work out?"

Millie sighed. "I guess you're right. It's just that I'm really excited. I thought it would be nice to share my news with her. After all, we'll be working in the same neighborhood." She smiled and grabbed Carolyn's hand. "Oh well, I have some great news. I have the perfect person to do the baking for us."

"Who? Tell me!" Carolyn took a nibble of her scone.

"Well, I'll give you a few hints. She loves to bake. Her parents own and operate a bakery, and best of all, she's moved in with my big brother, Bradley."

"Wow! MaryEllen is your baker? That's fantastic! And she's moved in with Bradley?" Carolyn giggled. "I still remember when you first met her. You decided right then she was perfect for Bradley, and you plotted to get them to meet."

"Yes, matching them up was so much fun!" Millie laughed. "I like to think they had no idea what I was up to. But let's talk about the bakery."

Millie leaned forward and stared into Carolyn's eyes. "I can't sit still any longer. I'm on pins and needles. What did you decide? Are you going to do this with me?"

Carolyn took hold of Millie's hand that was wrapped around her latte. "I'm sorry, Mil, but my answer is no. I'm not ready to jump into this venture with you. I talked with Richard, and he thinks I might be taking on too much responsibility, especially because we're thinking it's time to start a family."

Carolyn got up and walked around the small table to give her friend a hug. "You can do this without me, and now that you have MaryEllen, you're on your way. You'll find another good person to open the bakery with you. Millie, this is your dream. Follow through, and stop trying to convince me to do it with you."

Millie bit her lip, trying not to show her true feelings. She'd totally expected Carolyn to say yes. Her best friend had been by her side for so many years that she couldn't imagine doing this without her. She tried to remain upbeat, but no words came to her. Nothing. Her eyes were moist; she was devastated. She'd have time to think about what this meant later when she got home, but right now she only wanted to leave. She wasn't good at hiding her emotions—especially from Carolyn, who knew her so well.

"Ah, come on, Millie," Carolyn pleaded. "I told you I wasn't sure about this."

"I know. I was just so sure you'd say yes. And here I thought I'd ask our friend Todd to join up with us."

"Todd? Why?"

"He hates his job, and remember, he worked here at Miss Annabel's when she first opened. He has some experience that might be helpful. We always did make a good team, the three of us. And most of all, we love dogs."

"That's a great idea to hire Todd," Carolyn said as she glanced at her watch. "Look, I'm sorry. I have an appointment at the Knitting Needle."

"I'm ready to leave, too." Millie reached for her jacket as she looked around. She tried to carry on a normal conversation. "I wonder where Annabel is. We never saw her. Oh well, maybe next time. I might as well go to Bridget's to look for those Dummies books or whatever. I'll need them if I'm going to make my bakery a huge success." She winked and turned toward the door.

* * *

Annabel watched Millie and Carolyn leave. "Humph!" she said to herself as she stomped her foot. "So, my old high school friend Millie Myers Whitfield plans to open a bakery. She mentioned it was in this neighborhood. Boy, is she ever in for a surprise! I know all the properties around here. The only place up for sale is Christopher's building, and that building is going to be mine. I always thought she was jealous that I got to open this place. Figures she wants a business near here—it's the best locale in town. Lucky for me, she has no idea I heard her conversation. She thinks she can compete with me. We'll just see about that."

She grabbed her cell phone and punched in a number she knew well. "Hi, Christopher. I need to talk to you. I just overheard Millie Whitfield talking about buying your building. I expect you to sell the building to me."

"Annabel, I need to get the best price I can. I know we're friends, but you can't expect me to make a business decision based on that."

"Well, I have to say I am surprised. Not only have we been more than friends, but I've tried to help you out by encouraging people to go to your shop."

Annabel hung up and smacked the phone down on a table. She thought he'd help her out. In the past, they had a good thing going. *What is it with people today?* Well, she'd have to make sure she got her bid in soon. She wasn't about to lose out to Millie, who would open a bakery that would eventually be competition for her.

CHAPTER FIVE

Get-Together

Millie woke up feeling invigorated. This morning's plan was for MaryEllen and Todd to come to her house to talk about the bakery.

After feeding Luke and Annie and snatching a corn muffin for herself, she figured she'd bake her famous brownies. They were her mother's recipe and one of the only desserts she did well, and baking them would keep her busy until her friends arrived.

As Millie walked toward the kitchen, she noticed Annie and Luke sprawled out in the dining room. She stopped in her tracks and giggled. Annie and Luke were front to back, back to front. *How cute they look.* While Annie was looking out the window, Luke faced the opposite direction, his head pointed toward the inside of the house with his head lying on Annie's rear end. Her two dogs were such good friends that they liked to be touching each other. She sped off in search of her iPad, determined to get a photo of this to show Carl. She snuck up on them and clicked away. "I got a good shot." She pumped her fist in the air. "Wait till Carl sees this!"

Thank goodness Millie got the photo when she did because, a moment later, Luke and Annie ran to the door at the first *ding-dong* of the doorbell. She wondered who was already here; MaryEllen and Todd were not expected for another half hour. Putting down her iPad, she glanced at her watch and followed her dogs. When she peeked out her sidelight, she saw Carolyn standing there. She grabbed the doorknob and pulled open the door.

"Carolyn, this is a surprise. What are you doing here?"

"I hope it's okay," Carolyn said meekly. "I came to talk to you. You mentioned MaryEllen and Todd were coming around eleven, and I wanted to talk to you before they got here."

Right away Millie figured something was wrong when she noticed Carolyn wasn't wearing anything pink. She threw her arm around her friend. "Come on in. Are you okay?"

"We'll see. We need to talk."

They sat at the kitchen table. Millie folded her hands in front of her, waiting for Carolyn to reveal what was on her mind.

Carolyn put her hands on top of Millie's. "I'm going to just spit it all out. After I left you at Annabel's, I felt terrible. We've been best friends forever, and I'd like to help you with your bakery—but I'm afraid to work for you."

Millie couldn't breathe. How could her best friend be saying this to her? She could barely swallow. "Then why come here today?" she asked cautiously.

"Listen to me. When we played tennis together, you always wanted to be the one in charge. You'd pick when and where we practiced, when we changed positions, and everything else. We were kids then, but I was afraid working for you as your employee might ruin our friendship. That's why I turned you down."

Millie pulled her hands back and put them in her lap. "I only took over the decision-making for us because I thought you wanted me to. So, what can I do to convince you I'd still love if you'd do this with me? You know we made a great team!"

"Yes, Mil, we were great together. I've thought about this a lot now. I have a proposal for you." Carolyn squirmed around and leaned forward. "I'll work with you at the bakery, but I have one condition. It's big. I want to be your partner, not your employee. That way, I have equal footing with you."

Millie couldn't believe what she was hearing. She let out the breath she felt she'd been holding in. "Is that all?"

Carolyn nodded.

Millie jumped up and ran around the table to hug her friend. "Hooray! You're in! You're going to do this with me!" Her shouting got the attention of Luke and Annie, who started barking. Millie barely heard the doorbell, but the dogs must have because they ran to the door.

"We'll talk more about this later. Come with me," Millie said to Carolyn as she got up to go open the door.

MaryEllen stood there, and before Millie could open her mouth, the dogs jumped all over her. Right away, MaryEllen got down on the floor to pet them. "Hi, Luke. Hi, Annie." She lifted her head and sniffed the air. "It smells like chocolate and vanilla. Oh good, I bet you made your yummy brownies."

As Millie nodded, she heard a car door shut. She couldn't wait until Todd walked through the door before she blurted out, "Wait till you two hear the news! Carolyn's changed her mind! She's here, and she's going to partner with us. Come on, let's all talk."

Millie started walking toward her kitchen when she realized Todd knew Bradley, but she wasn't sure he'd ever met MaryEllen. She turned back and introduced them. Todd mumbled, "Hi."

Millie hadn't seen Todd in a while. She almost laughed when she saw he had gotten his ears pierced and had a small heart tattoo on his forearm with an arrow through the center. If he was hoping to change his image of the studious geek type, it wasn't working. He couldn't change the fact that his face was covered in freckles and that his hair was short with a slight cowlick in the back, and the choice of vintage-style tortoiseshell glasses didn't help.

Millie saw Todd steal a glance at MaryEllen, who was gorgeous with her thick, dark brown hair cascading down her back and her glorious smile that lit up her green eyes. Maybe he was thinking how lucky Bradley was to have found her.

"Let's sit in there," Millie said, pointing to her kitchen.

Todd patted Carolyn on her back. "So happy you're onboard. It'll be great to spend time with you and Millie. Back to our high school roots."

The brownies Millie had baked earlier were already on her kitchen table. "Before we sit down, if anyone wants coffee, I put out mugs and you can help yourself."

Todd, MaryEllen, and Carolyn went to sit at the table while Millie poured herself some coffee, and when she joined them, Todd passed around the brownies. Everyone took one. Luke sauntered over and sat on her feet. "Ah, Luke, are you comfy?" Millie said as she ruffled his fur.

MaryEllen laughed. "Okay, now that Luke is present, I guess you can start."

"Fine." Millie smiled. "Well, let me start by saying that I feel really lucky to have the three most perfect people helping me achieve my dream. I also have news. Carl and I have an appointment to see Christopher's building tomorrow, so we're moving right along." She stuck her hand palm up in the air to high-five everyone. "Obviously, I'm planning for all to go well, and we'll submit a bid. Next up, I figured today would be good to begin talking about what we plan to bake."

Todd held up his hands. "Wait a minute. Did you say Christopher's building? What's going on? What's happening with his ice cream store?"

"He's closed. He's selling," Millie said.

"Man, that's crummy. I love his ice cream. Are you sure he'll go through with a sale? I remember what happened years ago. More importantly, are you sure you want to open a bakery there?"

Millie frowned. "I actually think it'll be great! What's your problem?"

Todd squirmed and almost choked on his brownie. "Well, it's not very far from Annabel's. If she even thinks of you as competition, she might get nasty."

"Oh, for goodness' sake. We've all known Annabel since high school," Millie said.

"I'm just telling you I've seen her make trouble for people she dislikes. When I first went to work for her, there were all sorts of rumors swirling around about how she'd ruined Sandy's toy business, and as you know, that store eventually closed. Remember, she's had her store for a while now, and she knows everyone. Maybe you should look for another spot."

For a moment, Millie considered what Todd was telling her. "Why would she care? We're opening a bakery that's for dogs."

Todd shook his head. "Doesn't matter. You need to watch out for her."

"I can just picture the expression on her face if someone asked to bring a dog inside her white tablecloth lunchroom. Her fancy patrons eating their cucumber and cream cheese tea sandwiches would be aghast," Millie laughed.

With her mouth full of brownie, Carolyn mumbled, "I agree with Millie. Lots of people love to walk their dogs, and Christopher's is the perfect spot with all the good shops around there. Carl's huge project down on the inlet will hopefully mean lots of new people with dogs, and I bet many of them will enjoy stopping to get their dogs a treat and at the same time a cup of coffee for themselves."

MaryEllen reached over Todd to take a brownie. "I agree with Carolyn and Millie. It's a great location."

"Okay. Just remember what I told you." Todd turned to MaryEllen. "So, tell us what you plan to bake for our furry friends."

"I'm checking it out," MaryEllen answered. "Bradley told me dogs are not allowed to have chocolate. I never knew that; I need to do my homework and find out the ingredients they can have. I have a good taster at home, and we certainly have a good taster right here." She leaned over to pet Luke and giggled. "Luke, are you going to try my cookies?"

Todd frowned. "Millie, maybe MaryEllen needs our help if she has no idea what to bake?"

Millie sighed. "Todd, relax. MaryEllen's parents own a bakery. She's helped them out for years. I couldn't have found a better person; her experience will be invaluable."

MaryEllen piped up, "Don't worry. I do know how to bake, and I'll figure it out. Look, we've got time. Millie doesn't even have the location yet. FYI, I have been thinking about what I want to bake. I'm planning to keep things fairly simple at first. I'll keep you posted and let you know when I'm ready for you to see and taste. I already know Millie wants to call the small cakes 'pupcakes.'"

"Yes, I like the word 'pupcakes.' I thought it sounded cute," Millie said as she tried to lighten the mood.

"If you want some help, I'll try a few recipes," Carolyn said. "You can tell me what to do, and I can try them out on Levi."

"I'm sorry, MaryEllen. I didn't mean to snap at you. I'll help you in any way I can," Todd said apologetically.

Millie nodded. "Sounds good. Now, before you leave, there is one other thing I want you all to think about." She wiggled around and sat up straight in her chair. She wanted to make a good argument in favor of the issue, which meant the world to her. "Once the bakery is open, I'd like for us to come up with a way to support the dog rescue community. For example, maybe once a month we could work with our local sheltie rescue group." She held up her hands. "Now promise not to laugh. I've been trying to come up with a catchy phrase, and I finally think I have. It's 'Pick Your Perfect Pooch Day.'" She paused and chewed her lip. "Here's my plan: Once a month, the sheltie rescue group brings their adoptable dogs to the bakery, and a lucky pooch finds a 'furever' home."

She glanced around the table to see everyone's reaction. Their nods made her smile. "We could give the rescuer coupons in exchange for free treats. Hopefully that would encourage them to visit the bakery, and we'd get to see how the dogs are doing in their new homes."

"Wow! You've really given this a lot of thought. Good for you. I'm impressed," Carolyn said enthusiastically.

"Yes, I'd like to think it could work well for everyone involved. It could generate goodwill within the rescue community and bring in more customers for the bakery."

"Hey, something just came to me," MaryEllen said excitedly. "We could nickname you HHH—Heroine of Houndsville's Hounds." She put her hand over her mouth. "Oops, just kidding," she added quickly. "I can see how much this means to you. We'll figure out a way to make it work."

* * *

Carl sat sipping his nightly glass of Johnnie Walker Black. The evening news was on TV. Millie sat on the ottoman in front of him and tapped his thigh.

"I've got great news to share. Carolyn's changed her mind, and she's decided to come onboard along with Todd and MaryEllen. It turns out that Carolyn was hesitant because she wanted to be a partner in the business, not an employee. She wanted us to be on equal footing. I told her that I was good with that, but then it would only be fair to include MaryEllen and Todd. What do you think?"

Millie waited for what seemed like an agonizing minute for Carl's response. He finally replied, "Yes, that should be okay. I'll want to think about it some more, but we can work it out that I'll buy the building and rent it to the four of you."

Millie hugged him. "Oh, I knew you'd figure a way to make it work. I'll go over the details with them, but I'm sure they'll be happy with that."

"Remember, Millie, this all depends on if I think the building doesn't need too much to make it workable for you, and that the price is right."

"I know," she said. "In the meantime, MaryEllen is researching ingredients dogs are allowed to eat, and she's going to find some recipes to try out. My only job right now is to nail down the location." She reached over to hug him, and she planted a big, sloppy kiss on his handsome face.

CHAPTER SIX

Location

Millie and Carl were set to meet with the real estate broker at eleven thirty. After a quick shower, she blow-dried her hair, applied some blush and lipstick, and slipped on a black cashmere sweater paired with black trousers and sheltie earrings.

As she and Carl drove to their appointment, Millie thought about Houndsville and how it was expanding with new developments springing up outward from the inlet. Tourists were coming to meander around, enjoy a good meal, and visit the one-of-a-kind shops. Recently the town had renamed the entire district and surrounding park the Houndsville Commons. She figured Christopher's would be a perfect location for the bakery. It was close to the shops but somewhat secluded, making it a pleasant walk for owners and their dogs.

Carl parked in a spot not far from Christopher's in a parking lot used by many of the shoppers who, like Millie, didn't live close enough to walk to the stores. They walked the short block to Frannie's Flowers, the go-to florist in town, then Julie's Jewels. The third store in that short block housed Bridget's Bookstop, Millie's favorite bookstore.

Across the street was what the locals called Houndsville Park. It was about an acre of green lawns interspersed with stone-paved interconnecting walkways that led to many of the other shops. In the middle it had a bronze plaque commemorating the hounds that had been brought into the town by the British to chase the foxes. That was how Houndsville derived its name. Even nowadays the residents still had some local hunts.

Millie liked to purchase a book from Bridget's Bookstop and then walk across the street to sit on one of the many wrought iron benches located on the walkways. Depending on the season, there were always some flowers or trees in bloom that made the park look really spectacular. Her favorites were the white dogwoods in the early spring. Sometimes she'd bring Luke and Annie, and they'd curl up on her feet. She'd read, and the dogs would watch the squirrels that they'd give anything to chase. The evenings that she could convince Carl to walk in the park, they'd hold hands and wander along the many paths loaded with strategically placed gaslights that created a magical, romantic ambiance.

After Thanksgiving, the town's chamber of commerce hired a landscaping firm to decorate the small bushes in the park with tiny white lights, and then a few weeks prior to Christmas, a tree farmer set up shop inside the park to sell his trees.

As they walked past Bridget's Bookstop, Carl turned to glance at Millie and said, "I always like to browse in the bookstore, but I forget Julie's Jewels is next door."

Millie giggled. "I don't mean to laugh, but I used to think one of the reasons you were reluctant to get ice cream was because I always wanted to drag you down the street to Julie's to see her original designs. She always has some small bauble I want you to buy for me."

Carl grinned, grabbing her hand in his. "Come on. Let's walk through the park. I know you come here often, but it's been a while for me."

They walked along a winding path from one side to the opposite end of the center square. Millie pointed out Karen's Knitting Needle and Cross-Stitch Studio and Harper McNeely's Art Gallery, two more of her favorite stores.

"You also know that Miss Annabel's Tea and Coffee Emporium is nearby, and of course the Buckshead Inn is at the bottom of the hill near your new project."

Carl chuckled. "Your favorite." He then glanced down at his watch. "We better head back. It's time to meet the broker."

Once she and Carl got close, Millie could see a tall, thin woman dressed in a black coat standing in front of the building. They walked up to her. She extended her gloved hand and introduced herself as Sandra. "Carl told me you're interested in opening a bakery."

"Yes, but to be more exact, it's a dog bakery."

"Oh, I didn't realize that," Sandra said. "That sounds like fun."

"Yes, it will be for sure." Millie smiled. She was glad Sandra hadn't dismissed her idea for a dog bakery as a zany idea. It made her feel good about working with her.

"Well, if you're ready, we should go look inside. Oh, before I forget, an interested party called to say they'd be bringing in a contract today."

Millie blanched and grabbed Carl. "Oh no! I have such good plans for this place."

Sandra stared at Millie. "Why would you make plans? You haven't seen the space yet."

Millie grabbed Carl's hand as her stomach flip-flopped at the thought that someone else's contract might be accepted first. "Sandra, I've been here zillions of times. This spot is perfect for the dog bakery I've dreamed of opening."

Carl squeezed her hand. "Calm down. Let's go inside. One offer doesn't necessarily mean anything."

Sandra unlocked the door and held it open. Millie stepped across the threshold and stood looking around. There was only a small foyer with a room on the right, a room on the left, and an old wooden staircase leading to the second floor. She thought she could smell the lingering aroma of cinnamon and vanilla wafting in the air. She peeked into the room on the right. In her mind she pictured collies, beagles, Labs, Old English sheepdogs, and golden retrievers sprawled around with people sitting and chatting nearby.

Millie felt a tap on her shoulder interrupting her silent reverie, and she remembered that Carl was with her and couldn't move until she walked farther into the space. She turned to him and grabbed him in a bear hug. "Oh, Carl, can't you see it? This place is wonderful!"

"Millie, we haven't seen it yet."

"Oh, Carl, I don't need to see another thing. This place is just right!"

"Okay! Let's just look around. You're not even focusing on what's here."

Millie suspected she'd see some peeling paint, old and filthy light fixtures, floors that needed buffing, and windows that were grimy. This place was far from spanking new and clean, but that didn't matter. It was what was in her heart and in her vision. That's what counted. The deal was sealed the minute she walked through the door. The Best Doggone Bakery was going to be here. She just knew it!

Now if only Carl could envision it as she did. She wandered down the skinny hallway and walked into the room on the back right. On the back wall was another door. She wandered over to open it, and when she did, her eyes widened with surprise. "Wow! Carl, come quick! You've got to see this."

Carl meandered down the hallway, his footsteps moving slowly as if he was assessing every little detail. Millie wished he'd move faster. This was going to surprise even him.

She watched his reaction as he stood next to her. She smiled. She knew had him when he said, "I didn't expect to see a new kitchen with high-end commercial equipment. Looks like Christopher just did all this."

"He did," Sandra confirmed, joining them in the kitchen. "He told me he wasn't planning this move. He'd wanted to add some new items to the menu, so he bought new kitchen equipment, but then something came up."

Millie winked at Carl. "I can see Luke and Annie eating their treats here. Can't you?"

Carl nodded. "Let's go upstairs."

"I'll leave you two alone," Sandra said. "I've got a phone call I need to return. I'll wait for you out front."

The second floor had a full bathroom and three more empty rooms. "Carl, can we put in our offer now that you've seen the property?"

"One thing we still need is an appraisal, and I'm curious to know about other properties that have recently sold around here."

"But what if the other offer is accepted?"

"I'll tell Sandra my plans, and she'll tell Christopher. Sellers wait to see all the offers. Let's stop and get lunch. Want to go to the inn? I can try to make some phone calls while we're there."

This was so difficult for Millie. She bit her lip. Of course, she'd hoped Carl would be ready to put in an offer now, but if she was being honest with herself, she knew that when it came to business, he was smart and cautious, especially after the bad deal that had cost him a fortune years ago. Carl would watch out for her and protect her, one of the many reasons she loved him so much. She'd have to hope it would all work out.

Sandra was just putting away her phone when Carl and Millie joined her outside on the sidewalk. "We're done for today. I've told Millie that before we make an offer, I have a few details to check out."

"I wouldn't wait too long," Sandra advised. "Christopher is anxious to sell, and I was just on the phone with another agent whose client is putting in a bid. They told me they'd be at the office with their contract later this afternoon."

Millie twisted her sheltie ring. Her stomach, as usual, was in knots. It wouldn't help to say anything, so she just kept quiet.

"Mil, let's grab lunch at the inn. I didn't have breakfast, and I'm hungry."

Carl said goodbye to Sandra while Millie called ahead to reserve a table, requesting to sit outside on the bluestone patio.

Ten minutes later, Millie and Carl arrived at the inn. The clear skies and the bright sun were helping to warm up the chilly air, but the spot chosen for them on the patio was still partly in the shade. Millie shivered and was thrilled when Carl sat close enough to put his arm around her, his body heat warming her.

"When our server comes, I'll get him to bring over one of the propane-fired heaters," he said as he huddled even closer to her.

They both ordered salads, but it wasn't until after they shared a piece of flourless chocolate cake and Carl had taken a few bites that he said, "I know you think this building is perfect, so I'm willing to build into the contract some contingencies about inspections and appraisals. If you research the prices that others paid for properties around the Commons, we can submit a contract later today."

Millie stared at Carl. He always came through for her. She leaned in and kissed him gently. "Hooray! I can't wait to tell Carolyn, MaryEllen, and Todd."

Carl laughed. "Maybe you should wait until we know something for sure."

At that moment, Carl's phone trilled. He showed Millie his phone. The caller ID said it was Sandra. He stared at Millie. She was smiling. She drummed her fingers on the table as her heart raced. He whispered, "Shh . . ." and laid the phone on the table before pressing the speaker button.

With no formalities, Sandra said, "Carl, I want you to know that Christopher accepted the offer he received earlier."

"No way!" Millie gasped, unable to control her response. She slumped in her chair, blinking back tears of disappointment. She grabbed Carl's hands. She squeaked out, "Why didn't he wait to see if we would be putting in a bid?"

"If I remember correctly, Carl said he had to check out some details before he would submit a contract. Christopher didn't want to wait to see what you decided. He was satisfied with the offer presented today, and he's in a hurry to sell."

"Sandra, can you tell us who put in the contract?" Carl asked. He stroked Millie's hands.

"Yes, it was Annabel Larson."

Millie clenched Carl's hand in a death grip. "Oh no! Todd warned me about her. He said she was trouble. But why does she want that spot? She already has a place nearby. I wonder if she knew I wanted it."

"Millie, did you and Carolyn talk about it when you met at her place?"

Millie pulled her hands from Carl's and ran her fingers through her hair. She rubbed her temple. "Yes, of course. That's why we met. But we didn't talk to Annabel. Actually, we never saw her. Oh no, I guess she must have eavesdropped. She's just ruined everything."

A tear trickled down her face.

CHAPTER SEVEN

Surprise

Millie lay in bed with a blanket pulled over her head. She had lost Christopher's building for the second time. She couldn't bear to talk to Annabel now, and she had to decide what to do about the bakery. She had some thinking to do. Would she wait for a year or so until Carl's project down by the inlet was done and take a space there? Would she rather look for an alternative site, or just decide to drop the idea altogether?

The choice was hers. How badly did she want this? Was she willing to keep trying? It took only a second for her to realize she'd be so disappointed in herself if she didn't continue to pursue her dream. Extra determined, she threw back the covers and hauled herself out of bed. She'd dreamed about this bakery for way too long to let the loss of Christopher's end it all. She needed to get moving.

"Come on, Luke and Annie, it's time to get you something to eat." They followed Millie as she walked toward the kitchen. "I promise you I am not giving up on my dog bakery. We will find somewhere to eat pupcakes."

She heard Carl's footsteps behind her. As he got close, he put his arm around her shoulder and whispered in her ear, "Good to hear you being so positive. I was thinking you might give up after yesterday."

Millie shook her head. "Honestly, I thought about it—not for long, but I did. It was an easy decision in the end. I've wanted to do this for too long to give up."

Carl hugged her. "Good. Now come sit down. I've got something to tell you."

"Is it good? Do you have another location in mind?"

"No, unfortunately not."

"You have a way to zap Annabel and make her go away."

Carl laughed. "Sit and be quiet." He sat across from her at their kitchen table. He leaned forward and grabbed her hands in his. "Look, I've planned something special for your birthday, but you could use something to look forward to. Since I have trouble keeping secrets from you, I'm going to tell you now."

"Are you taking me away?" Millie quizzed him, hoping she was correct. Right now, she'd be thrilled to have a weekend getaway.

"Millie, slow down. Patience. You're not even close." Carl wiggled his fingers at her. "Give me a chance and stop trying to guess. I'll tell you."

"Okay, I promise I'll be quiet, but *please* tell me." Millie wiggled her fingers back at him.

Carl smiled. "Just let get my coffee first."

"No fair." Millie tried to grab Carl's hands so he couldn't get up. "Tell me first and then get your coffee."

Carl laughed, pulled his hands free, and went to get his coffee. Millie sat fiddling with her fingers as she watched him fumbling to find exactly the right mug, all done on purpose, before pouring his coffee. He was great at teasing her, and she should have been used to his antics, but when she finally hit on a plan to tease him back, he interrupted her thoughts. "Remember the day we went to Harper McNeely's Art Gallery a while ago? We loved her dog portraits, and her process where she paints and colors directly onto her photographs," he said as he came back to the table and sat next to her. "Well, I commissioned her to do a portrait of Luke and Annie."

Millie was dumbfounded and slow to react, not knowing what to say. The realization that Carl had come up with this special gift overwhelmed her. She placed her hands on either side of his face, pulled his head close, peered into his eyes, and softly kissed him. She adored him, and she loved that he understood how much she loved Luke and Annie. This gift was one she'd treasure forever. In this moment, her heart told her that she shouldn't feel bummed about the many hours he worked. He didn't intentionally ignore her. After all, it was his business success that made it possible to receive this wonderful present.

If she ended up opening the bakery, she'd do her best to get his help so he'd be spending more time with her. Having him around made her happy. Of course, it was possible that having the bakery would require so much of her time that she wouldn't mind his work schedule as much.

CHAPTER EIGHT

More Locations

Over the next week, Sandra and Millie checked out several locations for the bakery. None tempted her, although she tried to convince herself that the space wasn't the important factor; it was what she did with it that counted.

One morning Millie was meeting Sandra at another spot. She crossed her fingers, hoping this location would be the one.

She threw on her favorite go-to clothes—black pants with a black sweater—and tied a cobalt scarf with a sheltie appliqué from her friend Joy around her neck. On her wrist she put her newest piece of sheltie jewelry: a watch with the head of a sheltie inside the case. Maybe it would help her be on time. She kissed Luke and Annie goodbye, got in her car, and drove to meet Sandra.

She arrived at the location early and had time to walk around the building. This particular space was in an older area of Houndsville. She could see by peeking in the window that it needed painting and some general sprucing up. Its biggest asset was the pet store down the block. Lots of people brought their pets to a pet store, so that was a detail in the positive column.

Sandra waved as she got out of her car. "Come on. I have a feeling this space will be the right one." She used a key to open the door, and out wafted a stale, musty smell. Millie held her nose and turned to Sandra. "Yuck. Doesn't look good."

In less than five minutes, they were done. It didn't matter that this could possibly be a good location; the store itself needed a ton of work, not to mention that the smell inside was nasty. "Sorry, Sandra," Millie said. "I really was hoping you were right. Maybe something else will turn up."

Sandra frowned. "Well, I've shown you four locations you considered a possibility. There's nothing else to show you right now."

"I keep telling myself not to be so picky." Millie shook her head. "If only Annabel hadn't bought Christopher's, or if there had been another location available in the Commons."

"Millie, I know how much you want to do this. Maybe you should reconsider one of the spaces we already looked at."

Millie absentmindedly said goodbye and drifted off to her car. She fished around in her handbag for her car keys, and after opening the door, she slid in, laid her head on the steering wheel, and closed her eyes. She refused to cry. That wouldn't help. *Darn Annabel.* Maybe she should go talk to Annabel and find out why she wanted Christopher's. They had a history. Maybe she could convince Annabel how much the dog bakery meant to her. She'd give that some more thought before she did anything. In the meantime, she decided to drive to Bridget's Bookstop to look for some new romances to read. A good book was a good diversion.

Ten minutes later, when she parked in the lot next to Christopher's, Millie was feeling sorry for herself. She just knew there wasn't a better location suited for the bakery. She banged her hands on the dashboard, and that's when her phone rang. She recognized Carl's ringtone and answered it. "Hi, what's up?"

"Where are you?" he asked calmly.

"I'm bummed out. Sitting in the car near Christopher's getting ready to walk to Bridget's. So sad . . ."

"About that. I have something to tell you. Sandra called me."

"I just left her."

"I know. She had a question for me."

"Oh?"

"Aren't you curious? You might want to be."

Silence greeted him.

He waited a moment. "Okay, since you're bummed, I might have something to get you unbummed. She wanted to know if I was ready to put in a contract for your proposed bakery."

"But I didn't like any of the locations we looked at."

"Are you sure about that?"

"Yes, absolutely sure."

"Oh, Millie, I thought you loved Christopher's." Carl's speech was deliberate, his voice teasing.

"All right. You've got me really curious. Come on, share."

Carl spoke slowly, drawing out each word. "Seems as soon as Sandra left you, she got a phone call from Christopher. The bank denied Annabel's loan application for a mortgage. She had no choice but to default on the contract. Sandra said Annabel's still trying to come up with a plan to buy the building, but she thought we should put in our offer quickly since right now Christopher is anxious to sell."

Millie froze. It took a minute to absorb what Carl was telling her. She hesitated and then softly said, "Does that mean we have a shot at getting the building after all?"

"I told Sandra to give me a few hours to type up a contract."

Silence again.

"Millie, are you there? You didn't pass out on me?"

"Are you kidding? I'm here! I'd scream, but I'm afraid I'd hurt your ears. Wow! This means I'm going to be opening The Best Doggone Bakery after all. When do we get to celebrate?"

"Don't you think you should wait for our contract to be accepted?"

CHAPTER NINE

Looking Good

Fifteen days later, Millie stood outside Christopher's. She could hardly believe that this building was going to be the site of The Best Doggone Bakery. She pranced around and recalled all the images she had of what she would do to make this place perfect. She glanced at her watch. Where was everyone? She wanted to share her news, and she wanted to tell her friends about the plan for Carl to buy the building and rent it back to them. She rubbed her hands together and wrapped her scarf tighter around her neck. *Brr, it is cold.* Winter sure was here now. She was just about to pull out her phone and start calling everyone when Carolyn, Todd, and MaryEllen arrived with Sandra moments later.

"Hurry! It's cold out here," Millie said, shivering.

Sandra used her key to open the door. They traipsed inside and stood inside the central hallway. Millie stamped her feet and wiggled her toes to warm them, and then she stood on the third step of the staircase and cleared her throat to get everyone's attention.

"All right, everyone, I can't keep the news to myself any longer. Listen up. Our bid was accepted. We settle in thirty days."

"Yippee!" Everyone yelled at once, and Millie's three friends pulled her into a group hug. They danced around till Millie felt herself getting dizzy.

Carolyn took a step backward. "This is great news, and I hate to be a killjoy, but the building isn't yours yet, is it?"

"Carl's handling the settlement. What could go wrong?"

"Oh, okay." Carolyn shrugged as she looked around. "The inside looks so much better than I remember. We always sat in that room off to the right, and it was filled up with those high-top round tables and ice cream parlor chairs. It looks much larger now that it's empty."

Millie bounced down the narrow hallway toward the room on the right, her stomach fluttering as she casually walked to the back of the room where there was a door. "Come take a look at this." She stood aside, holding her breath as she opened the door.

MaryEllen's face split into a wide smile, and she ran over to the ovens, opening each one slowly and attempting to take in all the details. There was a huge stainless steel refrigerator, a center island with a double sink, and even a window that looked out on the back lawn. She opened her arms wide. "Oh my goodness!" She turned toward Millie with a huge grin. "I will love baking here. I can't wait to get started. This all looks brand-new."

"It is. According to Sandra, Christopher hadn't expected to leave, and he just bought all this new equipment. Look around. There is everything you need right here."

Millie went over and put her arm around MaryEllen. She looked at the rest of her team; everyone was smiling. What she wouldn't give for her mom and dad to be here with her now. They'd be so proud of her. She turned away from everyone and wiped a tear from her face.

"Excuse me. I don't mean to interrupt, but I have an appointment scheduled in an hour," Sandra said. "You'll need to get ready to leave so I can lock up."

"Millie, you should chronicle the story of the bakery from today to our opening," Carolyn said.

Millie gave Carolyn a high five. "Super-duper idea. I'll take a few photos now." She retrieved her phone from her handbag. "I bet I can convince Carl to come with his camera. He loves to take photos and record videos."

She walked around taking loads of photos, and after she took the last one in the foyer, she said, "Before we leave, we have one very important piece of business to go over, which I hope will be okay with you. I want you all to think about what I have to say."

"You sound so serious, Millie. Is everything okay?" MaryEllen asked.

"Yes, this is just something we need to talk about," she said as she pointed to the steps. "Please sit. I'm pretty nervous, so I would rather stand." She realized she was biting her lip, so she stopped herself. "Carolyn told me that in order for her to open the bakery with me, she wanted to be a partner, not an employee. She thought it would be better if we were on equal footing. I agreed, and I told her that I would talk to Carl about it. Well, he came up with a plan that I hope will be good for all of us. It's very simple. Carl will buy the building and rent it to us, and the four of us will be equal partners. Is that okay? We tried to keep it simple."

"Millie, that's perfect," Carolyn said, smiling.

"Well, I know it will be fine with Bradley if it's Carl's idea. Bradley loves working with Carl. He thinks he's brilliant," MaryEllen said.

"Wow! That's great for me," Todd said as he got up and hugged Millie. "That's more than I expected."

Millie smiled. "Okay, then if that's settled, let's go, partners!"

She pulled the threesome in for a hug, and they laughed as they tried to hold onto each other, squishing and squeezing through the front door. Sandra closed and locked the door behind them. Millie walked down the few front steps and turned around to face the building. "Someone pinch me. I can't believe I'm actually going to be opening a dog bakery."

MaryEllen and Carolyn, who had followed her down the steps, pretended to pinch her upper arm. "Okay, you guys, I'm sure I'm not dreaming, but I am freezing." She rubbed her bare hands together. "It's too cold to stand out here. Let's go to Miss Annabel's."

"Millie, that's a terrible idea," Carolyn said, frowning.

"Why?" Millie asked. "We're just going there to get something to drink."

"Come on, Millie. She lost; you won. She's likely going to think you came there to gloat."

"Well, if we see her, I can try to talk to her," Millie said as she started walking.

The others exchanged glances as they reluctantly followed Millie to Miss Annabel's, where Millie found the only empty table in a back corner.

A waiter appeared and laid a menu on the table. As Millie handed him back the menu, she said, "Thanks, but we know we want four coffees and a plate of scones for the table, and can you tell me if Annabel is around?"

"She's out running a few errands. She'll be back later."

"Phew," Carolyn mumbled. She held her hand up to her face and whispered to Todd, "Thank goodness! Let's just hope she doesn't show up."

The waiter returned with the carafe of coffee and placed the scones in the middle of the table. Millie took one and put it on the edge of her saucer. "Before we dig in, I'd like to propose a coffee toast in anticipation of opening the bakery. This is getting exciting."

"I agree wholeheartedly." Todd tapped his china cup lightly to Millie's. "But we may not want to be here too long. I'm worried about Annabel."

"Well, she's got to see us sooner or later, and I'm so excited that I want to share some of my ideas of what we should do to get started. See if you agree. I want to begin with cleaning and painting. Then we'll pick out new lighting, and I think we should install bookshelves in the front room on the right. That's the largest room and the one I figure we'll be using the most."

"Gosh, Millie. That all sounds great!" MaryEllen said encouragingly.

"I have two old love seats at home that we're not using. Let's try them in the front room of the bakery," Carolyn suggested.

"What about the outside?" Todd asked as he poured milk into his drink.

Millie sipped her coffee. "We'll spruce it up. Paint the front door. I don't think the porch railing can be painted because it's vinyl, but we can surround it with huge clay pots filled with whatever flowers are in season. The windows will look good if we add shutters and window boxes with flowers."

MaryEllen nodded. "Well, that's all easy. We're right down the street from Frannie's Flowers."

"Can we leave now? Carolyn asked, peering around as if looking for someone.

"Carolyn, don't worry. I know you're looking for Annabel. She's not here. I can see the front door from here, and she hasn't walked in. We'll leave in a minute. I have one last idea to share." Millie leaned forward and held her breath, pausing before she blurted out, "I want to have dog birthday parties."

Todd choked on his coffee. "Okay. I'm going to keep my mouth shut."

"No, really," Millie answered. "I think dog birthday parties could be great. Right now, people have to have them at home. We can offer an alternative. We would charge a party fee for the use of the bakery and sell a birthday cake."

"You could be right. Oh no, look." Todd pointed.

Annabel was heading right for them. She appeared in front of their table. She leaned over the table so she was in Millie's space and loudly announced, "I hear you're planning to open a bakery."

Millie clasped her hands in her lap. She sat up straight, stiffening her spine. "Yes, but you know that already. I'm planning on opening a bakery for dogs. Isn't that great? We'll almost be neighbors. We hope you'll want to come and see us," she said softly.

Annabel's face turned bright red as she spit out, "For dogs? I thought it was for people!"

Millie wasn't there to make a scene, and it surprised her that Annabel was so outspoken. She quickly gazed around to see the couple sitting nearby staring in their direction. Millie wanted to tone it down. She held up her hands, stared at Annabel, and nonchalantly said, "Annabel, you should have asked me about my plans instead of relying on eavesdropping. I didn't try to deceive you or do anything wrong. My bakery is for dog people and their pets."

Millie watched Annabel shifting from one foot to the other, and when she spoke, it was meant only for Millie's ears. "You'll be sorry you messed with me." She turned around and stalked off.

"See, she thought you'd be competition," Carolyn whispered. "Maybe now that she knows it's a dog bakery, she'll calm down."

Todd shook his head. "Not likely. She's got a nasty streak."

"Do you think she'll try to ruin us?" MaryEllen asked. "That's scary."

Millie shrugged. "At this point, I don't know what to think. But if she's bent on stopping us, I guess I should expect her to continue to make trouble. I really didn't think I did anything wrong. I wish she'd just sit down and talk to me."

Carolyn frowned. "Ugh! A fight with Annabel. Not a great way to start. And here we thought she'd be okay with you opening a store nearby."

"We're lucky she didn't ask us to leave. She was really angry," Todd added.

Millie leaned forward, clasped her hands in her lap, and whispered, "I guess you all were right. I was just trying to make things better. I had hoped she would help us, her being here in the Commons. Forget that. I guess I'll have to deal with it. I don't understand how she can think a dog bakery will hurt her. Let's leave."

As quickly as possible, they gathered their coats and exited. It was too cold to stand around outside. Everyone started to disperse. "Wait!" Carolyn held up her hands. "We haven't talked about what it is we plan to sell. Have you checked out ingredients that dogs can eat, MaryEllen?"

CHAPTER TEN

Recipes

The next morning Millie knocked on Bradley and MaryEllen's door at exactly nine o'clock. The entire gang had agreed to meet there just before parting ways after the fiasco at Annabel's. They were going to try out some of MaryEllen's recipes.

"It's open!" MaryEllen called. "Come on in!"

Hickory, Bradley's dog, jumped up and put his paws on Millie's chest. "Oh, you look so handsome," Millie said as she scratched behind his ears. He wagged his tail and then, hearing a noise in the kitchen, ran off to investigate.

Millie followed Hickory. Her three partners already sat around the granite island, drinking coffee and eating biscotti.

Pointing to Millie's black sweater, MaryEllen giggled. "Oh no, Hickory welcomed you."

Millie glanced down at herself, noticing for the first time that her sweater was covered with doggie footprints.

"Sorry, I spilled flour," MaryEllen explained, a sheepish grin tilting up her mouth. "Hickory obviously stepped in it."

Millie dusted herself off. "Makes me feel right at home." She shrugged. "Seems I wear some ingredient or other whenever I bake. So, where's Bradley? I thought he might stick around to help us."

"He's planning on joining us," MaryEllen said. "He's running errands, but he promised me he'd be back soon."

Millie scanned the ingredients sitting on the counter: cooked bacon, carrots, apples, cinnamon, yogurt, eggs, and oats. There was also canned pumpkin, Parmesan cheese, and peanut butter.

"All of you, please listen up. This is important," Millie said as she went to sit next to Carolyn. "We will need an accurate list of ingredients in each recipe. Before we open the bakery, I have to get final approval from the state's department of agriculture to bake the treats. In order to do that, we need to send them a label for each treat. The person I spoke to told me it takes about two weeks to get approval."

MaryEllen shrugged. "That doesn't sound too difficult." She pointed to some file cards as she said, "So far, I have one recipe for a ball-shaped cookie, one for Millie's pupcakes, and one for a doggie doughnut, and all the ingredients are listed. They're the ones I thought we'd try today."

MaryEllen handed Millie a humongous, glossy, traditional white coffee cup trimmed in gold. Millie filed that detail away. She liked the large cup rather than a mug, and the trim added a nice feature. They could possibly use something like that at the bakery.

"Oh, and one other thing," MaryEllen said. "I'm not sure, but how about if we have a little something for the humans to munch on?"

"I don't know." Millie bit her lip. "I don't want to make this job too difficult for you."

"I love to bake biscotti," MaryEllen replied cheerfully. "I can make tons of it at one time. I've even mastered several different varieties."

Todd held up his half-eaten biscotti. "That's a great idea; these are delicious. But wait." He frowned. "That involves getting approval from the health department."

"What's one more approval? It's probably just more inspections and forms to fill out. I can do that if MaryEllen doesn't mind baking them," Millie said. "But now that you say you love to bake biscotti, I just had a great idea."

"What's that?" MaryEllen asked.

"Why not make some biscotti for the dogs, too? I bet you could make it with peanut butter."

MaryEllen smiled. "I'd be happy to try." She picked up a file card and quickly jotted down some notes.

"Perfect. Just remember I want to have birthday parties for dogs, so we need to have a cake recipe, too," Millie said.

"That's easy. The cakes can be made using the same ingredients as the pupcakes. Okay, before we get started," MaryEllen said as she grabbed some cookie trays from a cabinet, "if anyone wants more coffee or some biscotti, help yourself. I figured we'd split up into two groups and each group would work on a different recipe. I have two ovens, so that won't be a problem."

Millie nudged Carolyn. "I'll work with you."

"Okay, fine. I'll work with Todd," MaryEllen said. "Let's just decide what each group is going to make so we can figure out who needs which ingredients. I'll try the apple cinnamon pupcakes first, so we'll need the ingredients for them. What about you two?"

Millie glanced at Carolyn. "If it's okay with you, I want to make the ball cookie. I have an idea for them that I'd like to try, and I'm anxious to see if I can make it work."

"What exactly do you have in mind?" Todd asked. "Maybe we can help you."

"I want to make a round ball, but I want to try to hide something in the middle, like a piece of bacon. We could probably hide a piece of cheese in the middle, too, or even a piece of a vegetable. I'm not exactly sure. I've already named the cookie Luke's Hideaways. Every cookie has a hidden treasure inside—just like when I got Luke, I got a treasure. Now all I need is a cookie named for Annie."

"I like that idea," Todd confirmed. "Although I don't know why I thought I could help you. I have never baked anything without my mother's help."

Carolyn laughed. "Come on, Millie, just let me get coffee, and I'll make the dough."

Once Carolyn was done mixing the dough, Millie formed balls and stuck a small piece of bacon in the middle. As she placed them on the cookie tray, she realized she had a good idea. "We could make some cookies in animal shapes, and they could be called Annie's Animal Crackers."

Carolyn smiled. "That's a great idea. All we need are some cookie cutters in animal shapes—I wonder if MaryEllen has any. But let's save that for later. We have enough to do now."

Once the first batch was ready to bake, Millie and Carolyn put them in the oven and sat at the island. As Hickory wandered around, Millie snuck him bacon when MaryEllen's back was turned. He even brought his smelly tennis ball for her to throw. She threw it a bunch of times. She loved spoiling Hickory, but she needed to get back to work, so she hid the ball in her pocket and fed him a carrot, making sure to wash her hands afterwards.

Carolyn peeked in the oven. "I think they're done. Hand me a mitt."

Millie got up, watching over Carolyn's shoulder as she pulled the golden brown doggie treats from the oven. Right away, Millie was aware of the aroma of cinnamon and vanilla in the air. "I can't wait to see them. Hand me the spatula. Let's let Hickory try one."

Clasping the edge of the cookie sheet with one oven-gloved hand, Millie tried to lift the first cookie off the tray. "Uh-oh, that one crumbled."

"Here, let me try." Carolyn grabbed the spatula. She tried three. They all fell apart. "This whole batch is no good," she whispered. "Oh crap. This is not good."

"Shh," Millie said as her stomach sank. She chewed her lip. She needed a minute to process this. They were there to test the recipes, but MaryEllen could be so unsure of herself that she'd likely be devastated. Millie picked up one of the file cards. "I'm sure we followed the recipe. It probably just needed more eggs. They seemed dry." She peeked over at MaryEllen. "Do you think she noticed?"

At that moment, Bradley strolled in. He took one look around his usually spotless kitchen, which was now anything but spotless. Then he caught sight of Hickory. "What in the world is all over my beautiful collie? He's all white. I hope you guys haven't been testing too many of your recipes on him. He'll get sick later."

Hickory sauntered over to greet Bradley, who hugged him by pulling him close and burying his face in his fur. He shuddered. "He smells like cinnamon, and is that bacon I smell, too? Sis, have you been giving him bacon?" He shook his head. "I know I offered to help, but I just realized I forgot to go to the cleaners."

"Good excuse. Come on, Bradley. You're usually a big help in the kitchen," Millie teased.

"My sweet sister, this looks like a disaster. I'll pass. All I want to know is when are you planning to tell Nicholas and Grant what you're up to?"

"After we settle on the building and figure out what we're selling."

"Well, hurry up. It seems to be taking forever. Every time they call, they ask what's new." He turned and walked out of the room after saying goodbye to everyone.

"Well, so much for him helping us." Millie shook her head.

"It is kind of a mess in here," Todd said.

"He's not much of a help in the kitchen anyway," MaryEllen said as the oven timer dinged. She removed the pupcakes from the oven and placed the muffin pan on the counter. "Let them cool for a bit."

A minute later Todd pried one out as MaryEllen looked over his shoulder. He groaned. "This doesn't look too good. It's not puffed up like a cupcake should be, and the bottom is burnt." He put it down on the counter and blew on it, then he raised it in the air. "Wait a minute. Maybe all is not lost. Let's see how Hickory likes it. Maybe burnt cinnamon and apples will taste good to a dog."

MaryEllen blanched. "I need to get something. I'll be right back."

Carolyn glared at Todd. "Be quiet. You're not helping. MaryEllen has never baked for dogs."

"I was just teasing her."

Millie whispered. "Unfortunately, she didn't get your joke. Let's take a closer look at the recipes. We'll get it right." She tried to speak calmly, even though she could feel her stomach flip-flopping. "I wish we had a computer handy. I'm sure we could find some other recipes."

Carolyn whispered. "Maybe you should go see if she's okay."

Todd kept shifting in his chair, fiddling with the recipe cards and stealing glances at the open doorway that led to the powder room by way of the hallway. "Where do you think she is?"

A minute later, MaryEllen wandered back into the kitchen. Right away, Millie noticed that her eyes looked damp and she was holding a tissue. "I know you're disappointed, but maybe I'm just not any good at this. I don't see any point in baking more today. I'd rather you all leave. Millie, I need to reconsider whether I can do the baking for you. Maybe baking for dogs is not my thing, and it might be that I am not the best partner for you."

Millie ran over and hugged her. "Oh, MaryEllen, it's okay. Don't let our first attempt get you down. How many times have you goofed up a recipe? We just need to tweak these."

"You're right. I've messed up too many times to count, but this time you are all relying on me. I think the pressure might be too much. I don't mean to be rude, but I'd like you all to leave. Give me some time to rethink my decision, and I'll call you."

No one said a word. Instead they all exchanged glances. "Are you sure?" Millie mumbled.

MaryEllen nodded.

Millie gave MaryEllen one last hug. "I'll wait to hear from you, but please call me anytime."

Outside in the parking lot of the townhouse, Carolyn stopped Millie before she closed her car door to ask, "Do you think you should go back inside by yourself and talk to her?"

"I'm not sure that will help, and I certainly don't want to make things worse. She was really upset. I've noticed she has trouble making decisions. I don't want to make her feel like she has to do this. Then she might quit later on. I'll just have to wait and see."

"What are you going to do if she drops out?"

Millie hesitated. "I don't have a clue. But if I need to, I'll come up with something." She took a deep breath. "For now, I'm going home and asking

Carl to take me out to dinner. I'll just have to sit tight. No matter what, she's still my first choice, so I'm stuck waiting till she calls. Cross your fingers."

"Well, if you need to talk, I'm around."

* * *

Millie ran into the house right past Luke and Annie. She wanted so badly to talk to Carl, but he wasn't home. He must have gone to check on something at his jobsite. It was a good time to take Luke and Annie for a walk. She could think about what happened with MaryEllen and come up with a plan to convince her that she could do this job better than anyone. She really didn't want to lose MaryEllen as a partner.

When she sauntered back home fifteen minutes later, she hoped Carl would be there, but his car was still not in the garage. Now she had nothing but time to think. Today had certainly not gone as she'd expected, and she was anxious to hear his opinion, especially when it came to business. She knew she had a lot to learn.

An hour later, when Carl showed up, Millie didn't even give him a chance to say hello before she blurted out, "Nothing went as planned today. MaryEllen is thinking about dropping out."

He pulled her in for a hug. "I'm sorry I wasn't here for you. I figured you wouldn't be home all day. What happened?"

Millie winced. "None of her recipes worked. She was really upset and asked us to leave. She told me not to call her, that she wanted to reconsider being the baker and even a partner. She'll call when she's made a decision."

Carl held her for a minute, patting her back. "She's just frightened. She feels responsible for the success or failure of the bakery. Remember, she's a partner, so she wants it to succeed, too. She's never done anything like this before. Give her time to work it out."

"I got so nervous. I was tongue-tied. It was crummy, and I felt awful. I talked her into doing this with me, and now she feels terrible. I did give her a hug before we all left."

"That was most likely the best thing you could do. In the end, she'll want to help make the bakery a success. Problems come with running a business. Your job as their leader is to come up with solutions. You're smart and clever, so use those assets to help yourself solve this issue. In this case, MaryEllen asked you to leave, so that was the right thing to do."

Millie gave Carl a hug. "You know just the right thing to say to calm me down and make me feel better." She sighed. "I want to be tactful, but sometimes what I say comes out wrong. Because of that, I try not to say anything." She sat down and wrung her hands. "MaryEllen was adamant that we leave. I felt helpless."

"I know how to make you feel better. Let's go out to dinner."

"Oh, I'd love that." She hugged him again and brushed a kiss across his lips. It was as though he read her mind. Maybe tonight she could talk to him about how she wanted him to try to spend more time with her. She knew she'd be really busy with the bakery, but when she was home, she wished he were there, too.

CHAPTER ELEVEN

Trouble

The ringtone of the phone woke Millie. She lifted her head and squinted at the clock radio on Carl's night table. Eight a.m. Who would be calling this early? Maybe MaryEllen? She grabbed the phone and sat up gingerly so as not to wake Luke, who was sleeping soundly at the foot of the bed.

"Millie, it's Sandra. I realize it's early, but I didn't want to miss you. I have some bad news."

Millie clenched the phone, sighing. She felt as though she'd been clenching a lot of her body parts lately.

Sandra continued. "The settlement officer called yesterday. We can't settle on the building."

"What?" She jerked herself up and leaned against her pillow. "That's not possible!"

"Sorry, but it is. Christopher doesn't own the building. Some other name is on the deed. Until we figure out who it is, we cannot move forward. I tried to reach Christopher as soon as I got the call, but he never answered, and as of yet he hasn't called back."

"Can you please call him now? It's early—maybe you'll catch him like you caught me. He has to answer eventually." Millie could feel her head clenching now. She hadn't had a migraine in forever, but she sure could feel one coming. She could barely concentrate on what Sandra was telling her, but she tried to listen.

Sandra rattled on. "It is all so confusing. I can't imagine who owns the building since his family ice cream store has been there for years. I'll be sure to call you when I have more information to share."

The news left Millie feeling blindsided. Would she ever get her bakery opened? She tried to tell herself to keep calm. Everything would be okay.

Good thing she had Carl helping her, and after their talk last night, she knew he'd be more understanding.

At dinner the previous night, she'd broached the subject that at times she was lonely. She told him that since his construction business had started expanding, she had been having a difficult time adjusting. He was gone so many hours every day, and even when he was home, he was often doing work-related things.

With her best friend Joy moving to Colorado and Carl starting this huge townhouse project, Millie had too much time alone. Carl listened to her carefully, and after she finished, he held her hand under the table and reassured her. He promised to try to spend more time with her and to listen to her when she had concerns. Well, she certainly needed him now. He always answered his cell phone. She was sure he'd know what to do.

Millie vaguely remembered Carl kissing her goodbye and telling her that he was heading to his jobsite. She called his cell phone, and when he answered, she tried to speak calmly. "Carl, Sandra just called. You won't believe what she told me. She said we can't settle; there's a problem."

"Did she explain?" Carl asked.

"Only to say Christopher doesn't own the building," Millie replied.

"So who does?"

"She doesn't know. She tried to reach Christopher, but she has yet to talk to him."

"Okay. Mil, this may not be as bad as you think. Give me some time to call Sandra. I'll call you back."

Millie hung up. She hoped she hadn't sounded spoiled or whiny. She didn't want Carl to think that he'd need to hold her hand for every problem and issue that arose. It was important to her that he thought she had what it took to be a success at this. She wanted him to be proud of her.

Sandra's call had taken away Millie's appetite, but Annie and Luke needed to eat. Afterward, she sat with a cup of coffee, trying not to watch the minutes tick by. She needed something more to occupy her time, to keep her mind off this latest stumbling block. In stressful situations, she either ate or cleaned, and cleaning seemed like a better idea right now. She went to the closet and pulled out the vacuum. There was always dog hair to vacuum. She just had to listen carefully for the phone to ring. When it finally did, she ran to grab it.

"Okay," Carl said. "Sandra finally reached Christopher, and even he was shocked to find out he doesn't own the building. His parents assured him before they retired and took off to travel the world that they had transferred the title to him. We're trying to find out from the settlement people exactly whose name is on the deed. I'll call you back when I have more news."

Once Millie finished vacuuming, she had to decide how to keep busy for the rest of the day, or at least until Carl called with some news. She took Annie and Luke outside, and as they ran around, she thought about this newest development. It was nerve-racking, but she wasn't going to let anything derail her dream. Not MaryEllen, and not this mess. She thought back to her conversation with Carl when he had told her business was fraught with problems. Well, she sure was learning that fast.

Hours later, when neither Carl nor Sandra had called, Millie called Carolyn, who sometimes could be a worrywart but in times of trouble always managed to reassure her. Sure enough, she told Millie that there were always showers before the flowers bloomed, or some such saying. Millie laughed until her belly hurt. It was good having a friend like Carolyn.

That evening as Millie sat in bed watching TV, the phone rang. She was afraid to look at the caller ID. She didn't want to deal with any more bad news. It was MaryEllen. She crossed her fingers, not sure she wanted to hear what MaryEllen had to say, but sooner or later she had to know her plans.

"Hi," Millie said tentatively. "So, what's up?"

"Millie, I am so sorry I behaved the way I did yesterday. I hated that the recipes were no good. I just didn't expect that to happen."

Millie took a deep breath and let it out slowly before responding. "I tried to tell you it wasn't a problem—that together we'd figure it out."

"I know, but I needed to think this through by myself. After you left, I spent the rest of the day and night baking. Bradley never got dinner, although the kitchen was such a mess I don't think he much cared. Poor Hickory. He was my tester all night. He willingly tasted everything and never got sick or spit anything out. Anyway, I felt like I had some good recipes by the time I was done. I'd be happy to give them to you, but I still think this job is going to be more than I expected. You should find someone else."

Millie's heart dropped. She hoped the advice Carl had given her would serve her now. "Listen to me for a minute. I actually believe you are right. I've come up with a plan . . . so hear me out."

"I'm listening."

Millie took a deep breath and plunged in. "Instead of baking a bunch of cakes and cookies every day, we only sell one type of cookie per day. For instance, Mondays can be pupcakes, Tuesdays can be Annie's Animal Crackers, and so on. The dogs couldn't care less; they'll like whatever they are given. It will be your decision to bake whatever you want each day. We'll post on a menu board the special of the day. I'm betting that you can handle that. In time, we can expand if we want, but at least we can still do this together, which is what I would really like."

"Um . . . that might work, but what about Carolyn and Todd? They may not like your idea."

"MaryEllen," Millie said, "Carolyn and Todd will be thrilled you're not dropping out. Like me, I know they care much more about having you as part of the team."

Silence greeted her. She chewed her lip. Was her idea going to work?

"Well, I like your solution, and it will definitely make the job more doable, but I still want to think about it."

"Done. Take whatever time you need."

Millie hung up and crossed her fingers again, hoping this solution would work.

CHAPTER TWELVE

Ducks in a Row

The next morning as Carl put on his coat to leave for his jobsite, Millie asked him to please contact Sandra.

"If I don't hear from her by noon, I will," he said as he kissed her goodbye. A few hours later, after she had fed and walked the dogs and cleaned the kitchen, she tried opening a book, but even though she loved the romantic comedy she was reading, she couldn't concentrate.

Carl finally called Millie around eleven. "Good news, sort of. Sandra found out that it's Christopher's grandparents' names on the deed. Obviously, for some unknown reason, his parents and grandparents deceived him. Now she has to locate the grandparents. Sandra seems to remember Annabel was friendly with them and knows where they are."

"Oh no, that's terrible news. If Annabel knows them, she'll never tell Sandra where they are. And especially if she knows it's for me, you can forget it. There has to be another way to find them."

"Mil, hang tight. I explained everything to Sandra. She thinks she'll still be able to get the number. We'll just have to wait and see, but Sandra's good. Have faith. We'll get this worked out. I'm sure the grandparents don't want the building empty. When it comes to business, friends don't always count. They did give Annabel a shot at it, and she failed to deliver."

"That makes sense. I'll wait to hear from you."

Millie hated the feeling of not being in control of events. It reminded her of when her parents died in the car accident. It was difficult to know she couldn't control every aspect of her life. She had to work with the cards dealt to her and make the best of it. But even now, the ups and downs of the process were tricky for her to handle. She just wanted to be able to open the bakery and to have all the rough patches behind her. She reminded herself again that Carl had told her problems were going to be a constant part of being in business.

Trying not to be impetuous, Millie had held off from calling her younger brothers, but she really wanted to share her plans with them, even if the worst-case scenario happened and she didn't get the property. Bradley had told her that it was time to tell them. She decided to send a text message to both of them asking if they could call her when they were together. She knew they met up often, so she figured she wouldn't have long to wait for them to call.

Sure enough, within the hour her cell rang. "Hi, sis," said Nicholas. "Grant and I are together, and I have you on speaker. So, what's up?"

"I have news, and I want to share it with both of you."

"Okay, is it good or bad news?"

"As far as I'm concerned, it's great news. I'm planning to open a dog bakery, and I'm really excited about it."

"What?" they both said at once.

Millie giggled. She was rarely able to surprise them, but this time she surely had done a good job. They were obviously stunned because, other than that one word, there was silence for a few seconds.

"Wow! I'm not sure I know what to say except that sounds great. Tell us more," Nicholas said.

Before she could answer, Grant interrupted. "I'm impressed too, but wait, I do have one very important question. Did Luke have anything to do with your decision? Was it because he wants an unlimited supply of fresh cookies?"

Millie rolled her eyes. *Okay, I totally expected to be teased. Two can play this game.* "Yes," she replied. "He suggested the idea. One day a month ago, the pet store was out of his favorite treats. He came to me that night and pawed me. I had fallen asleep earlier than usual, and he was upset that he hadn't gotten his bedtime snack. He proposed a solution to solve his problem. He suggested I open a dog bakery to make sure he had an endless supply of cookies for the future." She bit her lip to keep from laughing.

"I knew it was Luke! He is the only one of us who can get you to do whatever he wants. But what about a location?" Grant continued to play with her.

"The perfect spot came on the market—Christopher's Ice Cream and Cookie Shoppe. He shut down, and Carl is in the process of helping me obtain the building. The Best Doggone Bakery will open there. MaryEllen is going to be the baker, and Carolyn and Todd are working with me, too."

"Jeez, sis, I know we don't talk often, but how did all of this happen so fast?" Nicholas asked.

"Okay, to be serious, it didn't seem to me that it happened so fast. It's just that I didn't want to tell you until I was pretty sure it would work out." Millie crossed her fingers, hoping that was true.

"I bet Luke will be thrilled. He will get to spend all his days with you and eat all the cookies he wants." Nicholas laughed. "So, I'm guessing Bradley is onboard with this?"

"Yes, and before you call him, just remember I asked him not to say anything. I know how you work, and I figured I'd rather be teased after I knew it was a reality."

"Sis, this will be so good for you," Grant said. "We all know how much you love dogs. Just think, once I'm a vet, hopefully I'll be practicing nearby, and I'll have lots of customers to send your way. I'm really happy for you. I bet you will make this a rousing success. So, when do you expect to open?"

"That's difficult to know yet. As soon as possible is the plan."

"Well, I can't wait to see photos. You can keep me and Nick in the loop that way."

"Of course. That's a great idea."

"One question. Does Luke know he'll be getting *free* cookies? Once he figures that out, he'll be constantly pawing you."

Millie giggled. Some things never changed; she was expecting this. "Absolutely. He's excited. He's even been asking if there will be a cookie named after him."

Grant laughed. "So did you?"

"Of course. Luke's Hideaways. Every cookie has a treasure hidden inside, just like Luke is my treasure. We'll also offer Annie's Animal Crackers."

"Well, we all know Luke is your favorite. Glad you thought about Annie, too. I have to say this all sounds great. One last very important question: Are Nicholas, Bradley, and I going to have cookies named for us?" Before she could answer, he added, "Just kidding."

Millie smiled. "I love you guys, you know that."

"Yes, and we love you back. Remember to send photos, and we'll talk soon."

Millie hung up.

* * *

Grant and Nicholas sat staring at each other. Nicholas spoke first. "Well, I guess you could say our sister really surprised us. I'm happy for her. This sounds good to me. She loves dogs, MaryEllen loves to bake, and Carolyn and Todd are really good people."

"I totally agree," Grant said, nodding. "Listen, I had a few minutes to think about this, and I have an idea. How about we surprise her and Carl and go home once she opens?"

"Great idea. I like it," Nicholas said, smiling at his brother. "Let's give it some thought and come up with a plan."

CHAPTER THIRTEEN

Meetings

Sandra had come through, and now Millie stared at the building that would become The Best Doggone Bakery. *This is really happening!* She stuck her key in the lock and pushed the door open.

All Millie knew was that Sandra had somehow managed to get the location of the grandparents and emailed them a new contract of sale. They'd signed it, the title company had changed the deed, and they had settled on the building yesterday. Carl now owned the building.

So, here she was standing in the center hallway, allowing herself to dream. She visualized opening the door and sniffing air filled with the aroma of vanilla, cinnamon, and maybe sometimes smelly dog fur. There were dogs plopped on the floors, dogs perched on people's laps, and one huge Great Dane with his feet up on the counter ordering his own cookie. It was fun to picture her partners walking around sporting baseball caps and aprons with a Best Doggone Bakery logo printed on them.

"Hi, we're here!" Todd said, walking through the door with Carolyn and disrupting Millie's dream.

"Oh good, you're here," Millie said, smiling. "I've been standing here visualizing all the dogs that will be coming here soon."

"And I can't wait to see them eating my treats," MaryEllen said, coming through the door behind Todd and Carolyn.

Millie giggled and pulled her in for a hug. "I'm so happy you decided to do this with us. We're a team, and we're all here to help each other."

"I know that, and having to think about whether I wanted to do this or not was, in the end, not such a difficult decision. I know you will all help me out, and when I finally decided to stay in, I did come up with what I think is a really good idea I want to run by you."

"We're listening," Millie said as Carolyn and Todd nodded, smiling.

"I want to put something on all my treats that serves as my signature, just like a designer puts a label on their clothes. My signature will be a strawberry. Strawberries are one of my favorite foods, and I'm always sharing mine with Hickory. I have a story to tell you about that. The first time he ate one, it was because it fell on the floor. Bradley wasn't home and I totally panicked, thinking he might die. You have to remember I never had a dog before, and the first thing that came to mind was Bradley warning me raisins and grapes are on the no-no list for dogs. So right away I googled 'Can dogs have strawberries?' Thank goodness the news was good. I found out that not only could they have them, they are also a nutritional powerhouse for them. They are full of antioxidants and boast high fiber and a lot of vitamin C.

"Fast forward to now. We'll put a strawberry on the top of Millie's pupcakes. Won't that be perfect? And when I cannot put a real strawberry on a treat, I'll use a pastry tool to draw a strawberry with red frosting. What do you think?"

Everyone tried to talk at once. They laughed.

Millie held up her hand. "Okay, let's vote on MaryEllen's idea. Do we all agree it's fantastic?"

"Yes!" they all chimed in together.

Once they all calmed down, they stood around until Carolyn murmured, "We certainly didn't think this through very well. We don't have anything to sit on. I have an old bridge table and some folding chairs at home. Todd can help me load them in my car, and I'll bring them next time we meet."

"Thanks!" Millie covered her face with her hands. "I never thought about needing those things, but I did bring two whiteboards with me. For now, let's sit on the stairs," she suggested as she walked over to sit on them. "We won't be here long. On one board, I thought we could draw up a preliminary rendering of how we think the bakery should look; on the second one, we should start to make a list of some of the things we need to do before we open."

"Good idea," MaryEllen said enthusiastically.

Todd nodded. "We should do some measurements so we know what will fit correctly."

Millie winced. "Yes, measuring would be a great idea—if only I had thought to bring a measuring tape. Sorry! I was so excited about finally getting started that I forgot everything else. I promise to plan better in the future. So, let's just decide on a general concept of how we want the space to look."

They were all huddled together on the staircase, gazing at Millie as if they expected her to reveal her next great idea. *Wow!* Even though they were all partners, they were looking to her to be their leader and their inspiration. *Well, so this is what it feels like to be a business owner. Pretty cool.*

"Okay, this is what I'm thinking. We want this place to feel like home to our furry friends and their owners, so our furniture should reflect that vision." Millie wrote "Furniture Pieces Needed" on the top of one of the whiteboards. "Now we need a list, I guess, of different items of furniture." She was waiting for someone to make a suggestion when, out of the corner of her eye, she spotted Annabel walking up to the door.

"Don't look now. You're not going to believe me, but Annabel is about to walk through the front door."

"Yikes!" Carolyn whispered. "What's she doing here?"

"We're about to find out," Todd said.

Annabel entered and marched up to Millie. "Oh look, the whole motley crew is here. What's wrong? You don't have anything to sit on but your asses!" she laughed.

"Annabel, if you're here to insult us, please leave."

"Nah, just here because I'm nosy. I think I'll walk around."

"Annabel, there's nothing here to see yet. We're having a meeting here, so I'd appreciate it if you'd leave." Millie pointed to the door.

"Well, that's disappointing. I walked here thinking I'd get a peek at what you were up to. I guess I can always come back." She turned around and stomped off. The door slammed shut behind her.

"What was that about?" MaryEllen asked, puzzled.

"I have no idea." Millie sighed. "I'm just glad she's gone."

"Don't count on it," Todd replied. "She harbors grudges. She'll be back."

"Great, can't wait," Millie quipped sarcastically. "You know, it's almost like she is still back in high school, and she's one of the mean girls. I don't get her. She's never said why she wanted this store. She seems to be doing well with the one she has, so why does she want another one?" She shrugged, adding, "I'm willing to try and talk to her, but I get the feeling that would only make her angrier. It's like she's jealous of me, but I don't believe I've ever done anything to make her dislike me as much as she seems to."

Carolyn put her arm around Millie. "Millie, you don't have to do anything. You have a husband who adores you and is now helping you open your own business. Everyone knows Carl is building that huge project down on the inlet. He's obviously successful. And none of us really knows how well her store is doing. For now, maybe the best you could do is to just try not to rile her up."

"Okay, that's fine with me. I'd really rather not have a problem with her."

Millie thought for a minute. "Look, I know the plan was to sit here and hash out some more ideas, but it might be better if we go home and think about our visions for this place. Let's plan to meet in a few days to share our ideas, okay?"

CHAPTER FOURTEEN

Back Again

Carolyn and Todd brought the table and chairs for the partners' second meeting. They set up in the room on the right, and Millie spread out each of their drawings. "Well," she said, "it looks like we all had similar ideas to make the bakery look like someone's old, comfy home with big sofas and chairs. The biggest difference is that I have one room with a table that's large enough for the birthday parties."

"Only you would think of that," Carolyn said as her partners glanced at each other and started giggling. "But won't putting a table in there be wasting space we might need every day?"

"Not really," Millie explained, pointing to her drawing. "The table doesn't need to be so large that it takes up the whole room, and even though I can't draw well, you can see I placed a few cozy chairs in there."

"I can't believe we're taking up a big space for dog parties. It's hard to imagine people might really do that here," Todd added disapprovingly.

"I think you're wrong," Millie said, shaking her head. "I think it can be a big source of revenue for us."

"Changing the subject," Carolyn said, "I have two love seats you might like to try. I even have someone who can help us move them here."

Todd shook his head. "I don't think that's a good idea. We have no idea if they'll fit well. Plus, how do we know if they will wear well?"

Millie chewed on her fingernail. "Todd, you might be right, but you have to stop nixing everything. It's a sure thing we're going to make mistakes, but we have to be open-minded. Let's try them. We have to start somewhere, and they're free after all."

"Okay, I get it. I'll try to be more positive."

"So, if you're doing that, I'd like to have some floor-to-ceiling bookshelves in this room. Can you do that?" Millie asked, pointing to the wall she had in mind.

"I think that's a good idea, Millie, and I have a buddy who's a great carpenter. I don't think I could do it by myself," Todd said, shaking his head. "I'll ask him."

"That's perfect," Millie said, tapping MaryEllen on her arm. "I'd like you to set up the kitchen. You'll know best what you want or need. One thing, though: You should set up a recipe book for all of us. That way we can always do the baking if you're not here."

Contemplating her next thought, Millie put her elbows on the table, propped her hands under her chin, and told the group, "My job will be to line up the carpenters, painters, electricians, and any other subs. Carl can give me all the names we'll need. I'll also take care of hiring someone to help us design a logo and a sign for outside. And most importantly, I'm going to make sure we have some way of knowing when anyone comes through the door.

"Oh, and one other thing: Does anyone have a suggestion of who I can call to get aprons made for us?" Millie looked at her partners.

Todd shook his head. "An apron? Seriously? I have to wear an apron?"

"Of course." Millie laughed. "Remember you're trying to be positive, and chefs always wear aprons. It'll be fine."

"I know someone who designs T-shirts," Carolyn said. "Maybe she knows someone. I'll call her."

"Thanks! Well then, I guess we're done for today," Millie said as she stood up and gathered all the drawings together. "I'll call you when I think we should meet again, but keep in mind our goal should be to open in three or four months."

CHAPTER FIFTEEN

The Space

Ten days later, Millie asked her partners meet her at the bakery around five p.m. She had been at the site every day watching over the construction work, and she was excited for them to see the progress on the building. Carl's help had been invaluable. He stopped by every day to make sure that the work was being done to his specifications. A bonus was getting to see him during the day, especially when they managed to slip away and enjoy a quiet lunch.

Carl had suggested some small changes which the carpenters had completed. The most complicated one had been changing the door to the kitchen from a swing door to a pocket door. The electricians had done such a superb job on the inside that Carl had asked them to do some work on the outside. He had asked them to add a lantern on the side of the front door and post lamps along the path that led from the street to the bakery. Christopher had used only a few lights up on the roofline, and it had always been tricky walking up the path when it started to get dark. Carl had insisted that the area be safe for everyone.

The night the work was done, the building looked fantastic with all the lights blazing. Millie and her partners had decided that they'd open only during the daytime, but their plan was to eventually open in the early evening, so the lighting would serve them well.

The interior of the old place was greatly improved, too. Already Millie could see her vision taking shape. The old lights had all been removed and replaced with wall sconces and recessed lighting.

By the time her partners were set to arrive, she was bouncing around and peeking out the side window looking for them. Finally, even though it was getting dark, she went outside and waited on the front porch. Todd was the first to walk up the path. As he got close to her, he pointed to the new lights. "Wow! Those look great. Nice touch."

A minute later, Carolyn and MaryEllen arrived. Together the foursome walked into the bakery to the sound of jangling bells.

"Oh, I like the sound of the bells," Carolyn said as she touched the large jingle bells on a bright red ribbon. "For some reason, when you mentioned we needed something to tell us when someone walked in the door, I thought you meant a buzzer. The bells are so much better. Can we hear them all throughout the place?"

"Yes, my worrywart partner," Millie said as she put her arm around Carolyn. "I tested it out myself. That's why there are several bells. One wouldn't have been loud enough if we were in one of the back rooms, but with several it's fine."

"How did you manage to get so much done so quickly?" MaryEllen asked as she walked over to peek into one of their front rooms.

"We have Carl to thank for that. He sent over his heating and air-conditioning guys so we could have heat that really works. He knew that was probably the most important sub to get here. Then, yesterday and today, the electricians and carpenters worked here, and tomorrow the painters start. Later this week, Carl is sending his landscapers to clean up the outside. Right now it has the look of an abandoned house."

"Not so much anymore," Carolyn said. "I can't wait to see it all done."

"So, come look at the kitchen. I can't wait for you see the lighting in there." Millie walked down the hallway and through the room on the right to the back wall, and then she opened the door. Holding out her hands with a wave, she said, "Ta-da!"

"Ah, Millie, this is so much better!" MaryEllen said as she strolled into the kitchen and looked around the space. "It's fun thinking about baking in here."

The bells on the door jangled, and a voice called out, "Hi! Anyone here?"

"Oh, you're right! We can hear the bells back here. That must be my friend Joey," Todd said. "I asked him to bring Carolyn's love seats since he has a truck. He'll need help." Todd started to walk to meet him. "It'll take us two trips to get them out of the truck. Thank goodness I reminded him to bring a hand truck. We'd have had a hard time carrying them up the path."

When the first love seat was placed inside, the foursome and Joey stood back and stared at it.

"Todd, can you and Joey move it slightly to the left, next to where we plan to put the bookshelves?" Millie asked, chewing on her lip.

"If we're using both, they should be at a ninety-degree angle to each other," MaryEllen suggested.

Carolyn frowned. "It doesn't look right. Maybe when we see the second one with it, they will look better."

"You know what?" Millie said with her hands on her hips. "Let's be honest. It looks terrible!"

"So, what do we do now?" Carolyn slumped down on the sofa.

"I tried to tell you they weren't going to work," Todd said hesitantly, trying not to sound judgmental.

Carolyn grimaced. "Joey, I guess—if you don't mind—can you take them back to my house?"

At that moment, the bells jangled again, and someone yelled out, "So, where's the party?"

"Oh no, you've got to be kidding," Carolyn whispered. "That sounds like Annabel."

"Jeez, it is her," MaryEllen said. "I would recognize that high-pitched voice anywhere. Why does she keep showing up here?"

"I hope you're ready for her insults," Todd whispered, rolling his eyes and shaking his head.

"Hello, darlings!" Annabel's shrill voice rang out as she and Bridget entered the bakery and walked over to where the group was huddled together. "Bridget and I were walking to our cars when we saw all the lights blazing.

It was my suggestion that we walk over to see what was going on. Oh, I see you've put in new lighting. Awfully bright, isn't it? And look at the pretty sofa. So cute, and what an interesting color! Do you mind if Bridget and I poke around?"

Millie held her breath, thinking that was an interesting choice of words, "poke around." Did Annabel intend to mean something nefarious? And what was with her other comments about the lights and the sofas? Obviously, Todd was right and Annabel was trying to insult her. She clenched her teeth and bit the inside of her lip. She'd love to ask Annabel to leave, but there was no way she'd say anything in front of Bridget, who was the bookstore owner and someone she liked.

Millie shrugged. "Annabel, you were just here a few days ago. How much do you think has been done since then? But if you must, suit yourself. Look around."

Annabel smiled. "Come on, Bridget. Let's see what a dog bakery looks like." She walked off with Bridget trailing behind. Bridget turned back toward Millie and gave her a sheepish look. She looked uncomfortable as she walked off down the hallway toward the kitchen.

The foursome stayed huddled together. Millie whispered, "One of you follow her around. Make sure she's not up to something. Bridget looks like she's uncomfortable. If Annabel is up to no good, I'm afraid she won't tell us."

"I'll do it," Todd said, being uncharacteristically agreeable. "If you remember, I'm the one who said she's trouble."

"I know, Todd, and I wish I had listened to you. I'm just not sure what I could have done differently."

Five minutes later, after Annabel and Bridget left, Millie and her group all sighed with relief. "So, did she ask you any questions?" Millie quizzed Todd.

"Just asked me about when we expect to open. Otherwise, they just looked around. Bridget loved the kitchen setup, but Annabel didn't say anything. Although when I tried to observe her expressions, she looked positively devious, if there's a look for that."

"I guess it was a good thing she was with Bridget." Millie sighed. "She probably wouldn't do anything in front of her. It made me keep my mouth shut. But enough about Annabel. Look, it's getting late. I was about to tell you guys something when we were rudely interrupted. When Carl bought the building, he took out a loan to cover both the purchase price and the remodeling cost. Now I understand how smart that was. There's enough money for new furniture. I'll review the numbers with Carl so we know what we can spend. We still need money for painters and some other things, but we need to get everything done ASAP if we're going to open soon. I'll get back to you."

* * *

As she drove home, Millie used her imagination to envision the furniture. She didn't want sleek or modern. She wanted puffy sofas and giant chairs big enough for humans and dogs. She knew that wasn't reasonable with dogs being their primary customers, but maybe she could find another option. Maybe thick leather would work and she could get big, puffy pillows. Those she could replace fairly often. What were her options? Well, she could try to do it herself. She rolled her eyes. Doing that meant it would probably look like a hodgepodge at best. *Better to call for help and get someone who is an expert at decorating.*

Once Millie reached that conclusion, it was easy to make a decision. She knew her partners would agree with her. She was going to call Alfred, another old friend who was now a designer. He'd helped her with her house. Hopefully, he'd help with the bakery.

Once at home, as usual Millie fed and walked the dogs. Luke started pawing her as soon as they got back inside. "Okay, Luke, give me a minute," she said as she found the phone and sat on the den sofa. Sure enough, he jumped up with her. After petting him and talking to him a bit, she called Alfred, who answered almost immediately.

"Alfred, it's Millie. I desperately need your assistance."

"Is Carl finally letting you do your bedroom?"

"I wish, but no. What I have in mind is much more interesting." Millie crammed in the next words really fast. "Carl bought a building. I'm opening a dog bakery with three partners, and we need help."

Silence greeted her. Millie shook her head. "Are you there? Did you hear me? Are you going to laugh at me like everyone else?"

"I was thinking about it."

"So . . ." Millie hesitated. "Will you please help?"

"Um, why don't you start at the beginning? When did this all come about?"

"Oh, it's always been something I've dreamed about doing. Recently, an opportunity came up to buy Christopher's Ice Cream and Cookie Shoppe. Now my partners and I are going to open The Best Doggone Bakery in that spot."

"I know that space. How perfect for you—but you know I don't do commercial interiors."

Millie chewed on her lip. "But you see, we don't want it to look commercial. I want it to look like an old English manor house, and you can do that. Please help us. I'll even give you an incentive. How about if your precious little Bonnie can have free pupcakes for the first six months after we open?"

Alfred laughed. "I gather pupcakes will be one of your bakery items, and you think if you can bribe me, I'll agree to help you."

Millie laughed. "Sort of."

"Millie, you don't need to bribe me. I'll do it, and together we'll knock everyone's socks off."

CHAPTER SIXTEEN

Dry Run

It was the day of the dry run, and Millie was having a serious case of butterflies. It was like being six years old and having a piano recital all over again. Whenever she had to be front and center, the butterflies took over, making her feel even more nervous. Today was no exception, and even her first-choice breakfast of an English muffin with her favorite stuffed-with-whole-blueberries blueberry jam wasn't enticing, especially knowing it would probably make her feel green.

Millie paced around the house, reciting inventory items in her head. Pupcakes, human biscotti, plates, napkins, cups—the list went on and on. That was all she could think about. *It's okay if you forget something. That's the whole purpose of today.* At least that's what she told herself. It was a practice day with invited friends and family. If only Carl was around to hug her, but he had already left for work, telling her he'd see her later, probably shortly after they opened at eleven.

Too fidgety at home, Millie found her handbag, told Luke and Annie to sit tight and that she'd save a pupcake for them, and drove off to the bakery. First to arrive, she sat in her car and stared up at the bold mustard yellow sign. It read "The Best Doggone Bakery." Excitement bubbled up like champagne. *I love it.* Honestly, it was like she was the birthday girl who had blown out the candles and had her wish come true.

Grabbing her cell phone, she got out of her car to take several photos of the outside to email to Nicholas and Grant. Maybe they'd find a weekend to come home from college. They'd be really proud of her—at least that's what she hoped.

The last photo she took was her favorite. It showed the banner tied to their porch announcing the grand opening in three days. How cool was that?

Finished, she breathed on her hands to warm them from the cold, wintry air and was just wondering where her partners were when they came into her view, walking up the path.

Carolyn ran up to her, her five-foot-two frame dressed mostly in her favorite color, powder pink, reminding Millie of cotton candy. She twirled around, showing off her outfit. "I can't believe our practice opening is today. It seems like it all happened so fast!"

"Jeez, Millie, where are Luke and Annie?" MaryEllen asked. "I hoped to give them a pupcake before everyone arrived. I wanted to make sure they were okay."

"They'll be here later. Carl's bringing them. But please don't worry; the pupcakes are absolutely perfect," Millie said as she squeezed MaryEllen's shoulder. "Remember, you gave them one yesterday." She turned her head, a giggle bubbling up that she didn't want MaryEllen to hear. For whatever reason, MaryEllen just couldn't get it through her head that dogs weren't all that picky. Quite honestly, the humans would like the pupcakes, too. Not surprisingly, since MaryEllen had worked in a people bakery, they looked like the cupcakes found in those specialty cupcake stores with sprinkles and icing piled up high and swirled to perfection with a big strawberry on top.

"Hey, you guys. Did you see our sign is up?" Millie pointed to the roof. "I had my doubts when the sign company said they weren't sure they'd get here yesterday. Good thing you weren't here to see me when I first saw it. You would have laughed at me. I strutted around like a penguin puffing up its chest. I knew for sure my dream had come true." Looking down at her watch, she saw it was almost eleven o'clock. "Let's head on in. We should make sure we're ready."

As Millie went to unlock the door, she glanced around the porch, checking to make sure that it was clean and that no leaves were lying around. She flipped on the lights and looked around proudly. A small, rectangular chest with a stylish lamp on top sat against the wall next to the stairs. She moved slightly to the left to look into one of the front rooms. This space was her personal favorite. Alfred had selected two sofas covered in thick brown leather that he hoped would withstand dogs' toenails and drool, and he had upholstered three big, puffy pillows in a red and green plaid. The sofas faced each other with a large wicker coffee table between them. A pair of oversized brown leather barrel chairs sat next to each other with a table between them as well. They faced the sofas and were purposely large enough for a human and a dog. A small, bell-shaped lamp sat on the table, the yellow shade covered with shelties of all different colors. On one wall were the floor-to-ceiling bookshelves that Todd had constructed with his friends' help. There wasn't much on them, other than a few dog-themed items, but she knew exactly what she would do with them.

Next, Millie peered into the room she considered the birthday party room. It contained a rectangular table that Alfred had painted a light brown with paisley bones and dog bowls painted on the surface. The neatest feature was that Alfred had cut the table legs and the chair legs so they were not so high off the ground. The two of them hoped this would work for their canine guests. He had applied a heavy coat of lacquer over the entire surface to preserve the painted design. For the chairs he had found tie-on striped cushions, as she had insisted they be washable. In front of the window, Alfred had positioned a seven-foot ficus tree in a huge ceramic pot. The tree brought some needed warmth to the space.

Walking toward the back and looking into what was now called the "order room," Millie shouted out to her team, "Come back here—Alfred just finished here late last night. He's pulled off the perfect setup!" This was the room where the customers would come to place their orders, and all they would see was a counter housing the coffee equipment, but there was also a hidden, custom-made drawer for accepting payments. There was a small area that looked out of a side window, and four tables and chairs were placed there. All the chairs were extra wide to fit humans as well as their dogs. The kitchen equipment, including the ovens, sink, and other baking utensils, were in the kitchen behind a new pocket door cleverly constructed at the back of the room.

"I agree, Mil," MaryEllen said as she came up behind Millie. "I can hide in my kitchen, and if the dogs spit out their treats, I'll never know."

Millie grinned and put her arm around MaryEllen. "All will be fine."

"What are you going to say if one of the dogs asks to give you his paw as a thank-you for making such wonderful goodies?" Todd said, smiling. "Are we allowed to come and get you?"

"All of you, just chill," Millie teased. She left them to spar with each other while she went on a last-minute check of the other rooms. To the left of the kitchen and order room was a room for overflow. That room was nothing special. She hadn't wanted to spend a lot more money, so she and Alfred had found picnic-style tables to put in there for now. They had tried to find extra-wide benches, better for the dogs, to put with the tables. But gazing around, one of Millie's favorite accoutrements were all the wall sconces placed in every room. They added to the warm, cozy atmosphere. Missing was some art for the walls, but she had a plan in mind. Harper's art gallery was down the street, and Millie hoped Harper might lend her some dog portraits to display.

She wandered back to the order room. They needed to give names to each room. She'd have to give that some thought. Calling it the "order room" sounded awful. Maybe to make it easy, they should name each room after a dog in literature or on TV. They could add a plaque outside each room to identify it.

"Todd, I packed up some books that we can put on the bookshelves. Let's go get them from my car," Millie said as she went to find her key fob.

A few minutes later, Todd placed the two boxes on the floor next to the bookcase.

"You sure brought a lot," Carolyn said as she peeked into one of the boxes. "Are they for display only?"

"I've got that covered," Millie said. She pulled out a small sign that she had printed telling the customers that the books were for their reading pleasure but to please leave them in the bakery so they'd be available for the next person. A postscript was added at the bottom telling everyone that the nearby bookstore, Bridget's Bookstop, would be happy to order them a copy of any of the books they saw there.

"Oh, look." Carolyn pulled out *Lassie Come Home*. "An oldie but goodie. I remember the movie with Elizabeth Taylor."

Millie smiled. She picked up *Lad: A Dog* by Albert Payson Terhune. That book had been a childhood favorite. She had read and reread that book, over and over again, trying to imagine what it was like to have a dog. Millie's mother had been afraid of dogs and had never allowed Millie to have one. As a child, she believed that was a tragedy, and it was certainly part of the reason for her deep love of dogs as an adult.

Next, she picked up *Mollie's Tail*. She displayed it facing out so people could easily see it. The story was one of her favorites. It was about a four-year-old sheltie rescued from being euthanized.

Millie's stomach growled. "Breakfast was a nonstarter this morning. Now I'm starving. Can I get some biscotti? Are there enough?"

"Wait up! I've got a surprise that I hid outside our front door." Todd smiled. "I brought champagne. And before you ask, we don't have to drink it out of coffee mugs, because I did remember flutes, even if they are plastic."

"Oh, how nice! Pink bubbles for us. Goody. Matches my outfit," Carolyn said as she danced around in her pink mohair sweater set and black pants.

Minutes later, when everyone's glass was full, Millie proposed a toast. "May our bakery be successful beyond our wildest dreams."

While everyone was clinking and sipping, Millie thought she heard a knock on the door. "Did you hear that?" Millie asked. "No one should be here yet." She put down her glass and walked over to open the door. Carolyn trailed behind her. A man was standing there in a starched white shirt and tie. *Weird.* "May I help you?" Millie asked.

"Yes. I'm from the health department. May I come in?" he said in a hoarse, commanding voice.

Millie held the door open for him. "Yes, of course. But may I ask why you're here?"

He held out a document for Millie. She hesitantly took it from him. She saw the word "Complaint" written at the top, and her stomach dropped. *What is this all about?* She bit her lip. She was afraid to open her mouth and possibly say the wrong thing. She waited for the gentleman to speak.

"The health department received a complaint about this address. I'm here to do a full inspection," he said gruffly.

Millie's head snapped back, and she took a step backward. "That's—" She clamped down her lips and put her fingers over her mouth. *Not a good way to start.* She took a deep breath and let it out slowly. She managed to get out what she wanted to say. "I don't understand. We've passed all our inspections. Are you saying someone complained when we aren't even officially open for three days yet? Maybe you have the wrong address."

He pointed to her address on the form he had handed her. "I'm at the right place."

Millie frowned. "Can you come back tomorrow? Today is our unofficial opening, and our first guests are just walking up behind you." She hoped she hadn't sounded whiny.

The inspector shook his head. "No." But in a conciliatory voice, he added, "I can try to be unobtrusive."

"As much as I appreciate that," Millie said as she pointed to his lanyard, "everyone can see who you are." She stood to the side of the door and waved him in. She was feeling sick. She leaned against the doorframe to gather her thoughts and said, "Go ahead. If you have any questions, please ask."

After he walked off, Carolyn put her hand on Millie's forearm. "We'll be okay, Mil. Think about it. Probably no one will even notice him or his ID. They'll be too concerned about how their dogs are behaving."

Millie just scoffed. "Are you kidding? A man in a shirt and tie? Of course, everyone will notice him. Well, there's nothing we can do to stop him. If anyone asks, just say he's here to do our final inspection. No one will question that."

Carolyn sighed. "I hope this is not a bad sign."

Millie stopped herself from making a negative comment. One of her most important jobs was to be a positive force for her crew. "Remember, today is our practice run. We'll be fine. Come on, isn't that one of your friends walking in now?" She pointed to the bottom of the outside steps.

Carolyn walked outside and stood on the porch waiting to greet her friend. It was Judy with her two adorable long-haired dachshunds, who were wearing small blue bows in their hair. On their heels came MaryEllen's friend with an adorable Jack Russell terrier. Next came Todd's cousin, who looked just like him with his tortoiseshell glasses, freckles, and short hair.

Millie smiled, left Carolyn with the guests, and headed back to the order room. "I'm here to help. Seems as if everyone is coming at the same time." She elbowed Todd and smiled at MaryEllen. "This is fun."

They worked side by side fixing drinks and serving pupcakes and biscotti. It was great to hear the oohs and aahs when everyone saw the decorated pupcakes and said, "Are these really for dogs? I didn't realize dogs ate strawberries."

"Millie, take off and go mingle. This is a very special day for you," Todd told her. "MaryEllen and I have this covered."

"I would if I wasn't so worried about the health inspector," Millie said as she peeked around to see if anyone had heard her. "I don't want him to come up and ask me a question while I'm talking to them. How about I stay here and you go say hi to your friends? You might just garner us some mighty good compliments."

Todd didn't appear to hear her; he seemed focused on something outside. Millie watched him walk over to the window. As he pressed his face against the glass, he cried out, "Oh, crap!"

"Huh? What's out there?" Millie asked, concerned.

Todd raised his hand and pointed out one of the order room windows. He appeared to be speechless. Even though the room was in the back, the windows were situated on the right side of the house. It allowed anyone in the order room to see who was walking up the path to the front door. "Look

95

who's walking up to our door! We may have an even bigger problem than the inspector," he stammered.

Carolyn snuck up to the window and peeked outside. "Oh no, this is a disaster waiting to happen." She flinched and drew back.

"Shh," Millie whispered, scanning the room and hoping no one was paying attention to Todd or Carolyn. "Tell me. What's going on?"

Not willing to wait for an answer, she hastened over to the window herself. She didn't have to look far to see the black-haired, sturdily built woman marching up to their door. "Yikes! What is she doing here?" She shook her head. "She sure has a lot of nerve. Oh no—what if she sees the health department inspector?"

The bells jangled as Annabel opened the door. Millie, having run up front, was there to stop her. "Annabel, this is a surprise. Any special reason why you're here today?"

"I've come to see how this place turned out," Annabel said, putting her hands on her hips.

Keeping her hands clasped at her sides, Millie managed to hold herself in check. "That's so nice, but today is only for friends and family. It's a practice opening for us."

"Well, I thought since we own shops in the same area, I could come," Annabel said defensively. "My place wasn't busy, so I walked on over here to observe the comings and goings."

Millie raised her eyebrow and glared directly into Annabel's eyes, trying to determine what Annabel's real motive was in coming today. She tried to remember that she'd promised not to rile up Annabel. For sure, she didn't want to cause a scene or worse. First the health inspector showed up, and now this. Maybe it would be good when this day was over. But now what? Should she follow Annabel around? She just didn't know.

"Hi, Millie." Alfred smiled and waved from the bottom of the steps outside. *Oh, thank goodness, a distraction.*

Seeing Bonnie, his sweet white Maltese, in Alfred's arms, Millie quickly walked down the steps, leaving Annabel. It was best if she stayed away from her. She strolled over to pet Bonnie. It was always fun to see what Alfred did to make Bonnie look fashionable. "Bonnie, you look ravishing. I absolutely love your diamond tiara and hot pink bow." She held Bonnie's chin up. "Let's go inside and get you a pupcake. The pink sprinkles and the red strawberry on top match perfectly with your outfit."

"Oh dear, I forgot to bring a bib for her." Alfred frowned. "And I just had her groomed. I'd hate for her to get sprinkles in her fur."

Millie burst out laughing. "Alfred, darling, we've thought of everything here. We had bibs made in all sizes for discerning customers just like you. Heaven forbid our fur babies couldn't have one of MaryEllen's marvelous concoctions because they might get messy. Come on, we'll get Bonnie her treat. Wait till you see the pupcakes. MaryEllen outdid herself today."

Walking with Alfred, Millie wondered where Annabel was. It'd be too much to hope she had wandered right out the door, never to return. Millie tapped Alfred's arm. "Hang on a sec. I'll grab a bib for Bonnie."

As Millie walked behind the counter, Carolyn pulled her aside. She whispered, "No one's said a word about the inspector. Amazing really, since he's walking around shining his flashlight everywhere."

"That's good. Have you seen Annabel?" Millie asked nervously.

"Nope," Carolyn said.

"Dare I hope she is gone?" Millie said as she rifled through the container of bibs to find one she thought would be good for Bonnie. Carolyn laughed.

Having found a small pink bib with strawberries on it, Millie tied it around Bonnie's neck. It matched impeccably with her bow. "Ah, too cute! You could be our advertising model," Millie said.

She watched while Carolyn placed a pupcake on a plate for Bonnie, and then she steered Alfred over to one of the sofas. Just as Alfred sat down, she felt a light tap on her shoulder. She turned around. "Hooray, my big brother is here," she said as she threw her arms around Bradley and hugged him tight. Having him here was like the icing on the pupcake. Now if only Carl showed up, there'd be sprinkles, too.

Bradley stepped back from Millie and waved his arms around. "Hey, did my one and only sister do this? This place looks amazing. Nice touch putting animal books on the bookshelves."

Millie blushed. "Well, Alfred helped. Bradley, meet Bonnie, his doggie extraordinaire."

Bradley tickled Bonnie under her neck. "Looks like you are enjoying your pupcake."

Millie chuckled. That was an understatement. Bonnie's bib was already covered in frosting and sprinkles. *What a priceless photo op.* Hopefully, Carl would be here in time to capture that. Then she could make a copy for Alfred and put one on the bookshelves here.

"Obviously, she likes it," MaryEllen said as she walked up behind Bradley. "Look at all my fans gobbling them up." She giggled as she pointed around the room.

"Hey, could you guys just hang out for a few minutes?" Millie asked. "I need to check on something."

She hated to leave Bradley so soon after he'd arrived, but she just had to find out what Annabel was up to. She shook off that thought, smiled, and relaxed. The reality hit her. She, Millie Whitfield, had opened a dog bakery. She looked around. Dogs sitting on chairs and gobbling treats with frosting all over their noses, and people smiling and chatting. She wasn't going to let Annabel ruin this day. *No way.*

Millie quietly wandered off. As she walked around, a feeling of warm fuzzies permeated her body. Despite the fact that the health inspector was there, she was still proud of her accomplishment—until her eyes rested on Annabel sitting with Sally, a friend of Todd's. They were sitting in the overflow room with their backs to her. *Yuck.* Just seeing Annabel sitting in her bakery gave her the creeps. Millie stopped to listen.

Luckily, or maybe not, Annabel was speaking loudly, and Millie could hear her clearly. "Did you notice that person with a lanyard on?" Annabel said, moving closer to Sally. "He's from the health department. Why do you think he would he be here?"

Millie took a deep breath and bit down on her lip to keep from speaking out. She wanted to hear what else Annabel had to say.

"Oh my, do you think they have a problem? I wouldn't want my dog to eat something bad," Sally said, hugging her dog.

"Who knows, but I'd be careful. There could be something bad in their pastries," Annabel said as she leaned over to pat Sally's Yorkshire terrier on his head.

Huh! Millie squeezed her hands into fists and started to march over to say something when a hand reached out and yanked her from behind. "Millie," Carolyn hissed, "I know you want to say something, but you can't."

"Jeez, I know you're right, and I'm really trying to be good, but did you see that smug look on her face? It's all so obvious now. She's the one who called the health department."

"You're most likely correct. Still, you can't say anything. It will only make the situation worse."

Before Millie could comment, Sally waved and called out, "Hi, Millie. Come on over and meet Gertie, my Yorkie."

Carolyn held onto Millie and through clenched teeth ground out, "Get over there and don't give Annabel the satisfaction of creating a scene. That's probably just what she wants."

Millie nodded. She plastered a smile on her face, and with a bounce in her step, she walked over. She made sure to stand with her back to Annabel as she fingered Gertie's pink hair bow.

"Ah, Gertie, you are too cute. And I see you have pink toenails, too."

Sally grinned. "I have no idea why, but people always think she is a boy, so I always put a pink bow in her hair and pink polish on her nails. No mistaking her now."

"You're right about that." Millie fidgeted. "So, why don't I take you to get her one of MaryEllen's pupcakes? Her pastries are a big hit. I'm sure Annabel will sit and wait for you." She smiled at Annabel, daring her to say anything.

Sally got up, holding onto Gertie. As they walked toward the order room, Millie turned around, and making sure Sally didn't see her, she glared at Annabel. She was proud of herself for staying in control, and by the angry stare, she was sure Annabel knew she had been overheard. Millie shook her head; Annabel's goal appeared to be to cause as much trouble for her as possible.

"Listen," Millie said, touching Sally's arm. "I heard Annabel saying something about the health department being here. Well, somehow there was a mix-up. Our final inspection was supposed to be yesterday, but the inspector showed up today. But I want to assure you this is a routine inspection. Nothing is amiss."

"Oh, I guess you overheard Annabel. Sorry about that. I think everyone who is here knows she has a reputation as a troublemaker. I'm so glad to hear that everything is okay. This looks like it will be a wonderful place to bring Gertie."

Millie smiled as she and Sally got up to the counter. "I hope you don't mind, but I'll leave you here with Todd. He'll get Gertie a pupcake. I need to go check on the inspector." She gave Gertie one last pat, and as she started to walk away, she pointed to the biscotti and said, "Try one of those for yourself. MaryEllen made them, too."

Even after her explanation, Millie hated to mention the health department guy, but it really made no difference now.

Back in the kitchen, behind closed doors, Millie popped one after another of MaryEllen's chocolate chip biscotti into her mouth.

"Okay, Mil, spill the beans. What or who got to you? You only start throwing stuff in your mouth in times of trouble." MaryEllen giggled.

"Annabel. She's out there telling Todd's friend Sally that the health department is here."

Millie stuffed another biscotti into her mouth and watched MaryEllen slop a huge glop of cleaning fluid on the steel baking counter and scrub. "How nuts are the two of us?" MaryEllen said as she burst out laughing. "I clean, and you eat."

Millie walked around the counter, took the sponge out of MaryEllen's hand, draped her arm around her, and burst out laughing. "Together we are a piece of work. And now that I've finished stuffing my face, I'm going to go watch for Carl." As she walked toward the door, she turned back. "By the way, thanks for making me laugh. I needed that."

No sooner had she slid the door to the kitchen closed when the inspector tapped Millie on her shoulder. "May I use one of your tables to sit and write my report? When I'm done, I'll go over it with you."

"We have an office upstairs. Could you please go there? There's a small round table that you can sit at. It's quiet, and no one will bother you. I'll be up in a minute." Millie watched him walking up the stairs and turned to go tell her teammates that she'd be there, too, but being so distracted, she bumped into Carolyn.

"Oops, I was just coming to find you. Do you think everything is okay?" Carolyn whispered.

Millie shrugged. "Honestly, there's no reason for it not to be. We passed all our inspections before. I was on my way to talk to the inspector now." She trudged up the steps and sat across from the inspector at the small conference table. Her hands trembled. She wished she had a pen or anything to keep them still. She pushed back a bit from the table and put them in her lap.

"Mrs. Whitfield, I'll get right to the point. You passed the inspection. I've filled out the necessary forms, and here they are." The inspector pushed them across the table to her.

Millie let out the breath she'd been holding in. "Oh, thank goodness, what a relief."

"Truthfully," the inspector added, "I really don't understand why we got a complaint about this place. It's pristine. I wish everyone made my job so easy."

Millie sighed. "My team and I thank you for that. At least it softens the blow from you being here." She gave him a weak smile. "I'm sorry to rush you, but if you're done, I'll walk you out." Now that this travesty was over, she suddenly felt tired. She'd be glad when the day was done.

He got up and plodded down the steps. She walked next to him, her hand squeezing the railing, her thoughts on Annabel. *What a piece of work.* "I truly am sorry, Mrs. Whitfield," the inspector said. "It looks like you have a good thing going here." He spoke gruffly as if he was a smoker, but he smiled when he said, "I've got my own dog, and after seeing how much fun everyone seems to be having here, don't be surprised if I show up myself one day."

"We'd like that." Millie managed to eke out a smile in return.

A minute later, Carolyn, Todd, and MaryEllen corralled Millie in the kitchen as she was searching in her handbag for her cell phone, trying to reach Carl.

"Well, hurry up. Tell us what the report says."

"We're good. We passed with flying colors. The way I see it, our only problem is Annabel. Her fingerprints are all over this complaint."

Todd piped up, "I warned you!"

MaryEllen wailed, "I can't deal with her! I was a nervous wreck while the inspector was checking out everything in my kitchen. I was scared to death he'd find something wrong and shut us down. I've got to go clean the counters or something to calm my nerves."

Millie lifted her eyebrow. She didn't dare laugh. Poor MaryEllen; this inspection had traumatized her more than anyone else on her team. She told herself that at least this had happened today with friends around. It could have been worse if it was opening day.

"Okay, listen up, you guys. It's all okay. We're good. The guests will all be leaving soon, so let's just go mingle. I am personally going to find Annabel and suggest she leave. Sorry, but I want her gone." Millie didn't give Carolyn a chance to stop her this time.

As Millie walked out, she heard footsteps behind her. Her dearest friend Carolyn would do anything to stop a brawl. She spotted Annabel at the door, ready to slip out. *Good, now I won't need to say anything.* That was for the best. She really didn't want to upset her partners or the remaining few guests. She stood at the door with her arms and legs crossed, making sure Annabel went on her way. Only that's not what Annabel did.

She meandered up to a small group of the guests who were standing outside chatting. Her back was to the bakery, so Millie remained to listen again. She shook her head as Annabel—in a sweet voice, like she was talking to her best friends—said, "Did you see the health inspector? Doesn't it strike you as odd that he was here today? I wonder if they have a problem?"

Millie was about to write it off and go back inside, but then she heard Annabel say in a conspiratorial tone, "You know, my place is nearby if you want something more to eat. I'm open."

Okay, that is it. Millie was going to confront Annabel. She started to stomp down the steps, and once again she was dragged back. She had forgotten that Carolyn had followed her. "Millie, that won't help, and if you stop and listen, Sally is sticking up for you."

"Annabel, we can't come to your shop. You don't allow dogs, and if I'm right, you don't even have any outside seating. Where would we leave our babies?" Sally said.

Millie fist-pumped the air. "Okay, I'll concede for today. Remind me to give Gertie an extra pupcake the next time they're here." Millie looped her arm around Carolyn's shoulders, and the two walked back inside, but not before they watched Annabel stomp off in an apparent huff.

Back inside Todd and MaryEllen were collapsed on the sofa. Millie wanted to plop down next to them, but it was important to tell them how well they'd done. "Okay, all of you can breathe. You were magnificent, and if I wasn't so wiped out, I'd give each of you what I call a special squishy Carl hug."

Millie hadn't seen Carl walk in, but she did hear the *tap, tap, tap* of a dog's paws. She turned, and there was her hunky husband with Luke and Annie. She ran over to him. She bent down to say hi to Luke and Annie and to give them each a hug. "I promise I saved you a pupcake," she said. She didn't bother to tell them that only one was left and they had to share. She giggled at herself. Of course, they wouldn't know.

Carl frowned. "Mil, where is everyone? Am I that late?"

"Yes and no. No one stayed that long. I didn't have time to call you to tell you we had a surprise visitor. The health department showed up. They received a complaint, and according to the inspector, they had to do an inspection. We're all convinced it came from none other than the conniving Annabel. And before you start asking questions, the answer is everything is okay." Millie stopped to take a breath. "And now, I'd like one of your special squishy hugs."

Carl squeezed all the air out of her, but it sure felt good when she was mashed against his chest. She let go only to reluctantly continue her story. "It was pretty stressful for a while there, but it turned out the inspector was a decent guy, and we passed with flying colors. I did have to smile when he told me he was so impressed with our place that he planned to come here with his dog. I hope he didn't hear me laugh when he said that."

"Well, sounds like you all handled it fine," Carl said.

"Yeah, I guess so. The only problem was that it put a damper on us, and I don't think we could really interact comfortably with our guests. They walked around, got their dogs a treat and themselves a drink, and then they left."

Carl hauled in Millie for an extra hug. "I'm sorry I didn't get here sooner. Problem at the job and couldn't leave when I expected."

"Is everything okay?"

"Yup."

"Then may I have one more squishy hug?" Millie giggled.

It was Carolyn who broke the silence and announced as she got up, "Whew, what a day. The only surprise is that no one peed on the floor."

Laughing and smiling, Millie stammered, "Oh my, you are so right. And with that statement, I do believe we are done here today."

PART TWO

CHAPTER SEVENTEEN

Opening Day

Millie and Carolyn were standing outside the bakery. Millie fished around in her handbag and checked the pockets of her jacket. "Oh no! I can't find the keys anywhere. I must have left them in my other handbag. How could I do this on opening day? I'll have to run home!"

Carl was shaking her. "Wake up, Millie, you're talking in your sleep."

She lifted her head off the pillow. "Yikes, I was dreaming I left the keys home today."

"I know. You were mumbling away. Good thing I was still here to wake you. You were twisting the sheets all over the bed."

Millie wiped her brow. "Jeez, I'm all sweaty." She threw the comforter off. "I might as well get up. I'm both too nervous and too excited to stay in bed."

Thank goodness everything had worked out okay for the dry run, even counting the fiasco with the health department. Now she told herself today would be perfect.

The only little nugget of doubt, or potential problem, was Annabel. What if she tried to pull a stunt today? Well, Millie just wasn't going to think about that at all. Not one bit.

Carl came to tell her that he was leaving for work. His plan was to go and make sure everything at the jobsite was in order, and then he'd be at the bakery to take on his role as photographer.

An hour later, dressed in a pair of black pants, a charcoal gray cashmere sweater, and as much sheltie jewelry as she could manage without looking ridiculous, Millie was ready to leave. "Come on, Luke and Annie. Before we go for a ride, I need to brush you. You want to look marvelous in your opening day photos. I even have special kerchiefs for you to wear."

The word "ride" was all Luke needed to hear. He started whining. Millie knew immediately she'd goofed. "Okay, I know you're ready to leave, but I'm not." *Darn.* She should have known not to say anything yet.

Not about to be left home, Luke pawed her. "Okay, I get it. You don't think your whining is working, so it's time to paw me. Just give me a minute to brush you both, and then we'll leave." As she brushed them, she told Luke, "If you weren't in such a rush, I could put your bandana on you. I'll take them with us and put them on you at the bakery."

Once Millie was done making Luke and Annie gorgeous, she grabbed her handbag, checking and rechecking to make sure her keys were inside. She also had an extra set to give to Carolyn. "Okay, I'm ready. Come on, you two."

Her cell phone rang. Bad timing—she always had trouble finding it in her handbag. Finally pulling it out, she saw it was Nicholas calling. Even before she said hello, he started talking. "Mil, Grant and I are so sorry, but neither one of us can get home today. We figured we'd be there for you, but we both have classes we can't miss."

"Nicholas, what can I say except this is crummy."

"I know, Mil. We both feel awful. We will try to get home soon. We're really proud of you, and we can't wait to see your bakery."

"Hey, I don't mean to cut you off, but I need to get to the bakery. I can't be late. I guess we'll talk soon." Millie hung up quickly. She didn't want Nicholas to hear her crying. She sat for a minute in her kitchen and tried to pull herself together. She had to leave. She couldn't think about this anymore right now. This was to be a special day, and she wouldn't even let this ruin it.

All she had to do was open the car door, and Luke jumped right up onto the backseat. Not so with Annie. Millie found her on the front lawn.

"Come on, Annie. We're going to be late."

With some coaxing, Annie came into the garage, but instead of going near the car, she skirted around it and ran back into the house.

"Annie, you're going to have to stay home then. I need to go."

Darn. She really wanted Annie to come with her. She'd call Carl. He'd probably have time to stop home and pick her up.

When Millie reached the path, she could see the Best Doggone Bakery sign through the straggly trees, and as she approached the farmhouse, she saw MaryEllen, Carolyn, and Todd all bundled up and standing outside. The puffy clouds hid the sun from view, and it was bitterly cold. She quickened her pace, and when she joined them, they all hugged and high-fived. No one moved to walk through the door.

Millie had mixed emotions. On the one hand, she was almost afraid to walk in because that meant they were opening for real. On the other hand, it was thrilling to know she had achieved her dream of opening a dog bakery. Who knew if they'd be successful? It was time to take the plunge. "Come on," she said. "Let's head inside. It's cold out here."

The partners walked up the steps together, and Millie fished the key out of her handbag. Before opening the door, she turned toward them and said excitedly, "I hope you three know how much I love that we're all in this together. Come on, let's do this!"

She heard Carolyn whisper to MaryEllen, "I know the dry run turned out okay, but that was with our friends and family. I'm still nervous about today. Who knows who our first customers will be, or even if we'll have any. And what if Annabel shows up again to cause trouble?"

"Well, I'm still wondering whether the dog customers will enjoy my baking." MaryEllen sighed.

Todd laughed. "Oh, MaryEllen, so far the dogs have loved your confections. Personally, I'm more concerned about the humans liking our coffee drinks since I'm the one concocting them."

Inside, Millie bent down to talk to Luke. "Your job is to make the furry friends feel at home." He gave her a soft *woof.* She snuggled him to her and stuck her nose in his fur. He looked so cute with his blue bandana, and the coconut shampoo she had used on him made him smell good enough to eat. *Actually, coconut might be a great ingredient to add to our list for the dogs.* She'd have to tell MaryEllen to check that out.

Carolyn walked up to her. "Come here, Millie; the logo on your baseball cap is faced sideways, and your apron needs an adjustment."

"That's okay. I've got it." Millie twisted her cap and untied and retied her apron, making sure her sheltie pin was still attached. She really liked the brick red color they all had agreed on. "Okay, everyone. Are you ready? Fifteen minutes to zero hour," she said as she nervously glanced at the clock and put her hand on her stomach. "Darn these butterflies. They don't help when they're zooming around."

"I'll just flip the sign on the door," Todd said.

"Todd, hold up a minute," MaryEllen said as she walked to the counter to make sure the display case looked perfect.

"Uh-oh, I'm sorry. There are two women outside that watched me flip the sign, and they are walking up to the door now."

"Oh, okay. Come quick, Carolyn, let's make sure the coffee is ready to be brewed," Millie said as she tied Luke's leash to the closest chair and told him, "Sit and stay."

Todd ran his fingers through his hair. "I never thought anyone would be here this early."

"It's okay; we'll be fine." Millie crossed her fingers and thought it was time to get this show on the road.

Meanwhile, the two women pushed the door open, the bells jangling.

"Welcome to the Best Doggone Bakery!" the four partners chimed together as they jockeyed their way to the door to greet their first customers. Each woman had two collies on leashes, and they were all gorgeously groomed to perfection with over-the-top fluffy fur.

Millie turned to Carolyn and whispered out of the side of her mouth, "How cool! I can't believe our very first customers have collies. So much like my beloved shelties, although I've never really seen collies that look like these. They're mostly all white."

"Hi!" one of the women said. "Your sign says you're open even though it's not quite ten. Is it okay that we're a few minutes early?

Millie started to answer that it was fine, but the woman kept talking. "It's really cold outside, and the smells of peanut butter and cinnamon were driving Journey crazy." She sniffed the air. "Jeez, it smells wonderful. We were so excited when we got a flyer in our newspaper that a dog bakery was coming here. A place for our dogs sounded great to us."

Millie stuck out her hand. "Hi, I'm Millie. You're not going to believe this, but I have two shelties. As a matter of fact, one is here, and the other one is coming later with my husband."

"Sit, Journey; you too, Starlight," the dark-haired woman told her dogs as she introduced herself and her friend to Millie. "I'm Diane, and my friend is Eva. All four dogs are mine. Starlight is the tricolored, Cambric is the one with big sable spots, Journey is the smallest one of the bunch, and Buddy has a sable spot on his rear."

Millie couldn't help herself. She got right down on the floor to pet the collies. She probably should have been concentrating on the humans, but she figured she could take a minute to pet the dogs. Going forward, she was going to have to watch that petting the dogs was not the only thing she focused on.

Millie turned around to introduce her partners, but they had left her. She was sure they were getting in place to take orders.

Eva peeked into the front room with the bookshelves. "Wow, it looks fabulous in here. We've been chomping at the leash"—she giggled—"to get in here. Oh, I can see your sheltie. Why don't you bring him over to meet Diane's dogs? They're really friendly."

"Okay, I'll get him, and thanks for the compliment. We love the way it turned out," Millie said as she walked over to get Luke. When she came back with him, he sat by her side and let all four dogs sniff him.

"Why don't you walk around?" Millie suggested. "You'll see the bakery bar is in the back on the right. My three partners are around here someplace, and they'll help you with your order. Today's treat is baked peanut butter mud pies for the dogs, and in deference to the humans who so kindly have brought them here, we have cinnamon biscotti."

"Mud pies for the dogs. What a hoot," Diane said.

The two women's glances slid from right to left as they meandered toward the back of the house. Millie listened to their sounds of oohs and aahs as she followed behind. Once she got back to the order room, she wrapped Luke's leash to a special hook installed just for him off in a corner and planted herself behind the counter.

Diane went to pet Luke. "My neighbor had a sheltie when I was growing up. Such a great dog."

"It's funny; everyone seems to know someone who had a sheltie," Millie said as she looked to see that the coffee was ready.

"It must be nice to be able to bring your dogs to work. My four would love to be with me all the time. Right now, I'd better order something for them before there's a mutiny."

"Sounds good. Would you and Eva like a drink?"

"Sure. Your blackboard menu says you have caramel lattes. May we have two of them? I'll get each dog a mud pie. I'm sure they will love them."

"Why don't you two find a place to sit?" Millie said with a smile. "We'll bring everything to you."

As Todd prepared the drinks, Carolyn put the mud pies on two plates and walked to the front room where Diane and Eva were sitting on one of the love seats and looking at the books on the shelves. Diane pointed. "Look, they have a copy of *Lad: A Dog*. As a child I never realized Sunnybank was a real place and that the author, Albert Payson Terhune, was writing about his own collies. Starlight and Journey are descendants of the great Sunnybank collies."

"Wow," Carolyn said. "That's really neat. I think I read all of his books. I loved them."

Eva picked up *Dewey the Library Cat*. "They're open-minded too. Here's a book about a cat."

Carolyn laughed. "Millie only brought dog books. I brought that book here. I'm the one partner who has a cat and a dog, and I felt cats needed some representation." As she handed them their bakery items, she added, "My cat, Oodles, and my dog, Levi, get along great. Maybe someday Millie will allow cats here."

"I'd sure like to be here on that day," Diane said, giggling.

Journey jumped up onto the sofa. "Oh no. Journey, get down," Diane told him.

"No, really, it's fine if he wants to sit with you. We want all guests to feel at home," Carolyn said. She petted Journey. He balanced his paws on her shoulders and gave her a kiss. She laughed. "Oh, what a friendly dog. I guess he's happy I said it was okay for him to stay on the sofa."

"He knows how to get what he wants. Smart boy," Diane added.

Starlight moved closer to Diane and stared up at her. "My beauty, you want attention." She reached down to pet her. "Maybe someday you'll show off your singing and dancing skills."

"So tell me, how did you end up with four collies?" Carolyn asked.

"Well, Cambric and Buddy are rescues. They needed me, and I was thrilled to adopt them. Cambric is my athlete. Eva takes him for agility. Buddy is my special baby. I rescued him when he was four months old. Unfortunately, he has many neurological issues that are very frightening to me. He is only three. I keep hoping he will be okay. Buddy and Starlight are best friends. She looks out for him, like a good big sister."

Carolyn looked around. "I wonder where Millie went? She loves her shelties, but she talks about getting a collie someday. I'm surprised she's not here trying to get to know your dogs better."

"She'll get a chance. This place is great," Diane said enthusiastically. "We'll be back soon, maybe even tomorrow. You are going to have a big hit on your hands."

Eva petted Buddy and added, "All my friends have dogs. I can't wait to tell them how great this place is. You'll be swamped."

* * *

Millie stood in the foyer while Luke sat by her side. Every time the bells jangled, she felt goose bumps on her arms. What a special day! She loved greeting everyone and their dogs. When she left her post at the front door, one goldendoodle caught her attention. He couldn't seem to figure out how to eat the strawberry that topped off his mud pie. She burst out laughing.

The next time the bells jangled, Millie looked up to see Carl with Annie. She ran over and whispered in his ear, "Did you see all the people in here? We've already sold a bunch of stuff."

Carl laughed. "Wasn't that the plan?"

"Of course!" Millie giggled. "I'm just surprised we're so busy so soon. Can you take photos? I'd like lots of them."

Carl held up his iPad. "I'm ready to start now if you want. Just take Annie."

"Come on with me and Luke," Millie said as she took Annie's leash from Carl's hands.

Diane and Eva stopped Millie as she and Annie walked by. "We're leaving, but we're planning to come back tomorrow," Diane said. "We used to go to Miss Annabel's every morning to pick up coffee. Now that we have a place where our dogs are welcome, we'll definitely be stopping here instead."

Millie stood at the door watching dog tails wagging and women chatting as they faded off in the distance. A woman walking toward the bakery was forced off the narrow path until they passed her. Millie could see she was fairly tall with straight, shoulder-length blonde hair and bangs. She wore a long, fur-collared, black coat and a fluffy white fur headband. As she walked, she stood tall and straight, and with her long neck, she appeared almost regal. Millie expected her to walk up to the door, but she stopped midway up the path. She didn't have a dog, leaving Millie to question why she was there. Was the stranger wondering the same thing? Should she call out to the stranger or walk up to her?

"Hello, welcome to The Best Doggone Bakery." Millie's friendly side won out.

"Hi," the woman replied tentatively.

Millie chewed her lip. "Would you like to come in?"

"Sure. To be honest, I'm not sure why I'm here except I saw you outside earlier this morning with a sheltie. I was wondering if I could pet him or her?"

"Oh, so you saw my beloved Luke. Of course, come on in. He's inside with his doggie sister, Annie."

Millie held the door open, and as the woman walked up the steps and through the door, Millie pointed to the right. "Luke's over there with Annie."

As they stood next to Luke and Annie, Millie watched the stranger's gaze move from one dog to the other. Just for a moment, Millie thought she glimpsed a hint of a tear in the stranger's eye.

"This is Luke, and I'm Millie," she said as she held out her hand for the stranger to shake, expecting her to respond likewise.

"Hi, I'm Samantha. May I pet them?"

"Of course; Luke loves attention. Annie is more reserved."

Millie watched Samantha remove her coat, sit cross-legged on the floor, and gently extend her hand as if to let Luke smell it. Abruptly she pulled it back, covered her face with her hands, and burst into sobs. "Oh, I am so sorry. I should leave."

Millie was silent. She chewed the inside of her lip. What to say? She had the feeling no words would be satisfactory right now. Instead she slipped down on the floor, put her arms around Samantha, placed Samantha's head on her shoulder, and just held on. They stayed locked like that until Samantha lifted her tear-streaked face. "Again, I am so sorry. I should have known this would happen. I had a sheltie named George. He looked a lot like your Luke; he even had the same four stocking legs. When he died twenty-eight days ago, I lost my best friend. I miss him so very much. I thought it would help to pet another sheltie like him. I better go. I'm spoiling your day."

"Don't be ridiculous. Stay and pet Luke. He loves it, although I have to say it seems like you were putting yourself in an uncomfortable situation by coming here."

"I didn't really intend to come here. I just moved to Houndsville, and today I had some time to take a walk around my new neighborhood. When I saw your sign down by the street, it was a spur-of-the-moment decision to see what a dog bakery looked like; I've never lived anywhere that had one. As I got close to the bakery, I saw you outside with Luke. I never expected to see a sheltie that looked so much like George. I turned around and left. After walking around for the last half hour, I couldn't help myself and I came back, thinking it would be nice to pet another sheltie. Maybe not a good decision, huh?"

"Why did you move here? Boyfriend or husband here?"

"No. I moved here for a job."

"Oh, is your job near here?"

"Actually, yes. I'm going to be working at the Buckshead Inn."

"Oh, that's great. My husband and I love it there. Hey, sit here for a minute and pet Luke. I'll find Carl and bring him over so you can meet him."

"That's okay. I really need to leave. I still have unpacking to do before work tomorrow."

"Wait, it'll only take a minute. He can take our photo."

Millie found Carl talking to Todd. "Excuse me, I want you to meet someone," she said as she grabbed his hand and dragged him with her. "Her name is Samantha. She just moved here, and she's going to work at the inn. She seems really nice."

Samantha had already gotten up and was heading for the door. Millie caught up with her. "Wait, here's Carl. We can talk later, but for now let him take a photo of us with Luke and Annie."

"Look, Mil," Carl said. "MaryEllen is waving furiously at you. She must need you."

"I'll go see what she wants. Wait here; I'll be right back." Millie trotted off.

"So, Samantha, does anyone call you Sam?" Carl asked her.

"Uh, no! Not really."

"Millie mentioned you just moved here. From where?"

"Listen, I better go. I really should have left already," Samantha said as she handed him Luke's leash.

* * *

Wow, what a day. Samantha leaned her back against the door of her new condo. She fished in her handbag for her key with tears pouring down her face, making the task nearly impossible. Opening the door meant dealing with not seeing George waiting with a nonstop wiggle-waggle and a kiss. Would the tears ever stop? Would her new condo ever feel like home without him? Would she ever get over his death? She took a deep breath and shook off those thoughts. Sooner or later, she had to go inside.

Having purchased a bottle of white wine on her first "look and see" of her new neighborhood, she'd pour a drink for herself. *Maybe that will help.* After washing her hands, Samantha walked over to her favorite chair with goblet in hand and plopped down, putting her feet up on the matching ottoman. Setting her glass down on a small, round, wooden table next to some treasured photos of her dad and George, she took in the breathtaking view of Houndsville through her large plate glass window. Later she'd finish emptying and collapsing the last of her moving boxes. For now, she just wanted to relax, have a glass of wine, and think about things—today, for instance.

Going to the bakery to pet Luke had been impulsive, in some ways a good idea and in some ways not. There were pluses and minuses; on the plus side, she had met Millie, and that quite honestly was great. Millie had been warm and inviting, and Samantha had felt an immediate bond with her. At first, the connection was due to Luke and their mutual love of shelties, but then when she had started crying, what Millie did *not* say made her realize that she'd found a soul mate. When George died, some insensitive people had suggested that she'd get over him—that he was just a dog—but for her, George had been one of the best things in her life, and nothing could replace him. Thank goodness Millie had not repeated that platitude; instead she had hugged her, a complete stranger—a sure sign of understanding. As far as Samantha was concerned, Millie was the best thing to happen to her in a long time.

Samantha swirled her glass of wine and tapped her fingers on the rim. Another plus, a big one, was her new job at the Buckshead Inn. Getting hired at the renowned inn was the first step toward someday owning and operating a boutique hotel that was hers. She'd learn everything she could from Brenda, the longtime owner, and then branch out. Along the way, she'd prove to herself and someone she loved that she was capable of standing on her own.

Samantha got up from her chair and paced in front of her window. On the minus side, she hadn't wanted Millie to take her photograph. She preferred to have no photos of her floating around. Her preference was to keep a low-key presence and fly under the radar. She had her reasons for that, although they were certainly in no way life-threatening—just a conscious choice on her part.

Samantha sat down again, looked at the photos of George and her dad, and sighed. She hoped Millie didn't think it strange that she'd bolted out of the bakery without saying goodbye.

CHAPTER EIGHTEEN

Busy

Millie jumped out of bed and flew into the bathroom to take a shower. Afterward she dried her hair, applied lipstick and blush, and dressed for a wintry day in a hooded black cashmere sweater, black pants, and warm, fur-lined boots.

She ticked off a list of items she wanted to get accomplished at the bakery. First, fix a malfunctioning thermostat on one of the ovens. Second, come up with names for each of the rooms. Third, plan a party. But before she left home, she went scrounging for her dog brush.

After finding it in her top drawer, Millie sat on the floor. "Come here, Luke," she said before she ran the brush through his hair and talked to him. "My cutie pie, you have a birthday soon, and we're going to celebrate with a 'paw-ty' at the bakery." She giggled. Luke tilted his head from side to side while listening to her. He was such a sweetie—her huggable, lovable Luke. "I've got your paw-ty all figured out. We'll invite Annie; MaryEllen and Bradley's dog, Hickory; Carolyn's dog, Levi; and Todd's dog, Artie."

Just then, Carl walked into the bedroom, snuck up on Millie, and tapped her shoulder. "Are you serious? You're having a birthday party for Luke at the bakery? I know you love him, but . . ."

"Oh, Carl, my plan is to have birthday parties for other dogs eventually. Luke's will just be the first one, a dry run for birthday parties." Millie winked.

Carl rolled his eyes. "I'm not going to say another word. It will just get me in trouble."

"That's for sure!" Millie laughed. "And don't think you can get out of coming. You're our resident photographer."

"Of course; if you are seriously going to do this, I'll be there. I love Luke, and knowing your party-planning capabilities, his party will be a hoot."

"Well, hopefully my partners will agree. They might think it's too soon." Millie went back to brushing Luke, and then she remembered she had something to discuss with Carl. "So, listen to this. Annabel has a new trick up her sleeve. If she can't shut us down, she'll try competing instead. One of her employees told Todd that Annabel is going to put tables outside, hoping to get people with dogs to eat there. They also said she may try serving some dog treats. Wonder where she plans to get them? So, I have a question. Does she need a zoning variance to put tables outside?"

"The short answer is yes, and if you're wondering why, it's because there's lots of issues. When you apply for a zoning variance, it goes through all the different county departments—planning and zoning, health department, and fire department, to name a few. They will check the parking, and safety is an issue. They'll want to know how people will walk by her place if the sidewalk is filled with tables."

Carl ruffled the top of her head. "So, don't worry your cute little self about this yet. All in all, it will most likely take her ninety to one hundred twenty days to get the variance, and that is *if* it is approved."

"Not much I can do anyway. At least that might keep her mind off of other nefarious plans." Kissing Carl, Millie laughed and ruffled his hair. "I'm off to the bakery."

She stared down at Luke and Annie and pointed her finger at them. "You two be good, and just maybe I'll bring you home some Woof-a-Roos."

Thirty minutes later, when Millie opened the bakery door, she figured MaryEllen would know by the jangling bells that she was there, but she still hollered out, "Hi, everyone. I'm here!"

MaryEllen yelled back, "Good! Carolyn and I are baking. Come help."

Millie joined them in the kitchen. "Tell me what to do."

"Well, we could use more peanut butter filling," MaryEllen said. "I'll get the ingredients for you."

Millie went to the sink to wash her hands. "Sometime today, if we have time, we really need to come up with names for our rooms. Calling our rooms 'front room' and 'order room' sounds stupid. We can do better."

"Mil, you're right about that." MaryEllen laid the peanut butter, cream cheese, and olive oil next to the mixer. "Here's everything you need. Oh, I meant to ask, who was that pretty blonde you were talking with yesterday? Sure seemed like you two were having an intense conversation."

Millie unscrewed the top of the peanut butter jar and started to measure out two cups. "She was telling me about her sheltie that just died. It was really sad."

"How do you know her?" Carolyn asked.

"I don't. I just met her yesterday. She saw us outside in the morning with Luke. She thought it would make her feel better if she got to pet another sheltie. It didn't work out that way—turned out, petting Luke made her cry."

"Did she tell you her name or any other personal info?"

"Only that her name is Samantha, and she just moved here to work at the Buckshead Inn. Why so curious?"

"She looks familiar, like I've seen her before. I figured I'd seen you two together before."

"Nope." Millie shook her head. "Like I said, I just met her."

"Well, she's definitely Harry's type: tall, thin, and blonde. You know I'm always on the lookout for women for my adorable, eligible brother. If she just moved here, that could work out." MaryEllen grabbed one of the wicker baskets off a shelf to put the finished cookies in. "Remember Rebecca? Well, thank goodness she's gone. She didn't like our small town and tried to get him to move up north. He gave her the boot. Boy, I'm glad about that."

Millie took a lick of the frosting. She laughed and shrugged; peanut butter dog frosting was tasty. "Yeah, that would have been awful if he'd left town. He's such a great vet. Actually, Luke wouldn't have liked it either. He loves Harry. Wait! I have an idea!" She smiled. "I'll get Samantha's number and give it to you, and you can pass it along to Harry. Coming from his younger sister, he'll take it from you."

"Are you kidding?" MaryEllen frowned. "Harry hates when I get involved in his social life. We'll just have to come up with a clever way to introduce them."

Millie clapped, sending frosting flying everywhere. "Oops, sorry!" she said as she placed her hands back on the counter. "This is serious. You mean I get to use my matchmaking skills? Oh, fun! I'll come up with a great plan. I can be really sneaky when it's called for."

MaryEllen put her hands on her hips and stared at Millie. "Like you were with me and Bradley?"

"What are you talking about?" Millie squeaked and looked down at the floor.

MaryEllen raised an eyebrow and tilted her head. "Bradley is totally unaware of your meddling. I am not. But who cares? It worked out great."

Millie looked down at the floor to avoid answering. When she looked back up, she said, "I'll finish the Woof-a-Roos, and Carolyn can get the red frosting out of the refrigerator and use the pastry tool to paint the strawberries. And while we're working, let's try to come up with the room names."

"Mil, how about we run a contest?" Carolyn proposed. "We can ask our customers to recommend names, then whoever suggests the best names wins a prize."

"Wow, that's a great idea," MaryEllen said excitedly.

"I second that," Millie added as she glanced at the clock. "Where's Todd? It's just about time to open."

A minute later, they heard the doorbells jangle. "I'm here!" Todd burst through the kitchen door. He held up his hands. "Now don't holler, because I promise I won't open the door till you tell me it's okay, but there's someone waiting outside with the biggest dog you have ever seen. I told him we'd be opening soon."

"I'm done baking for now." MaryEllen wiped her hands on a paper towel. "I'll go let them in." She headed up front, flipped the sign, and opened the door. Waiting there was an enormous sheepdog with his male owner, who had on a faded dark green sweatshirt with the wording *Proud Parent of a Rescued Sheepdog*.

MaryEllen stood to the side, staring at the humongous dog. "Wow! Todd wasn't kidding when he said there was a big dog waiting to come in. Anyway, welcome, you're our first guest today— and an early one, too."

"We live nearby, and I swear Woodrow Wilson—or as I call him, Woody— dragged me here. Are you baking something with peanut butter? Woody's a peanut butter kind of guy."

MaryEllen got in Woody's face. "I'd high-five you if you were a person. Got a paw instead?" She picked up Woody's paw and shook it. "Good job, Woody, bringing your person here. If more fur babies do that, we'll be a huge success," she laughed.

"Did you just call my dog a fur baby? I never heard that before." Woody's owner tapped Woody on the head and laughingly said, "Woody, did you know you are a fur baby?"

"Well, if Woody would like a peanut butter treat, he needs to follow me. I was just getting really to fill up our display case."

"Woody, follow the lady. She's got the goodies."

Woody and his owner followed MaryEllen to the order room, where she signaled to Millie. "Can you help them while I get my Woof-a-Roos and fill up the case?"

"Sure." Millie offered to get Woody's owner something to drink while they waited for MaryEllen to bring out her peanut butter Woof-a-Roos. "We serve a great mocha latte, or if you want, I just brewed fresh coffee."

"Coffee sounds good. I won't have to go to Miss Annabel's then." While Millie found a mug and poured the coffee, she found out that Woody's owner's name was Peter and that he worked nearby as an architect.

When MaryEllen walked up beside them carrying a tray loaded up with Oreo-style cookies, Peter asked, "What are those?"

"The treat that brought Woody here—my special for today, Woof-a-Roos. And the cream in the middle is delicious: delectable peanut butter."

"Ah, that sounds good, even to me. Is that a strawberry painted on them?"

"Yes," MaryEllen said as she started filling up a wicker basket with Woof-a-Roos. "We put a real strawberry on some of our treats, but on our cookies, we paint a frosting strawberry using a pastry tool."

"Wow! I didn't know dogs eat strawberries."

"My dog, Hickory, loves them, and it turns out they are a really healthy treat for dogs."

"I wonder if Woody will like them? When we come back, hopefully you'll have a real strawberry on the treat that day."

"We always put them on our pupcakes, which I bake a few times a week," MaryEllen said, pointing to herself.

"Well, for now," Peter said, "I'll take two of the Woof-a-Roos for Woody, and we'll sit for a minute. Woody can gobble his treats while I drink my coffee."

"Just FYI, dogs are allowed on the furniture," Millie told him.

"You're kidding. If huge old Woody decided to pick the sofa, there wouldn't be much room left for anyone, human or otherwise. The floor is fine for him." Millie handed Peter his coffee and a plate with Woody's cookies, and as he took them, he turned to MaryEllen, who'd just finished putting the basket of Woof-a-Roos in the glass case. "I remember being here a few times when this was the ice cream shop. It's impressive what you've done. This place is awesome."

"Thanks. We think so, too." MaryEllen smiled.

"Come on, Woody." Peter held Woody's cookies up for him to see. "You come sit, and you can have your treats."

As Peter and Woody walked toward the front room, Millie went to talk to MaryEllen, who she knew had disappeared into the kitchen. She found her getting ready to whip up some more cookie batter, so she sat on the stool at the steel counter and watched her. "Peter sure likes our place, but I think he liked you even better," Millie said teasingly.

"Oh, come on, Millie. He just wanted someone to talk to."

"Nah, I don't think so. He was definitely checking you out. I watched him."

MaryEllen shook her head. "I hope you're wrong. That could make things awkward if he comes back." She stopped the twirling mixer and held up her left hand, wiggling her fourth finger. "Between you and me, I'm hoping Bradley gets around to giving me a ring. Then I won't have to say anything."

"MaryEllen, you silly woman. You know me by now. I will casually mention to my brother that some guy was here checking you out. I'll act like it was nothing, but you can be sure I'll manage to mention that this person was no slouch in the looks department."

MaryEllen came around the counter and wrapped her arms around Millie while being careful to keep her floured hands away from Millie's clothes. Millie adored MaryEllen and couldn't wait to have her as her sister-in-law. It really wouldn't change anything; it just would be nice to officially have another woman in the family. She also knew her parents would have loved her.

The rest of the morning flew by. Dogs and their human companions kept the bakery hopping. During a lull in the afternoon, while everyone was sitting on the sofas taking a breather, Millie cleared her throat. "Okay, everyone. Listen up. We got interrupted earlier, but we really need names for our rooms. If we come up with good ones, we won't need a contest. That might take too long anyway."

Millie smiled and checked out her team. Todd was tapping his fingers on the edge of the sofa, Carolyn was twirling her hair, and MaryEllen was lying back with her eyes closed. She shrugged. Things didn't look good for them to come up with some names anytime soon, but then Todd sat forward and said, "Okay, I've got a few. Labrador Lounge, Mixed Breed Center, and Milk-Bone Galley."

MaryEllen piped up, "I like Milk-Bone Galley, but I came up with my own name for the kitchen and order room: Collie Counter."

"Oh, I love that." Millie gave MaryEllen a high five. "Bradley will like that, too. He'll think you were thinking of Hickory."

"Well, I was." MaryEllen laughed.

"I can't come up with anything!" Carolyn wailed. "You guys are way more creative than me."

"That's okay. We still love you." Millie slung one arm around her friend's shoulder and pulled her close. "I've got a few names to share. For the front room, how about Lassie's Library, and for the birthday room, the Doggie Diner."

"Oh, those are good, Mil." Carolyn clapped her hands.

"Okay then, if everyone is in agreement, let's name the main room Lassie's Library, the order room will be Collie Counter, the birthday room will be Doggie Diner, and the last room will be Labrador Lounge."

Carolyn raised her hand. "Wait, wait, I've got one: Puppy Parlor. That's good, right?"

"See, you did good, Carolyn." Millie smiled. "So, let's go with Puppy Parlor instead of Labrador Lounge. Is that okay will all of you?"

In unison they hollered out, "Yes!"

"Carolyn, can you get us the plaques made to place on the walls next to the designated rooms?"

"Sure. I can do that tomorrow."

Millie cleared her throat. "One more item is on my agenda."

Todd started tapping his fingers once more. "Uh-oh, you sound serious. Is Annabel up to no good again?"

"I'm sure she is, but that's not what I want to talk about now. In just a week from Saturday, we will be hosting our first birthday party."

"That was quick. We just talked about this. How did anyone know to ask you about having a birthday party here?" Carolyn asked, surprised.

"Well, that was easy." Millie giggled. "The birthday party is for Luke. So, here's the deal. I've been trying to figure out the best time to have it. How about two thirty? We close at three thirty, and it seems that the last hour is pretty quiet. If a customer does come in, we can include them. I may be crazy, but I do realize that Luke won't know if there is a strange dog at his party."

"Well, that's a relief," Todd bantered. "For a minute I was worried. I was expecting you to say Luke only wants to share his cake with friends and family."

"All right." Millie smiled. "Laugh at me all you want. When Luke's party is a raging success and you want to have a party for your fur babies, I'll have the last laugh. In the meantime, I'll be sending invitations to your fur babies. I'm sure all of them will be happy to come to Luke's 'paw-ty' and eat cake. Presents expected."

"Oh, you've got to be kidding," MaryEllen said. "You aren't going to give up teasing us, are you?"

"Nope," Millie said. "But seriously, all gifts will be donated to our local sheltie rescue." She heard the bells jingle. "Saved by the bells. Look, someone's got a beagle. He's wearing a kerchief. How adorable."

The bells kept jangling; the bakery was bustling. Millie and her partners shared smiles across the room.

A few minutes later, Millie spotted Julie Starr, owner of Julie's Jewels, walking through the door. She waved, but Julie didn't appear to see her as she walked over to a group that included Carolyn, who was oohing and aahing over another customer's little white fluff ball.

Millie walked over to the group, but before she could say anything, Julie tapped her arm and pulled her off to the side. "I'm so sorry. I had hoped to stop by yesterday, but I never had time. It was crazy busy at my store. Lots of my regular customers who have dogs stopped in to say hello and to tell me they were on the way to see the new dog bakery. I bet you were swamped. If it was such a good day for me, I can only imagine how much fun you all had here."

Millie put her arm around Julie's shoulder and guided her to a corner to talk privately. "Yes, it has been great—except for earlier this week, when the health department showed up courtesy of Annabel Larson. She tried to get us shut down."

"What?" Julie said, grabbing hold of Millie's hands. "That's awful. I do know she's busy telling anyone who will listen that you stole the building from her, and now you're trying to put her out of business."

"She's obsessed with this idea that I'm out to ruin her. For now, I'm trying to ignore her. We're the new kids on the block, and I don't want to make trouble. I have to admit it's not easy being harassed constantly. Carolyn has had to stop me from wanting to retaliate. I find it really hard not to respond to her taunts."

"Carolyn's right, Millie. Most of us have been here a long time and know about her penchant to make trouble for newcomers."

"But we've known each other since high school. I would have thought she'd welcome someone she knew."

"She's a strange person, so who knows? Anyway, some of us know you really well. We'll watch out for you. So listen, I have some great news. My niece is coming to work with me. She's always been interested in jewelry design, and she asked to apprentice with me. She'll be here soon. I'm really excited, and guess what? She just rescued a dog, so now I'll actually have a reason to come here."

"Jeez, Julie, you're welcome here anytime, dog or not."

After Julie left, Millie sat and called the refrigeration company Carl recommended. She got an appointment for them to repair the thermostat at the end of the week.

Next order of business: Millie was sure something was bothering Carolyn. She went up to her and asked, "Are you still worried about Annabel?"

"Yes. She's a threat to you, and since I'm one of your partners and best friends, I'm really concerned."

"Well, like MaryEllen likes to say, 'Spill the beans.'"

"Diane and Eva told you they used to go to Annabel's every morning, and now they said they're coming here instead. Today, I heard Peter say the same thing. Annabel is positive we are taking away her customers, and in some cases, it turns out she is right."

Millie sighed. "I promise you I will try to make the situation better if it will get you to stop worrying. In the meantime, Annabel has a great breakfast and lunch crowd, and we are not consciously trying to take away any of her customers. It's a two-way street. I'd be willing to work with her if she would just stop her antics."

Carolyn shook her head. "Quite honestly, if she had talked to you, I am not sure there is anything that could have been done differently. This is your dream come true. In her mind, you are her competition. Her only shot was to make it so you never got to open, and when that didn't work, her next move was to make it so no one would want to come here. It's almost like she is a little crazy where you're concerned."

"If you're right, she's not going to stop."

* * *

MaryEllen took advantage of Millie being distracted to run into the kitchen to find her cell phone. It was in her handbag. She quickly did a group text message to Nicholas and Grant. *Luke's party a week from Saturday. Bradley and I will call you guys later.*

Then she quickly punched in Bradley's number. "Hi," she whispered. "I can't really talk, but your sister just told us about the birthday party for Luke. It'll be next Saturday, but I better go. Your sister can be very nosy, and I don't want her to ask who I was on the phone with. I never lie very convincingly."

MaryEllen started to hang up, and then she remembered to say, "Oh yeah, I texted the date to Nicholas and Grant and told them we should talk later."

MaryEllen heard Bradley laughing as she ended the call.

* * *

Hickory greeted MaryEllen at her door. "Oh, I guess that means you need a walk. Okay, let's go!" she said, grabbing his leash from its hook near the door. She enjoyed walking Hickory. He was so well-behaved, and people always stopped to pet him.

Fifteen minutes later, when MaryEllen and Hickory walked into the kitchen, Bradley was on his cell phone to one of his brothers. She tried to hear what he was saying, but Hickory kept bringing her his squeaky tennis ball to throw, and he barked when she didn't throw it quickly enough, making it impossible to hear anything.

"Gosh, I thought you'd never hang up." MaryEllen sat on her barstool. "So tell me, what's the plan?"

"They want to surprise Mil, although we all agreed to tell Carl. They'll arrive late Friday night and crash here. We've got a great plan for Saturday for Luke's party. Carl can make dinner reservations for Saturday night and brunch on Sunday. That will make Millie happy."

"I don't envy Carl. If Millie is the least bit suspicious, she will nag him to death to find out what he's not telling her," MaryEllen said.

Bradley laughed. "Yeah, I know all about that."

CHAPTER NINETEEN

Party

The week flew by quickly. Saturday afternoon was Luke's birthday "paw-ty." Millie peeked out the bakery window. She breathed a sigh of relief to see no rain falling. Earlier in the week, the weather forecast had predicted rain. Of course, the party was inside, but it would have been a mess with wet dogs all over the place.

A constant barrage of people and dogs kept the bakery humming all morning. Millie couldn't get herself to concentrate on any tasks. She constantly caught herself looking at the clock on the wall. Around two, when she walked around, there were still a few dogs and humans, but hopefully everything would work out. Luke's party would be held in the newly named Doggie Diner, which they would have to themselves.

Millie positioned herself outside the front door to wait for Carl. It was cold. She wrapped her arms around herself and bounced up and down to help keep warm. *Thank goodness.* She could finally see Carl walking up the path with Luke and Annie. She waved, and as they got closer, she saw Luke was sporting a blue paisley kerchief and a white baseball cap that said "Birthday Boy" in a handwriting that looked suspiciously like Carl's. Annie looked perky in a pink kerchief. "Wow! You did this?" Millie hooted and whistled.

"Yes, I came up with this all on my own," Carl chuckled.

Millie got down on her knees to pet her dogs. "Ah, I better take care. I don't want to mess you two up."

"Don't worry; I took photos of them before we left the house," Carl bragged.

"Well, you sure did think of everything," Millie said as she got up and hugged Carl. "Come see the decorations." She took his free hand as she steered him to the Doggie Diner. He walked through the door and stopped in his tracks.

"Wow!" Carl said, gazing around the room.

Millie had balloons hanging from the small brass chandelier that hung over the table and others around the crown molding attached to crepe paper streamers. Posters with photos of Luke wearing a cowboy hat and a red kerchief had been blown up and placed around the room.

"Do you like it?" Millie asked.

"Are you kidding? It's typical Millie. Over the top but fantastic."

Millie threw herself at Carl. "Squishy hug, please." As usual, the hug made her feel especially cherished, and she reveled in it until she heard footsteps.

"Ahem, we're here." Carolyn walked into the room with her husband, Richard, and Levi, who sported an unusually bright pink paisley tie. Todd followed them in.

"Oh, hi." Millie blushed as she and Carl split apart. "I see Levi has on the prerequisite color pink even though he is a boy."

"Boys can wear pink," Carolyn said defiantly as she petted Levi.

Carl burst out laughing and pointed to the door.

Todd's close childhood friend, Michelle, walked into the Doggie Diner with Artie, his corgi, who was sporting a baseball cap and a tie.

Todd smiled. "Oh, Artie. You got dressed up for the party. How appropriate. Did you pick out your tie or did Michelle?"

Michelle grinned. "I picked it right out of your closet. With M&Ms all over it, I thought it looked birthday party ready. I did have trouble finding a baseball cap to match, so he's wearing one of mine."

"I knew that tie looked familiar. Good, you picked a nice one," Todd said as he looked at his dog, shook his head, and rolled his eyes.

Michelle touched his arm and batted her eyelashes. "Anything for you, my good friend."

Millie listened to their exchange. It was apparent—at least to her—that Michelle definitely thought of Todd as more than just a friend. It also appeared to her that Todd was clueless.

"So, we're still waiting for Woody—I invited him the other day—and Hickory. I would have thought Bradley would be here already." Millie looked at MaryEllen.

"Me too. By the way, Harry said he'd try to stop by and wish Luke happy birthday."

"Oh, what a nice treat for Luke." Millie smiled and looked more closely at MaryEllen. "You're very fidgety. What's up?"

"Oh, nothing. Just worried if the dogs will like Luke's birthday cake," MaryEllen answered cryptically.

That didn't make much sense, but Millie was too happy to care, and she shrugged it off.

Carl glanced at his watch. "Oh, I just realized I left the iPad and the camera in the car. I better hurry up and get them."

The door swung open. Bradley walked in alone.

"Oh no, where's Hickory? Is he sick or something?" Millie asked, concerned. "Don't tell me he's not coming to Luke's party."

"Don't worry. He's here. He's coming with his friends."

"What friends?" Millie exclaimed. "There's no extra room at the table. It only seats six."

"Well, I think you will want to find room for these particular friends."

As he said that, Nicholas and Grant walked in with Hickory. The two boys yelled, "*Surprise!* We're here to celebrate our fur brother's birthday."

Millie was speechless for only a second, and then she launched herself at the twins, grabbing them tight to her. She finally let go and looked at both of them. This was turning out to be one special day. "For once in my life, I don't know what to say."

She looked at Carl. He was grinning from ear to ear. "You knew about this?"

"Yup. I even kept the secret," he said as he gave her the crinkly smile she knew and loved.

She then stared at Bradley and MaryEllen. "And of course, both of you knew, too?"

MaryEllen looked down at her feet. "Yes."

"Hi!" Peter hollered as he and Woody entered the room, interrupting the conversation. Everyone turned to look. Woody was all decked out in a tie, fancy red high-top sneakers with white laces, and even a birthday hat.

"Woody, you look divine!" Millie burst out laughing.

"Come meet Bradley and his brothers," MaryEllen said, holding onto Bradley's hand.

Millie found it interesting to observe all the interplay among the guests. She couldn't miss the disappointment in Peter's eyes when he was introduced to Bradley, who draped his arm over MaryEllen's shoulder. MaryEllen's response was to smile meekly at Peter. In a nice way, she had made Peter see where her heart lay. Millie was impressed with the way MaryEllen had handled the awkward moment.

"Okay! Attention, everyone. It's party time!" Millie announced loudly. She kind of wished she could just sit down and talk to her brothers, but that would have to wait until later.

She walked over to the rectangular table she had prepared for Luke's party. She had placed six chairs around the table. "Artie and Levi get the booster seats because they're small. Luke gets to sit at the head of the table." Millie picked him up and put him in his chair.

"Okay, Carl, give me a minute. I've got some stuff to get before you start the video."

"Oh, this should be interesting. Hurry up!" Carl shook his head.

Millie went to the small closet in the kitchen and came back to hand out cowboy hats and red kerchiefs. Carl started his video. She overheard him say, "In whose world is this normal?"

"MaryEllen, can you get the cake so we can sing 'Happy Birthday' to Luke?" Millie asked as she stood next to Luke.

Luke's cake, designed and made especially for him by MaryEllen, was a round white cake surrounded on the edges with strawberries. It turned out that Luke loved strawberries. If he so much as smelled them, he begged for one. In the center of the cake was a photo of Luke with a cowboy hat on his head. Instead of candles, Millie had placed tiny photos of Luke all around the cake. The photos were stuck on stakes about three inches high and were Millie's favorite photos of Luke from the time she had rescued him to the present.

Millie had purchased clear plastic dog bowls and decorated them on the outside with cowboy stickers. The bowls were for each dog's piece of cake and vanilla yogurt.

MaryEllen placed the cake in front of Luke. "Okay, we're ready."

Millie smiled and got down close to Luke. "Happy birthday to you . . ." she sang with everyone joining in, until Woody belted out a singsong howl. *What the heck? Was Woody singing along?* Sure seemed that way. Everyone else stopped and burst out laughing.

Once everyone had calmed down, Millie went to cut the cake when, out of the corner of her eye, she watched Woody leap out of his chair and launch himself onto the tabletop. "Someone grab Woody!" she hollered.

It was too late. Woody's eyes were on the cake. Sliding and slipping, he tried to gain traction with his sneakers. With everyone's attention on Woody, no one noticed when Levi and Hickory jumped up to join him, and all the dogs skidded into one another.

In the meantime, the cake got pushed around until Luke stopped it with his front paw and stuck his nose and mouth into it. The other dogs, except for Annie and Artie, who amazingly stayed in their seats, skittered to a stop and gingerly pushed themselves next to Luke so that they could get to the cake, too. *What a mess!* Millie didn't know whether to laugh or cry. Obviously, Carl thought it was a riot. He was laughing his head off but still managed to shoot the video. Looking around, Millie saw that her friends' faces reflected wide-eyed disbelief. She froze. She didn't have a clue what to do.

Peter managed to pull Woody off the table by leashing him, but not before his shirt was covered with frosting. Hickory and Levi continued to consume the cake. Bradley got a hold of Hickory, and Richard got a hold of Levi. The best was watching Hickory jump up and place his paws on MaryEllen's shoulders to give her a kiss.

"Ah, so cute!" Millie exclaimed. "He's thanking you for baking such a good cake for his friend Luke."

"That would be nice," MaryEllen said, licking her frosting-covered lips. "Yum, that's good."

Todd frowned. "Millie, I hate to say this now, but maybe the birthday party idea won't work after all?"

"Oh, come on. Artie was a perfect angel, and Woody's rendition of 'Happy Birthday' was hilarious. We just need to do the next party a little differently."

"The next party? You are kidding, right?" Todd sighed.

"Nope." Millie grinned. "For the next party, we'll just leash the dogs and have their owners stand behind the chairs their dogs are sitting in. That will solve the whole problem."

Bradley, Nicholas, and Grant stood around shaking their heads. Judging from the smirks on their faces, Millie knew they thought she would ultimately prevail. Growing up, she was used to hearing them say to her, "Like, yeah, Mil, whatever you say." She stalked off laughing.

Cleaning off the table, Peter said, "I kind of expected Woody to sing, but I wanted him to surprise everyone. I certainly didn't expect him to climb on the table. Actually, he is usually very well-behaved. I guess the smell of that cake combined with the strawberries was too difficult to ignore. Ever since we started coming here and getting pupcakes, he loves strawberries. I really feel terrible. Woody singlehandedly ruined Luke's party."

"Oh, don't be silly. Woody was afraid he wouldn't get a piece of cake since it was put in front of Luke. He was just making sure he got his 'just desserts.'" Millie giggled at her pun.

* * *

When Millie climbed into bed later that night, Carl smiled, turned on the TV, and pulled her close to him. She leaned over to give him a kiss, and that's when she heard the theme to *Bonanza*. Right away, she knew Carl had one last surprise for her.

"Oh, Carl, the video—you got it done. How did you manage that?"

"It wasn't easy, but I did it when you changed your clothes and went outside with Luke and Annie."

Watching the video, Millie got to see her face when Nicholas and Grant surprised her.

"Wow! I'll have this memory forever." Millie sweetly brushed her lips against Carl's. "What a perfect day." She rested her head on his shoulder. "And how clever to use the theme songs from *Bonanza* and *Gunsmoke* as the background music."

Millie watched Luke climb onto Carl's stomach and cover his face with wet kisses. She was exhausted, but sleep was elusive, and she lay awake thinking about the last several months. Carl had been so attentive lately. He obviously enjoyed helping her, and throughout the process of opening the bakery, they had grown more in tune with each other. His work schedule didn't seem to intrude on them nearly as much. She knew having her own business helped tremendously. She was so busy herself that she didn't notice quite so much if he was working. All good stuff was happening. Now if she could only get Annabel to stop her antics.

CHAPTER TWENTY

Memories

On Sunday morning, Millie woke up to the sound of raindrops pounding on the roof.

She and Carl were supposed to meet her brothers and MaryEllen at the inn for brunch. Her plan was to bring Luke and Annie and sit outside on the outdoor patio with the propane heaters running. Now the dogs would have to stay home.

Making a concerted effort to be on time, Millie got ready quickly. Her outfit was only slightly different than her usual black pants and black cashmere sweater. She switched out black for gray, and her jewelry was the epitome of casual elegance with simple diamond studs.

Millie didn't want to squander any time she could spend with her brothers, so at exactly ten thirty, she and Carl arrived at the inn. It was only a minute later when she spotted everyone but Bradley walking through the door, and while MaryEllen was explaining that Bradley was taking care of the valets, Samantha waved and called them over. "Sorry about the rain. I know you wanted to sit outside, but I picked a good table in the main dining room that overlooks the patio." She picked up menus off a side table and said, "Follow me."

While they walked to their table, Millie watched Grant elbow Bradley and point to Samantha. "Who's that?" she heard Grant whisper.

Bradley shrugged and murmured, "Good-looking, right?"

As promised, Samantha seated them at a corner table looking out at the rain-covered patio. "Enjoy the brunch. I've made some changes to the menu." She handed a menu to each of them and started to walk away.

"Wait a minute," Grant said. "Do you still have pancakes?"

Samantha stopped and turned toward him. "Of course, and I added blueberry ones, as you'll see when you read the menu."

After she walked off, Bradley snickered at Grant. "I don't think she realized you were trying to get her attention. She just thought you were asking a stupid question."

"Grant, did you ever get a chance to talk to my brother?" MaryEllen asked before Grant could respond.

"Yes, I spoke to him this morning."

Millie's ears perked up.

"He told me he was open to having another vet join his practice. He said he's getting to the point where he needs help."

Millie exchanged a glance with Carl. Her family knew she would love to have her brother join Harry's vet practice.

"So, are you two going to get together and talk?" Bradley asked.

"He couldn't see me until this afternoon, and that wasn't going to work, so the plan is that we'll meet the next time I manage to get home."

Millie smiled. "And when is that?"

Nicholas winked at Grant. "So, sis, now that Luke's party is over, do you have another project in the works?"

Millie gave them her knitted brow look—her favorite expression when they were younger and in trouble—tempered with a smile. "I do know you are trying to change the subject, and for now I'll let you succeed, because I do have a new goal. Now that the bakery is open and doing well, my plan is to have a different event, maybe every Tuesday, to bring in more customers. One week it could be an event to benefit our local sheltie rescue group. I'm thinking I can have them bring some adoptable dogs to the bakery. Then the next week, maybe we could have someone come in and talk to us . . . like a dog trainer. Another week, a group of us could meet to share dog stories."

"Oh no, that first idea may not be a good one," Nicholas and Grant chimed together.

"And why is that?" Millie asked innocently.

"Oh, come on, sis. You'll want to bring one home."

Carl shook his head. "That is not happening."

"I told you we were going to nickname you HHH," MaryEllen joked.

"What does that stand for?" Bradley asked.

MaryEllen giggled. "Heroine of Houndsville's Hounds."

Nicholas and Grant nudged each other and burst out laughing. "That's perfect for our sister."

Millie saw Carl frowning. "These rescue events you're planning"—he raised an eyebrow and stared at her—"will require quite a bit of work."

Millie laid her hand on his arm and said, "I'm determined to do this, and I'll get help."

MaryEllen stared at Millie. "Don't look at me. I've got more than I can handle with the baking."

"So, when are you planning to do these events?" Carl asked carefully.

"As soon as I can. There are so many dogs that need help."

"Be cautious with this, Millie," Carl admonished. "Too much time spent on rescue events can hurt the bakery. Remember, it's still new. You need to concentrate on it."

"Changing the subject, this time in your favor," Grant teased. "How do you know Samantha?"

"We met the day we opened, but I don't know her all that well."

"She's walking this way now," MaryEllen whispered. "Your sister will fill you in later."

"Got it," Grant said as he winked.

Samantha walked over to Millie. "I'm sorry I couldn't stay and talk to you before. Everything got a little confusing. We weren't expecting rain. It meant at the last minute we had to rearrange some tables to accommodate all the reservations."

"No problem. I could see you were busy. Let me introduce everyone." Millie pointed to Grant and Nicholas, identifying them as her younger twin brothers. Then she pointed to MaryEllen. "She's our baker—I don't believe you saw her opening day. She lives with Bradley, my wonderful older brother, who is sitting next to her."

Millie watched Samantha's eyes roam from Nicholas to Grant. She wondered what Samantha was thinking. She knew they were quite attractive with their dark, wavy hair, green eyes, and square jaws. Could Samantha be interested in one of them?

"Are you here in Houndsville for long?" Samantha asked Nicholas. It was Grant who answered, "Just long enough to celebrate our fur brother's cowboy birthday at the bakery, which was really fun." He smiled and asked her, "What kind of dog do you have?"

Samantha looked down at her feet and mumbled, "I don't have a dog. Listen, I have to get back to work." She turned and walked away.

Millie wanted to get up and go after her, but she needed to talk to her sometimes-clueless brother. "Oh my goodness, Grant," Millie said. "Didn't you see me rolling my eyes and my hand signals to cut it off? Samantha had a dog, but he died not that long ago!"

"How was I to know that? You said you met at the *dog* bakery. I assumed that meant she had a dog."

"Yeah, brother." Bradley nudged him. "You totally blew it. Now she'll never want to get to know you better."

"Maybe she'll like me instead." Nicholas chuckled. "After all, we are identical."

"Oh, be quiet, Nicholas. How was I supposed to know her dog died?" Grant replied sarcastically.

MaryEllen butted in. "You weren't, but if you were even slightly observant, you would have seen her face when you mentioned Luke's party."

"All right, all of you." Grant held up his hands. "Should I go tell her I'm sorry?"

"*No!*" Bradley said. "Just leave it alone."

"I think this is a good time for us to go up to the buffet," Nicholas said. "I'm starving."

MaryEllen looked at Bradley. "Yes, let's go get some of their yummy French toast."

"Mil, I know you plan to see Samantha at some point. Please tell her I'm sorry, and make sure you tell her I'm not usually a jerk," Grant said.

"I will," Millie promised. "I'm sure she knows you didn't mean anything. It's just that she misses her dog a lot, and to make things worse, he was a sheltie. I gather from her comments about him he looked like Luke."

"Oh, crap. I really screwed up. Are you sure I shouldn't apologize?"

"Yes. Now is not the right time." Millie pushed back her chair and stood with her plate in her hand. "Come on, let's get some food."

Forty-five minutes later, Millie looked around the table at all the empty plates. She knew that Nicholas and Grant would want to leave soon. She gazed long and hard at them. "This weekend has been perfect. Maybe you could get home again soon. You do know my birthday is coming up."

"Sis, your birthday is in a couple of weeks. I'm sorry, but there is no way I'll be able to get here again so soon," Nicholas said.

"That goes for me too," Grant added.

"Well, at least Bradley and MaryEllen are here." Millie smiled at them.

"And I'm here!" Carl teased.

"And don't forget your other kids." Grant laughed. "Your fur babies will be happy to eat cake with you."

"So true." Millie laughed too. "Plus, Carl planned a fabulous surprise for me. He just couldn't keep it a secret until my birthday."

Everyone asked at once, "What's the surprise?"

Millie beamed. "He's commissioned Harper McNeely to do a portrait of Luke and Annie."

Grant stared at Carl. "Oh no! You didn't!"

Carl smiled and draped his arm around Millie's shoulder. "Actually, I did. Your sister saw her dog portraits and loved them."

"So now you're going to have a portrait of Luke and Annie hanging in your house and none of us three." Bradley shook his head.

"Oh, come on, you guys." Millie said. "There are photos of you three everywhere. Every bookshelf is covered with them."

"Mil, honestly, you are so easy to tease. We can't resist." Nicholas got up and came around the table to hug her.

"Yes, I know." Millie sighed. "I hate to admit it, but sometimes I miss it."

Carl glanced at his watch. "You guys better get going."

Millie's eyes roamed over her brothers and MaryEllen, whom she also considered part of the family. "It's been wonderful having everyone together."

"So, let's get this over with." Grant kissed Millie and hugged Carl, and gave MaryEllen and Bradley a hug, too. Nicholas did the same. In a minute they all walked away from their table.

Millie linked her arm with Carl's arm, and they walked slowly to their car. She was recalling the entire weekend in her head. *What good memories.*

"Hey, look. What's that paper on the front window?" Millie asked.

"Looks like a flyer of some sort."

Millie took the flyer from underneath the windshield wiper. She read it quickly and crumpled it up. She really wanted to stomp on it, but that didn't seem very mature. "Listen to this. Annabel is putting out these flyers. She is starting what she calls 'specialty Tuesdays.' If you go to her place and buy a coffee on Tuesdays, you can get a free refill. Of course, she is trying to get people to choose her place over ours, but that's okay. We're going to have our own events. She must be getting nervous. In this case, I can be nice and pick a different weekday for our events."

CHAPTER TWENTY-ONE

Photos

Millie woke up on Saturday, the day of the photo shoot with Harper. She jumped out of bed while Luke and Annie were still sleeping and peeked outside. It was going to be a sunny day. That was great. Maybe Harper would take some outside photos.

She had bathed both dogs yesterday. They weren't really fond of getting bathed and had tired themselves out twisting, turning, and generally making bath time exhausting. Now she had to wake them so she could feed them before Harper arrived. But first she blew her hair dry, put on some makeup, and dressed in black sweatpants and a gray sweatshirt. She wanted to be comfortable for the photo shoot.

By nine thirty Millie had glued herself to the dining room window, waiting to see Harper's car. It was just about ten when Millie saw a black SUV cruising up the driveway. "Carl, Harper's here."

With Luke and Annie barking in her wake, Millie walked to the front door and peeked through the sidelight to watch as Harper retrieved her camera equipment from the trunk of her SUV. When Millie couldn't wait any longer, she opened the front door. Luke and Annie ran out and rushed up to Harper, yapping.

"Hello, you two." Harper used her free hand to pet them. "Oh, they're gorgeous."

"Thanks!" Millie said. "You two quiet down. Come in. Sorry to bombard you outside, but I am just really excited about this."

Waiting just inside the door was Carl, who reached out to help Harper with her camera case and placed it on the foyer floor. "It sure is nice to finally meet you."

"Yes, it is nice to meet you, too," Harper said as she squatted to better greet Annie and Luke. She looked up at Millie. "What are their names?"

"The sable one is Luke, Annie is the tri, and they love posing for the camera."

"And Millie made sure they are clean and fluffy. So, do you have a plan as to where we should start?" Carl asked.

"Do you mind if I walk around the house to see where I think I might get my best shots?"

"Of course not," Millie said. "Just leave your equipment here, and we'll show you around."

Millie led the way with Carl, Luke, and Annie following. The last room they looked at was the master bedroom. Harper immediately stopped in front of an overstuffed creamy beige chair with a matching ottoman in front of the glass patio doors. Her face lit up.

"Let's start here. The beige color in this chair and the creamy wall color will set off Luke and Annie perfectly. I'll get my camera. Why don't you get some treats to encourage Luke and Annie to pose for me," Harper suggested.

Five minutes later, Harper had finished setting up and was ready to start. Millie instructed Luke and Annie to get up on the lounge chair—they had never sat on it, yet they jumped right up and sat crunched together like two good friends. Only a few times did Millie have to tell them to sit still. They were really good, and Millie felt like a proud mom. Harper shot a lot of photos there, then she took some with them lying on the bed. She completed the photo shoot with them sitting outside on the deck.

The photo shoot was all over much more quickly than Millie expected. Harper explained that was because her subjects were very cooperative. So, about an hour after she arrived, Harper packed up her equipment and, with Carl's help, loaded up her car.

As Harper's SUV disappeared down the driveway, Carl nudged Millie. He put his arm around her waist and smiled, "That went well."

"Yes, it did. The dogs were great! I can't believe how they sat and posed. I can't wait to see how the photos come out."

"Me too," Carl said. "Listen, I have an idea for you. Why don't you ask Harper to come see the bakery? Once she sees it, she might be interested in having you hang some of her dog portraits. If she's smart, she'll realize it could get her some new clients. At the same time, she could meet your partners."

"Spill the beans," Millie laughed. She felt like she had been using that expression a lot lately. "Why would you want her to meet my partners? Come on, I know you have an ulterior motive besides just having her come to see the bakery. Would you like to share?"

Carl laughed. "Well, I was thinking Todd might find her attractive."

"Oh, now the truth is revealed," Millie giggled.

"I know." Carl grinned back at Millie and gave her a little squeeze. "See, you're not the only matchmaker in the family."

"We'll have to figure out a way to introduce them without being obvious."

"Of course," Carl said. "But I have the utmost faith that you'll come up with something."

Millie bit her lip. She didn't want to give herself away and let on that she had her own list of people she was thinking about matching up. She slipped her arm through his, and the two of them walked back into their house.

CHAPTER TWENTY-TWO

Romance

It was a gray, wintry day, and snow was in the forecast. Millie wanted to go to the bakery early. She was the first to arrive. Luke and Annie were with her. She hadn't really brought them as much as she'd expected. She was sorry for that, but she was always a little nervous that Luke would walk out the door. She knew Annie wouldn't, but Luke was curious enough to try it.

That day, the special was Luke's Hideaways, so Millie got started on the dough. The only problem she encountered was that Luke kept pawing her, and she had to keep telling him he couldn't have the raw dough. Finally, she said, "Luke, you are not getting any cookies yet. They need to be baked first. Go sit with Annie and relax."

It took her a while with all the Luke interruptions, but Millie finally placed the first tray in the oven and sat at the counter after brewing herself a mug of coffee. MaryEllen and Carolyn, along with Levi, came in a few minutes later.

Millie smiled. "Oh good, you brought Levi. You really should bring him more often."

"I know you're right." Carolyn sighed and bent to hug her dog. "I just feel bad when he gets underfoot. I don't want anyone to trip over him."

MaryEllen glanced around. "Thanks for baking. Any problems?"

"Nah, it's been good. Luke and Annie are having a blast eating the extra bacon and cheese pieces that fell on the floor." Millie bent down to let Levi lick her bacon-flavored fingers. "You know, you should bring Hickory here, too. He did fine at Luke's party."

"I know. It's just that I'm usually baking, and we all know that if the health department finds out dogs are near the food prep, we'll jeopardize the bakery. Can you imagine if the day I bring him, Annabel decides to show up?

She'll get us shut down for sure. Besides, he's a lap sitter, and none of us really has time to indulge him."

Millie grinned. "Oh, a beautiful collie that looks like Lassie? I bet we could easily find someone who'd like him in their lap."

"Yeah, I guess so. Maybe I'll give it a try one day soon."

"Oh no, I just heard the bells chime. One of us must have left the door unlocked, and someone came in." Millie pointed to the clock. "I didn't realize what time it is. The first batch of Luke's Hideaways is ready to come out of the oven. Can one of you go out front? I'd like to make a quick phone call."

Rummaging around, Millie finally found her cell phone in her handbag and punched in the number for Harper's gallery. She planned to put her matchmaking skills to work and was chomping at the bit to get started. It might be too early to call, but she figured she'd take a chance.

When the phone was answered almost immediately, Millie was sure it was an answering machine, and she started to leave a message when Harper said in a rushed voice, "Hello, hello."

"Oh, hi Harper, it's Millie Whitfield. Carl said you called to tell him the photos are ready for us to review."

"Yes, I haven't been particularly busy, so I had time to get them done."

"Well, I was wondering if you might have some free time this afternoon."

"I probably do. What are you thinking?" Harper asked.

"When you were at our house, I didn't mention that I'd just opened a business near you."

"You did? What business? The only new store that I heard about is a dog bakery. Oh my!" Harper burst out laughing. "That's yours, isn't it?"

"Sure is. Anyway, I was wondering if you would come here and bring the photos."

"Sure, I'd love to see the bakery. I just need to wait until my assistant gets here. Then I'll walk over."

It was a crazy morning. Every time Millie turned around, another new customer walked through the door, and whenever someone ordered a Luke's Hideaway, Luke pawed her leg. At first Millie couldn't stop laughing. Luke would hear his name and think he was supposed to get a treat. After a while, though, she was telling him no, and before she knew it, he was going up to the customers and planting himself right beside them and their fur babies. She finally got to the point where she had to tell him to stop begging for cookies and to go sit with Annie, who was being a perfect angel.

Right about the time Millie was expecting Harper, the bells jangled as a new customer and her dog walked in. The person stopped to look around and then walked into Lassie's Library.

Millie wandered over to greet her. "Welcome. Can I help you?"

"Hi, I'm Susie," the stranger said as she smiled. "My aunt is Julie. She told me to ask for Millie when I got here."

"That's me. How nice to meet you!" Millie said as she pointed to herself. "Your aunt mentioned you'd be here soon. I bet you're excited to work with her. She is so talented." She held up her arm and jangled her newest sheltie charm bracelet. "As you can see, I love her jewelry."

Before Millie could say anything else, Todd snuck in next to her and planted himself next to Susie. Millie chewed her lip to keep from giggling. Todd was being rather obvious that he wanted to meet Susie. "Hello, I'm Todd. I'm one of Millie's partners. I assume that's your dog."

"Yes." Susie picked up her small dog and held her up for Todd to pet. "Meet Eloise. I've only had her a few weeks."

"Ah, she's cute. So, I overheard you say you're Julie's niece and you'll be working with her. That's great." Todd smiled. "Want to get a treat for Eloise?"

Somehow, Todd twisted around and nudged Millie out of the way. *Good for Todd for making a move on Susie if she appealed to him.* No surprise really. She was cute with her perky nose and curly red hair, her alabaster complexion enhanced by her green eyes. Millie had never seen Todd flirt before; it was fun to watch him.

Of course, right then the bells chimed, and Harper walked in. *Figures. Now what should I do?* Millie's plan was to introduce Harper to Todd, but he was busy chatting up Susie. Millie laughed. Matchmaking never totally followed her rules.

She sighed and went to greet Harper. "Hi!" She put her arm around Harper's shoulder. "Come on, I'll show you around, and then we'll get something to drink and look at the photos."

Five minutes later, after they had wandered through the whole bakery, they sat next to each other on the sofa in Lassie's Library. Harper agreed to try a mocha latte, but before Millie could get up to get it for her, Luke jumped up on the sofa to join them. He settled his head on Millie's knee. "Ah, Luke, you cutie, you need a cuddle." Millie ruffled his fur and hugged him. "Luke, you sit here with Harper while I go get something to drink."

When Millie returned and placed the drinks on the table, Harper handed her a folder that she had in her tote bag. Not wanting to wait another minute, Millie opened the folder and began to look at each photo. *Wow!* As she reviewed each one, what struck her was how good they all were, but it was one in particular with Luke and Annie in the bedroom that really got her attention. "Oh, I love this one! Look how Luke is looking at Annie, and Annie is curled up next to him. I can't wait to show these to Carl. I wonder which will be his favorite," she said as she carefully placed the photos back in the folder.

The whole time she sat with Harper, Millie could hear the jangling bells in the background. She didn't think she would ever tire of that sound. Sometimes when she heard them, she felt like pinching herself to make sure she wasn't dreaming. She, Millie Whitfield, had really achieved her dream and opened a dog bakery, and it was turning out to be quite a success story. She peered around the room, and her gaze lit fondly on each one of her partners. If it wasn't for their total support, and Carl's too, this never would have happened. She had a lot to be thankful for, and she knew it.

A minute later, Woody and Peter wandered into the library. Millie smiled and hollered out to Peter, "Where have you been? We haven't seen you since Luke's party. Are you embarrassed to return to the scene of Woody's bad behavior?"

Peter laughed. "No, not at all. Work has been crazy busy."

Luke jumped off the sofa and wandered over to say hi to the sheepdog. Peter bent down to pet him. "Hi there, Luke. Have you forgiven your friend Woody for eating your cake?"

Harper leaned over and whispered to Millie, "Jeez, who is that hot guy with the great dog?"

Millie smiled. "Oh, that's Peter and his sidekick, Woody. Yeah, he is tempting with his dirty blond hair and day-old stubble. I guess having a dog that complements his messy looks helps, too. Peter's one of our favorite customers. I really don't know much about him. I believe he mentioned one time that he's an architect. Woody is a major character. He even sings!"

"Mmm . . .'" Harper batted her eyes. "Have him come sit with us, please."

Millie laughed. "Ah, so you're interested." She called out, "Peter, come join me. I have someone to introduce you to."

Peter and Woody marched over with Luke following. Millie scooted over to the end of the sofa, leaving room for Peter to sit next to Harper, but Luke sprang up to take the spot at her knee.

Peter laughed. "Okay, Luke, I see you get preferential seating. I'll sit in the chair."

Harper leaned forward to pet Woody. "What a great-looking sheepdog. I've never seen one with a gray circle around his eye." She stuck out her hand. "I'm Harper."

"Hi, Harper. I'm Peter, and this is the infamous Woodrow Wilson," he said as he tousled Woody's fur. "Better known around here as Woody. Do you have a dog?"

"No. I came to see Millie. I own a business around the corner."

Millie started twisting her ring as she tried to think of a polite way to leave the two alone. "It looks like Carolyn needs help. Please excuse me."

Peter turned toward Millie. "What did you say?"

"Oh, nothing; it just seems as if we are having a full house today. I better go help out." She grabbed the photos and got up.

Peter looked at Millie with wide eyes. "That's great!" She laughed to herself. Peter was so distracted that he had no idea what she'd said. *Interesting. Peter and Harper.*

Millie ambled over to the bookshelves, pretending to straighten the books, where she could possibly eavesdrop. She smiled when she heard their conversation.

"That dog adores her. He doesn't allow her out of his sight."

"I sort of gathered that from the photos I took of them. Seems she feels the same about him," Harper said.

Peter snapped his fingers. "Of course! Now I know why you look so familiar. You own the gallery around the corner. I love your dog portraits."

Harper blushed, bent down to pet Woody again, and glanced at her watch. "I need to go. Come see me at my gallery sometime."

"How about me and Woody walk you back?"

Millie grinned and rubbed her hands together. *Todd likes Susie. Harper likes Peter. And I didn't even interfere!*

* * *

Carl sat down on the den sofa and opened the manila folder containing Harper's photos of Luke and Annie. Millie joined him. "I can't wait for you to see them. They're fantastic!"

Carl had barely started to look at them when Millie said, "So what do you think? They're fabulous, aren't they?"

"Why don't you give me a minute to look at them—maybe even two minutes?" He tickled her, slung his arm around her shoulder to pull her close, and continued thumbing through the photos one-handed. "Gosh, these are even better than I expected!"

Millie snuggled closer and twisted her head up to look at Carl. "I already have a favorite. Now you need to hurry up and pick which one you like best."

"You know me. It might take me a while to decide. I want to go through them more carefully."

She squirmed around to face him and touched his arm. "Carl, there is something else I want to tell you. But first, do you think cupids really exist?"

"Uh-oh! What's this all about?" Carl burst out laughing and put the photos down on the table. "All right, Millie. Where are you going with this?"

"Well, sometimes I feel like there's a cupid slinging arrows around the bakery and randomly matching up people."

Carl couldn't stop laughing. "Millie, I have a feeling the cupid has a name, and it begins with an M."

Millie sat up straight. "Maybe. But it was really fun at the bakery today. You knew Harper was coming, and I was supposed to introduce her to Todd, but events took their own turn. Before Harper even got there, Todd met Susie, Julie's niece. She came over to introduce herself and her rescued dog, and let's just say Todd was smitten. Then Harper showed up, and I wasn't sure what to do, but as luck would have it, Peter and Woody came in a few minutes later. Harper took one look at Peter and told me she wanted to meet him. They clicked."

She grinned. "Two matchups in the same day! It feels like the bakery is turning out to be a hotbed for romance." She burst out laughing. "I can't wait to see who meets whom next."

Carl shook his head, although she did see he was smiling. "Millie, promise me you aren't going to get involved in matchmaking customers at the bakery."

"Honestly, I haven't had anything to do with this." Millie held up her hands. "It's just happening."

Carl gave her one of his looks that said he knew better. "I know you. You love to see everyone partnered up and happy."

"Yes, of course, you're right. But honestly, so far I haven't done anything to encourage this." She hid her hands behind her back and crossed her fingers. She'd have to be careful. Good thing she'd never mentioned she wanted to introduce Samantha to Harry.

Carl just shook his head again. "I know you like to meddle, but please try to refrain. Things can get messy."

He picked the photos back up. Millie watched him taking his time to look at each one. "So far, my favorites are the ones taken in our bedroom." He handed her five photos. "Here, look at these. I like these best."

She smiled. "Maybe this process will be easier than I thought. One of those is my first choice. I won't tell you which one yet. I'll wait to see what you decide."

CHAPTER TWENTY-THREE

Plans

"What's on your schedule for today?" Carl absentmindedly asked Millie as he stared at his computer screen.

"Usual stuff. Going to the bakery. I would like to sit with my crew if there's some downtime and brainstorm suggestions to bring in new customers. So, I'd like a yellow legal pad to make notes on."

Carl pushed back his chair, opened a cabinet underneath his computer, and removed one from a stack. He handed it to Millie. "I thought you had some good ideas yourself?"

"I guess. I've thought of having a Halloween party or a Thanksgiving feast, and of course a plan to hook up with the sheltie rescue folks and have them bring some adoptable dogs."

"Um." Carl flipped around to face Millie, his hands still. "I'm telling you, don't come home crying because no one adopted the sad little sheltie sitting by itself in the corner."

"I wouldn't think of it." She crossed her fingers behind her back and raised her eyebrow, although he couldn't see it. He had quickly turned back to his computer after delivering his speech. She knew he had said that only because he was a softie. He couldn't look at a homeless dog and not take it home any more than she could. She breezily kissed his cheek and left his office.

Meandering her way to the kitchen for coffee, Millie watched Luke trying his best to encourage Annie to play with him. He was at one end of the sofa, peeking at her and whining. Millie laughed. "Annie, are you going to play hide-and-seek with Luke?"

Sure enough, Annie peeked at Luke from the opposite end of the sofa. That was all it took. They peeked at each other, and then Annie ran to Luke's side as if to say, "I caught you!" The next thing Millie knew, they were zooming at lightning speed from room to room until they tired themselves out.

After filling her mug with coffee, Millie sat and opened the local paper, the *Houndsville Times*. As she read the paper, she came across a story about a community having a charity drive to help its citizens whose homes had been destroyed in a wildfire. It had a nice ending that told of people putting together a gala after the charity drive to raise even more money to help the impoverished families.

Carl walked into the kitchen. "I'm leaving for the jobsite," he said as he walked over to Millie and kissed her lightly on her lips. "I'll see you later."

Putting down the paper, Millie glanced at the clock over the sink. It was later than she thought; she needed to leave soon. Instead of taking Luke and Annie for a walk, she'd take them with her to the bakery; she hadn't taken them much lately. Maybe Annie would actually want to come for a change.

Fifteen minutes later, Millie was in her car driving to the bakery, and as she drove, she talked to her dogs. "You guys will have to sit quietly today. I have to get some work done. I'll take you upstairs with me, and you can keep me company. I'll try not to take too long so you can meet and greet whoever comes in today."

As soon as Millie, Luke, and Annie arrived at the bakery, MaryEllen asked Millie to put the strawberries on top of the pupcakes. With Luke and Annie sitting by her side, Millie fed them a few of the imperfect ones. As she worked, she mentioned to MaryEllen that she'd like to have everyone discuss upcoming events, but MaryEllen was so busy baking that she paid no attention. When Todd and Carolyn came in, they had other tasks they wanted to get done, so Millie didn't bother telling them about her plan, and instead she made up her mind to try to work on the list by herself. After she finished helping MaryEllen, she said, "Come on, Luke and Annie, let's go upstairs."

Millie's office upstairs had been designed for her. She and Alfred had chosen a small writing desk that was sized perfectly for her. On it she had her computer, a lamp, a few Steuben handheld crystal pieces, and a small dish with paper clips. She also displayed several treasured photos that she looked at as she sat in her high-backed chair. Some of the photos were ones of her with her brothers and her parents, but her favorites were the ones with her beloved Carl and her dogs. Staring at the photos now, she felt warm fuzzies in her belly. She got down on the floor and hugged her dogs. She was one lucky person. Ultimately, she knew life was a series of memories stored in the heart, and she certainly had many wonderful ones.

Time to start my list. With Luke on her feet and Annie nearby, Millie picked up her pen. Her plan was to start out small with a few events: a Halloween party with a prize for the best doggie costume, and possibly a Thanksgiving feast with turkey, gravy, and a canine pumpkin pie. She hoped to get calls for birthday parties too, but most importantly, she wanted to have a small rescue event.

Millie could hear the bells jangling again and again. *The bakery must be getting busy.* She needed to get done so she could go and help out. Besides, she was missing all the fun.

Footsteps on the stairs and a knock on the door distracted her. Millie looked up to see Carolyn standing there. "Mil, can you come downstairs for a minute?"

"Oh no, you sound upset." Millie put her pen down. "Don't tell me Annabel's here again; I can't deal with her today." Her partners knew that if she was upstairs, she was trying to get some work done; they wouldn't interrupt her unless it was important.

"No, it's actually someone you'd like to see."

Millie patted Luke, then Annie. "Come on, you two. Let's go. You'll be happy. I'm sure you'll find some stray crumbs around, and if MaryEllen sees you, I bet she'll have a sample of some new morsel she needs you to taste."

Millie stored her pen and yellow pad in the desk's front middle drawer. Her time upstairs hadn't been at all productive. *Oh well.* She shrugged; she'd have a better chance of getting this done at home one evening. Thankfully, it was nothing urgent.

Millie walked down the steps; Luke was on her left, pulling on the leash, and Annie was next to the banister, stepping more sedately. Annie was going up and down the stairs more slowly lately; maybe her eyesight was not so good now that she was getting older. Millie made a mental note to mention this to Harry the next time she had a vet appointment to make sure it was only old age creeping up on her.

When they got to the bottom step, and right before Millie stepped onto the floor, Charlotte Giery threw herself at Millie. "Oh, thank goodness I found you! Millie, we need help. The rescue is in big trouble."

Millie held Charlotte for a moment and then stepped back. She could see Charlotte had been crying. Her eyes were red-rimmed and swollen. Charlotte was usually impeccably dressed. Today, her cardigan sweater was buttoned incorrectly, leaving a gape between holes. Her reddish-brown hair was combed, but her usual dangling earrings were missing, and her face was devoid of makeup and definitely blotchy.

"Oh no, what's wrong?" Millie put her arm around Charlotte. "Come on, let's go sit down and talk. You can fill me in."

Millie led Charlotte into Lassie's Library, and they sat on the two leather armchairs off in the corner. They'd added the chairs at Todd's suggestion that some people might like to have a private conversation; now that space was a godsend. Millie made sure to see that Luke and Annie were stationed nearby. She leaned forward, her hands clenched in her lap. "So, tell me what's going on."

Charlotte took a deep breath and let it out with a sigh. "Oh, Millie, there were eighty-seven shelties that we seized from a local backyard breeder. We're not even sure we have an accurate count; there could be more." Charlotte stared up at Millie. "I'll spare you their conditions, but just know they need vet care ASAP."

Charlotte sat wringing her hands until Millie put hers on top to still them. Charlotte grabbed and squeezed Millie's hands as she continued, "Of course, this all has to be paid for, and we are at a loss as to what to do with so many dogs needing help at once. And to top it off, we are reeling from the death of our benefactress, Betty Townsend, who died unexpectedly. She always assured us she would leave money in a trust for the rescue, but now her lawyer has informed us that's not happening. We always counted on her for help in situations like this. Without it, I am not sure what we can accomplish."

Millie sat and absorbed Charlotte's words. Obviously, the rescue group wanted her help, and she'd be first in line to do something. But what? She chewed on her thumbnail and tapped her foot.

"I'm not sure I know how to help. I'd be happy to host an event at the bakery to help you get the dogs adopted out, but if the dogs are in bad shape, that's not what you need now. Carl and I can send a check, but I'm guessing you came here hoping for something else."

"We're not sure either. Our group is so small; it seemed like a good idea to come talk to you. Maybe you could put up a sign asking for volunteers to help foster the dogs or to send us a donation. We also need help with grooming them, although I have to warn you that what's matted in their fur is not nice."

"Putting up a sign is easy. Consider that done. I also believe I'll be able to find people to help groom the dogs. Meanwhile, I'll also try to think of something else to do. While you're here, can I get you a drink?"

"Thanks, but no. I only took a break to come talk to you. I was at a loss as to what to do, and you and Carl have always been there for us. I'm sorry I nearly attacked you when I saw you. Seeing all these shelties in deplorable condition is gut-wrenching."

Millie felt her own stomach clenching at the thought of all those poor dogs. She got up and hugged Charlotte. "I'll try to think of a special way to help you."

"Thanks, Millie. I better go. I need to get back to help with them. Wish us luck."

Millie walked Charlotte to the door, gave her one last hug, and watched as she walked away from the bakery. Her shoulders were hunched and droopy. It was obvious to Millie that Charlotte was totally overwhelmed. It was sad. Millie would do her best to think of a way to help her. First, though, she wanted to give Luke and Annie a hug—she needed that. However, she discovered Luke was not where she had left him, only Annie. *Darn that dog.* He kept her in a constant state of worry. She loved him so much and loved bringing him here. The problem was she never liked to tie him up, but leaving him loose was not always a good idea. Like now. She had been distracted, and he had disappeared. Grabbing Annie's leash, she thought, *Okay, he's fine. He's probably with MaryEllen begging for extra treats.*

Seeing Todd and Carolyn, Millie asked them if they'd seen Luke. They both shook their heads. She sped to the kitchen and opened the door. Seeing MaryEllen, she asked, her voice quivering, "Is Luke with you?"

"Of course, where else would he be?" MaryEllen laughed.

Sure enough, Luke stood with his head cocked, watching MaryEllen fill a wicker basket full of Annie's Animal Crackers. *Thank goodness he is okay.* Millie took in some deep breaths, knowing she had been careless and Luke could have just as easily walked out the door. She went over and ruffled his fur, trying to lighten her mood. "Luke, you have had enough tastes for today. Save some of Annie's Animal Crackers for Annie." She grabbed several of the animal crackers, admiring the way MaryEllen had cleverly painted a strawberry in red frosting on each animal cracker in the area of the heart. She fed them to Annie before she sat at the kitchen barstool.

After a moment of thinking about Charlotte's situation, Millie got up and grabbed a few biscotti out of the jar where MaryEllen kept the extras and stuffed them into her mouth.

"Okay, Millie," MaryEllen said. "You're stuffing food in your mouth. Something's wrong. Talk."

"Charlotte Giery was just here. Her rescue group just rescued eighty-seven shelties from a backyard breeder situation. She needs to raise money ASAP to get them help. I have to try and come up with some ideas."

If Millie hadn't been so sad, she would have laughed at MaryEllen, who was about to slice some apples but froze with the knife in midair and pointed it at her. "Oh no, what are you planning in that little head of yours?"

"Just some flyers asking for help. Nothing more." Millie grinned surreptitiously.

Millie turned around, hearing footsteps. Todd and Carolyn rushed into the kitchen and stopped in their tracks. "We wanted to make sure Luke was okay," Carolyn said. "But I happened to hear your conversation with Charlotte."

"Me too," Todd chimed in. "Oh, come on, Mil. None of us are going to believe you are going to be happy only doing flyers. I do have an idea, though. I've seen where they do online auctions that can be done by *others*. Please notice I'm emphasizing the word *others*. Seriously, you have a bakery to run."

"Okay, I get it. I need to stay focused on the bakery. And an online auction is a possibility. I'll pass on that idea to Charlotte, although they're going to need a lot of money fast, and that may take a while."

Nothing more was said, and the afternoon passed by swiftly. It was during the short drive home from the bakery, with Luke and Annie sleeping in the backseat, that Millie had some quiet time to think. It was a good time to review the events of the day in her head. *I've got it! Why didn't I think of this before?*

* * *

When Millie drove into the garage, Carl's car was not there. She was hoping he'd be home already. She walked into the house with Annie and Luke following her. She figured she'd feed them and watch TV while she prepared dinner, but when she turned on the TV, she ended up being transfixed by what was on the screen. There were a few emaciated shelties being held by what she assumed were rescue workers, while the newscaster spoke and the camera panned over wire cages. Standing on their hind legs and crowded against the wire fence were many more shelties looking forlornly into the camera. The image brought tears to her eyes and was one she knew she'd never forget. *Why aren't there laws to prevent this? It is so distressing.*

In the background Millie heard footsteps and then felt a hand on her shoulder. It was Carl. She pointed to the TV. Together they listened to the reporter. "So I missed most of the story. What's up?" Carl asked, concerned.

"Well, you saw all the shelties." Millie grimaced. "They looked so helpless, like they were begging to get out of those awful enclosures." She laid her head on his chest, tears pouring down her face. She attempted to wipe them with the bottom of her T-shirt.

"Okay, Mil, calm down. It'll be okay." He gave her one of his squishy hugs, which soothed her frayed nerves. "Let me get a drink, and we can sit and talk. Do you want something, too?"

"Maybe later." Millie knew Carl so well. He wanted some whiskey because he wanted to brace himself. He'd be thinking she'd want to rescue some of the dogs. Actually, maybe she would want one or even two eventually, but that was not what she was thinking about now.

He grabbed her hand, pulled her with him, and nudged her down onto their sofa. She waited while he fixed himself a drink. With his whiskey in hand, he scrunched in next to her, put his arm around her shoulders, and said, "Now tell me: What's going on?"

It was his unruffled demeanor that allowed her to keep calm and to choose her words carefully. "Charlotte came to see me today. Those shelties you saw on the TV—well, that's why she came to see me. Her group is rescuing them. They're in deplorable condition and desperately need vet care. She was hoping we might be able to help. I assured her I'd be happy to print up flyers asking for donations, but while I drove home, I came up with a grand scheme to do something special. I want to know what you think."

"Okay. Should I be worried you want to bring some of them here?" Carl peered into Millie's eyes.

She smiled and patted his knee. "You're safe. Not right now. I believe I can be more helpful in another way. I got my idea from an article that I read in the newspaper this morning. It involves a charity drive and a gala. It will take a lot of my time, and I need to know if you think I can do that and run the bakery at the same time."

Carl tapped his fingers on his glass and picked it up. Millie watched as he swirled the pale gold liquid, hearing the tinkling sound of the ice hitting the edges of the glass. He was making her wait to hear his response. She put her hands on his glass and took it from him, putting it on the table. "Come on, you're torturing me here."

"Millie, I know helping Charlotte with the shelties is of utmost important to you. Of course, I have some reservations, but I truly believe you have a great team in place. If you are aware of the pitfalls of ignoring the bakery, you will be watching carefully to avoid them." With that said, Carl turned Millie to face him, put his hands on her face, and gently kissed her. His mouth tasted of whiskey laced with sherry.

That did it for her; that was all she needed to know. If the person she loved best supported her decision, she knew she would ultimately succeed. His words confirmed it.

He squeezed her tight. "You're going to do an amazing job."

CHAPTER TWENTY-FOUR

Eighty-Seven Shelties

Millie arrived at the bakery extra early. After losing track of Luke the day before, and with so much on her mind, she'd left him and Annie home.

It was good she lived near the bakery. It never took long to drive there, and today she wanted to get everything set up for the day before contacting Samantha and hopefully seeing her at the inn. The idea Millie had percolating in her brain had only intensified after she'd read post after post of the seizure all over Facebook.

Time was of the essence. Her highly ambitious plan involved the inn and lots of local participation to pull it off. She'd call Samantha as soon as she could, and hopefully get to see her face-to-face. In the meantime, she couldn't sit still, and she didn't want to stuff her face, so she pulled out the broom and swept the floor while waiting for her crew to show up.

Next up, Millie grabbed a tray of Luke's Hideaways out of the freezer, and as she placed each one in the display case, she felt a pang of guilt that Luke wasn't here pawing her for one of the cookies named after him. He would never wander off when food was nearby.

Millie glanced at the clock. It was still early, and her partners wouldn't be arriving for an hour or so yet. She wanted to keep busy until then. An idea for the Woof-a-Roos had been percolating in her mind lately, so she went in search of some red food coloring and the ingredients for the cream filling of the Woof-a-Roos. It was no problem locating everything she needed with a neat freak like MaryEllen in charge of the kitchen. She spent the next fifteen minutes making the cream filling for the Woof-a-Roos. When the bells chimed, she had just started pouring red food coloring into the mixer. *Uh-oh. I better hurry before MaryEllen sees what I am up to.* Who knew what

MaryEllen would think of her inspiration? She turned on the mixer. Now the cream filling of the Woof-a-Roos would be red. How fun was that?

"Mil, what are you doing?" MaryEllen asked as she peered into the mixer.

"Oh, I thought it might be fun to color the filling of the cookies. This way the filling matches the strawberries you paint on top."

"You make me laugh. You may not like to bake, but you are certainly creative. Interesting. Might be fun to try other colors, too."

"Oh good, you like my idea. I wasn't sure you would." Millie turned off the mixer. "Want to finish up for me?"

"Sure."

"Thanks, that would be great. I want to . . ." Millie trailed off, realizing MaryEllen was so focused on baking that she had already zoned out. She'd share her plan with her later. Quietly, she slid open and shut the kitchen door and sat at one of the small tables by the window in the Collie Counter room. Earlier she had put her cell phone in her pocket. She pulled it out and speed dialed the number she had for the inn. She tapped her fingers on the table, impatiently waiting for Samantha to answer.

Finally, Samantha breathlessly said, "Hi, Millie. Is everything okay?"

"Yes, but if you have time, I'd like to come talk to you today. I have a proposal for you."

"Oh, this sounds interesting. Come over anytime. I'll be here."

"Super," Millie said. "MaryEllen's already here. As soon as Carolyn and Todd get here, I'll walk over."

By the time Carolyn arrived ten minutes later, Millie grabbed her best friend and told her the plan she had come up with. Carolyn thought her plan was brilliant, but she also believed it was quite an undertaking to get done quickly.

A half hour later, as she was striding to the inn, Millie concentrated on how she'd present her case to Samantha. She knew that how she conveyed her vision was vitally important. She thought about the many dogs that needed help. She knew how happy Annie and Luke were, and if not for the sheltie group, who knows what their fate would have been? *Still, if I convinced Carl about the bakery, I can do this, too.*

Entering the inn, Millie stopped midstride. *Wow! What had happened here?* New paint, new furniture—it looked amazing. She couldn't wait for Carl to see it. She'd have him bring her here for lunch or dinner. He'd be impressed, too.

Millie automatically assumed Samantha was responsible for the improvements because Brenda hadn't changed a thing for years. If so, she was good—really good. She'd have to tell her so. Looking around, she spotted Samantha rearranging flowers in a vase on a console table. She walked over and tapped her shoulder. "Hi."

"Oops." Samantha caught the vase as it almost slipped from her hands. "You surprised me! I was concentrating on arranging the flowers and I never heard you. Flower arranging has never been my strong point." She smiled. "You got here quick; you must really have something on your mind."

"Yes, I do."

"Well, then just give me a minute to finish up." Samantha fiddled with the flowers. Millie watched her, although she thought they already looked wonderful.

Samantha stood back and wiped her hands. "Come on then. Let's sit over there," she said as she pointed to a small sitting area near a window overlooking the patio. "It's quiet and out of the way. No one will bother us there."

"I assume you're responsible for all the changes around here." Millie sank into one of the two buttery soft, gray-blue, velvet-upholstered barrel chairs. "It's difficult to believe this is even the same room as before. I'm impressed."

Samantha grinned. "Thanks. I feel good about what I've done, especially when returning guests express their approval."

"I guess Brenda likes what you've done?"

"Truthfully, she's hardly ever here." Samantha shrugged. "And when she is here, she seems distracted and happy not to be bothered. Listen, I'm thirsty; can I get you something to drink?"

"Sure, a soda would be nice. Lately, all I drink are lattes."

Samantha laughed. "Give me a minute, and I'll grab us both one."

While Samantha went to get the sodas, Millie got up to peek at the main dining room. A huge crystal bowl brimming with white lilies, white roses, and a touch of baby's breath took center stage in the room, where even the tables looked different. *Wow!* She really couldn't wait to come and eat here with Carl. He'd be so surprised. She went back to wait for Samantha.

"Here's your soda." Samantha sat and passed a straw to Millie. "So, I'm dying of curiosity. What's on your mind that you felt the need to talk to me in person?"

Millie bit her lip before she blurted out, "I want to do a dog rescue event with you."

"Ah. Now I get why you're here in person. You knew this would make me think about George." Samantha folded her hands in her lap and paused, staring right into Millie's eyes with such intensity that it made her wish for the power to bring George back. "Listen, not a day goes by that I don't think about George."

Millie placed her hands on Samantha's shaking ones. "Samantha, you know George will always be with you in your heart. And if you rescue, you will be helping another dog that needs your love. I believe that trumps everything."

Samantha sighed. "This is so difficult for me to even utter, but lately I've been thinking George would want me to have another dog to love like I loved him. So, tell me what you want me to do. I'm not sure how I can help."

"Well, I believe when you hear my plan you'll understand. I have what I consider a great idea, but I need help, lots of it. Knowing Brenda hired you to organize some social events at the inn, I think you'd be the perfect one to help make my plan a reality." Millie reached out for her soda and took a sip. "I'll start by telling you that there were eighty-seven shelties that were rescued from a backyard breeder. Charlotte Giery, the head of the local sheltie group, came to me for assistance. Obviously I would love to help her and the dogs."

"Oh no! I remember a few years ago when the news covered a story in Texas about more than a hundred collies being seized from a really bad situation. It was scandalous. At the time, I wished I lived nearby. The Houston rescue pulled all the dogs, had lots of volunteers, and worked to rehabilitate every single one. If I remember correctly, some were even pregnant. They called it Camp Collie. I wonder if they will model this rescue after that one. We could volunteer to help. I'd really like that."

"I'd like that too, but they will also need lots of financial assistance. I have been thinking about this nonstop, and here's what I've come up with." Millie paused. "I want to have a charity drive. We start by asking the local merchants around here to help us raise money. Here's what I think might work. Take Bridget's Bookstop; for every kid's book she sells, she donates a dollar, or at the bakery, every time we sell a latte, we donate 10 percent of our profit. If we're successful in rounding up a lot of the merchants around here to participate, we could raise a lot of money to help the dogs." She thought as she chewed her lip that by purposely changing the pronoun from "I" to "we," Samantha would think of herself as already involved.

Samantha smiled broadly. "So far, I love it! Your idea sounds fabulous. I'd like very much to participate."

"There's more," Millie said. "What I have in my mind is to have a blowout gala at the end of the weeklong charity drive." Here she paused again and took a deep breath before letting it out and continuing really quickly. "Let's have our gala right here at the inn and announce the results of our charity drive and hand over a check to the recipients."

Millie stared at Samantha. She was expecting a lot. Was Samantha still onboard? She wasn't at all sure. Well, she might as well divulge the one major detail that she was a little bit nervous about revealing. It could be the deal breaker. "Samantha, the biggest problem, as I see it, is that we need to do this really soon. These dogs need our help now."

Samantha's face was no longer all smiley. Had Millie's request to have the gala at the inn really soon derailed everything? *Darn, I hope not.* Millie really believed in her vision, but then again, like envisioning the bakery, she could picture this all so clearly in her mind. It really could be fantastic, and she would personally work tirelessly to make it happen.

Samantha sighed. "Oh, Millie. I'd be happy to have it here, but it's not up to me. Brenda has to make that call. She is, after all, the owner of this place. Even if she says yes, putting together an event of this proportion and doing it well, which I know is your aim, might be difficult to pull off quickly. What's the rush?"

"It's all about those shelties needing vet care. To do that, the rescue group needs money now."

"That makes good sense. I can try to convince Brenda, but I have no idea what she'll say."

"Tell her the story of the dogs living in squalor. I know Brenda likes dogs. She allows them to be guests and to eat on the patio. Maybe that will sway her."

"Good point, Millie. That might work."

Millie chewed her lip again. She needed to stop herself; if she did not, it might start bleeding because she was gnawing it so hard. In her haste to put this event together, she hadn't really considered that Samantha would need Brenda's consent. Now she'd have to wait to see if Brenda agreed to have the gala at the inn. Obviously, Brenda could nix her whole plan. In the past, Brenda had never seemed interested in having affairs at the inn. What if she still felt that way? But then why had she hired Samantha? Millie had no answers, and all she could think to say was "I'll be waiting to hear from you after you talk to Brenda."

Samantha seemed to sense Millie's frustration and tried to console her. "Come on, Millie, have faith. I will give it my best shot, and I will get back to you as soon as Brenda gives me an answer. I too would like to do this for those poor dogs."

Millie took one last sip of her soda and then got up to leave. "Okay, I'll wait to hear from you. Hopefully, you'll have good news."

Millie trudged out the front door of the inn, smiled absentmindedly at the doorman who held the door for her, and headed back to the bakery. She couldn't help but worry about the fate of the eighty-seven shelties.

CHAPTER TWENTY-FIVE

The Answer

The rain pounding on the roof woke Millie up. *Yuck!* She'd rather have snow. She didn't like rain as an adult, and she hadn't liked it as a child. It made her think of when she couldn't go outside and play in her beloved sandbox. Luke and Annie didn't like the rain either. Actually, Luke hated it so much that Millie had bought him a waterproof khaki rain jacket with a hood. And although he didn't like it when she put it on him, he seemed to understand that it kept him dry. She'd be putting it on him today; it sounded like it was pouring.

The smell of coffee brewing finally enticed Millie to get out of bed. She strolled into the kitchen with Luke, as usual, on her heels. Carl was sitting at the table, and she watched as he got up to put his coffee mug in the sink. He came over to give her a quick kiss. "Call me after you talk to Samantha," he said as he grabbed his rain jacket from the back of the kitchen chair.

She nodded. "Today will creep along until I hear from her. I'm hoping the bakery will be really busy. That'll help keep me from watching the clock."

"Well, if it's not busy, you can always find some biscotti to munch on," she heard him teasingly say as he walked away.

Millie waited until she saw the taillights on his car before she took the dogs outside. Because of the rain, they stayed out just long enough to go to the bathroom. She wanted to see if there were any more stories about the shelties, but she was not curious enough to walk down the driveway in the pouring rain to get the newspaper.

As she walked back into the house, Millie heard the phone ringing, but it had stopped by the time she got to the kitchen. *Crap.* Had she missed an important call? Luckily when she looked at the phone, she saw there was voicemail. She tapped in her password and listened to the message. "Hi, Millie, it's Samantha. I'm sorry . . ."

She bit her lip, sank into the nearest chair, and braced herself, figuring she should at least listen to the entire message. It went on: "Sorry it took me so long to call you, but when I called Brenda yesterday, she was too busy to talk. I convinced her to listen to me for a minute. She wouldn't commit to anything, but said she'd be at the inn all afternoon. I told her I was going to have you come give her your proposal in person."

Samantha's message sank in. *Okay, at least it wasn't bad news.* Millie still had a chance to fulfill her vision. She crossed her fingers as she went off to get dressed.

* * *

The first to arrive at the bakery, Millie kept busy straightening and vacuuming until her partners showed up. MaryEllen checked to see if there were enough pupcakes, and when she wasn't sure, everyone pitched in to help her get more baked quickly. Unfortunately, Carolyn wasn't watching the oven carefully, and the first batch burned.

"Oh, don't worry, MaryEllen," Todd said teasingly. "The dogs won't know if they're not right."

"Todd, I refuse to serve less than perfect pupcakes to my best customers."

"Well, you might not have a choice; it's time to open," Carolyn piped up.

From the moment they switched their sign to Open, the bakery was a beehive of activity. Fortunately, MaryEllen was a pro in the kitchen, and she had more pupcakes baked before they had to use any of the burnt ones.

At ten thirty, Millie peeked out the kitchen door and saw Todd serving a customer and her Great Dane. She couldn't help herself; she just had to pet the humongous dog. He was so tall that she could stand behind the counter and didn't even have to reach across to pet him. He just stuck his head into her outreached hand. Not many people had Great Danes, and she loved that one was at the bakery.

When Millie finally remembered to check the time, it was already after twelve o'clock, and she eagerly wanted to go see Brenda. She tapped Carolyn's arm. "Can you come into the kitchen for a minute?"

"Sure."

Millie slid open the door and walked over to the island. Carolyn followed her. "Okay, what's up?" Carolyn asked as she sat at one of the two stools at the baking counter.

"I need to get to the inn. I am so sorry, I wanted to tell you earlier, but it's been crazy busy ever since you got here. Samantha expects me to convince Brenda to have the gala at the inn. I hate to leave you again. Will you be okay?"

"Mil, that's fine. What's the big deal?"

"I don't want you guys to get annoyed with me because I'm not here to help."

"Mil, as long as you don't do it too often, we'll be fine. We all know this is something you are passionate about, and this is certainly an unusual situation."

* * *

Brenda and Samantha were seated at a round table in the corner of the dining room. As Millie got closer to the table, Brenda waved, and Millie could see she looked different—more relaxed. She had cut her gray hair more stylishly in a short bob, and she was wearing a pretty navy blue sweater set with a traditional pearl necklace around her neck. Millie waved back. She was all set to give Brenda a description of a dazzling gala that would have her happy to agree to having the event at the inn.

"Good to see you, Millie," Brenda said as Millie slipped into a chair across from her. "I hope you don't mind that we already ordered. I took the liberty of ordering the chicken salad platter for you. I know that's your favorite."

While the group was waiting for their food, Millie jumped right in with her plans. If she wanted to eat anything, she had to get her pitch done first. At the moment, she had no appetite and her hands were trembling. She had only this one chance to get it right, and even if it wasn't totally true, she felt that eighty-seven shelties were counting on her. She tried to make it short and sweet. She explained just the key elements by telling Brenda that her goal was to involve the local shopkeepers in their area to raise money for the sheltie rescue group. She'd do it by having a weeklong charity drive, culminating with a gala at the inn that would keep people talking for months.

Millie reached across the table to grab Brenda's hand. "I bet Samantha could put together a great party." When Samantha added that she was ready and willing to help, Millie started to breathe easier.

The waitress came to deliver their food, so the conversation halted. Millie picked at her food, her stomach still all twisted in knots.

"Millie, you're not eating. Is the chicken salad okay?" Samantha asked anxiously.

"It's perfect, as always. I'm just nervous waiting to find out Brenda's decision," she said. "I'm so worried about these shelties. I really want to help them."

Brenda placed her fork on her plate and locked eyes with Millie. "Well, at first, when Samantha asked me, I was going to say no. I didn't really want to get involved, but after listening to you today, I realized that was pretty selfish of me. The dogs need help, and the inn could use the advertising. Go ahead with your plans. It's your show, you two. I'll be at that gala ready to have my fancy silver pumps knocked off."

Millie dropped her fork, and it clattered loudly on her plate as she got up and ran around the table to drape her arms around both women. "This is going to be so good! You'll see!"

CHAPTER TWENTY-SIX

Ready, Set, Go

As Millie raced back to the bakery, her mind swirled in a good way. Now she knew for sure that she had a real chance to change the outcome for eighty-seven shelties. She wanted to share the good news with her coworkers, she wanted to dance around, she wanted to pump her fists in the air, and yes, she wanted to call Charlotte. She pulled her cell phone from her handbag, found Charlotte's number in her contacts, and tapped it. Unfortunately, she had to leave a voicemail, but certainly Charlotte would be thrilled at the news.

Millie skipped up the bakery steps, threw open the door—letting off a rush of jangling bells—and ran to find her teammates. She stopped in her tracks. The bakery was overcrowded with dogs and humans—it was so good to see, but it meant she would have to wait to share her good news. Since it looked like her team had everything under control, she'd take the opportunity to make a list of all the ideas floating around in her head.

Millie slipped upstairs and retrieved her yellow pad from the desk. The first thing to do was to make a list of merchants to participate in the fundraising, starting with those she knew best, including Julie's Jewels, Bridget's Bookstop, Frannie's Flowers, and Harper McNeely's gallery. She'd need to convince them to serve on a committee and ask them to help her to get other merchants involved. Bridget and Frannie had been around forever, and they could reach out to some of the other merchants for her. She planned to include Harry, too. She had several reasons for that. He would know the group that had rescued the shelties. Besides, there was her plan to match him up with Samantha. Never one to lose an opportunity, Millie would work every angle.

* * *

Just two days later, Millie had arranged with Samantha to have the first meeting of her newly formed gala committee at the inn. It was set for 8:30 a.m. She left her car at the bakery and walked over to the inn, arriving at eight to help Samantha set up for the meeting.

Walking up the steps to the inn, she was impressed once again with the changes Samantha had made. At the front door were two beautiful ceramic pots filled with some exotic plant she didn't recognize and a huge doormat with a logo, presumably made expressly for the inn.

Hilary, Samantha's assistant, waved to Millie from the reception desk and pointed toward the morning room. "Samantha is in there waiting for you."

What a pretty room this is now, Millie thought as she walked in to find Samantha placing a carafe of coffee on a sideboard piled high with bagels, their fixings, and pastries. "Wow, you did all this for our meeting? And I came early thinking I'd help you. Obviously, that's unnecessary. The food looks yummy—thanks!"

Millie looked for a place to put her handbag and saw Samantha had set a rectangular table with place settings. "I gather that's for us, too."

"Yup. This room is great for small meetings."

Millie had brought a yellow pad with her. The only problem was that she had rolled it up so it would fit in her handbag, and now it was all bent out of shape. At least she could still read her notes. She placed it at the head of the table and went to join Samantha, who was standing in the doorway and presumably waiting for the others to arrive.

Millie waved when she saw Frannie and Julie heading her way. She was pleasantly surprised to see Julie, who had told her she wasn't sure she could attend due to a previous appointment.

"So, where's Luke?" Julie asked as she walked up to Millie. "I'm not used to seeing one of you without the other."

Millie laughed. "Ah, you mean my best buddy. I left him home today with Annie. To be honest, I feel guilty because I always seem to leave Annie home alone. She likes his company, too, and if I had brought him here, he certainly would have kept tapping me with his paw. He likes to have my full attention."

"Oh really! You think?" Julie said as she and Frannie looked at each other and burst out giggling.

Millie laughed with them until she looked up and saw—*oh no!*—Bridget walking down the hallway with Annabel. "Crap."

Samantha raised her eyebrows. "Did you just say 'crap'?"

"Yup. Annabel is walking this way, and to put it nicely, we are not getting along these days. Bridget must have invited her to come. I certainly did not. I told everyone I invited they could bring other shopkeepers with them—the more the merrier." Millie shook her head. "This could definitely turn out not to be merry."

"I'll save you for now," Samantha whispered. "Go grab yourself something to eat. I'll deal with this."

That would work for now, but how was Millie going to handle it with Annabel sitting at the meeting table? Annabel had spread rumors about her. How many of the people here had heard the rumors? *Oh no! What if she is here to make trouble?* She shook her head. Well, there was no way she'd allow Annabel to get in the way of her goal to help the rescued shelties. It was better to be quiet and allow Annabel to make the first move.

Millie took a plate and used the tongs to help herself to a sesame bagel. Next up, some cream cheese. She loved just about everything Samantha had put out, and she might have taken more, but thanks to Annabel, she had pretty much lost her appetite.

Grace, the grocery store owner, and Harper strolled in. As Samantha corralled everyone over to the buffet, she said, "Help yourselves. After we're all seated, a waiter will come by to see if there's anything you want to drink besides coffee, which is here."

Millie looked at her watch. It was time to start the meeting. She took her plate and sat. *Darn, Harry is not here yet.* That could mean he had an emergency at his practice. Maybe he'd still show up. Her plan was for him to meet Samantha and to be instantly smitten.

Once she saw everyone was seated, Millie used her hand as a makeshift gavel and banged it on the table. "Okay, everyone. You eat; I'll talk. I'll start by saying I'm thrilled you all agreed to come to this meeting. Unfortunately, Charlotte Giery, the person who is in charge of the seizure of the eighty-seven shelties, could not be here. She is struggling every day simply to keep some of the shelties alive. So, moving on, I'll get to all the details about the charity drive. First, I hope you don't mind, but I picked myself to be chairman of the committee, and I've chosen Harry, whom I think you all know as one of our local vets, and Samantha as the two co-chairmen. The secretary will be Julie. I hope the rest of you will serve on this committee."

Millie took the time to look at each person for approval, and it was no surprise that everyone but Annabel was nodding in agreement. She shrugged. It wasn't unexpected.

"Okay, so here's my grand plan. We start our fundraising two weeks from Monday and culminate six days later with the First Annual Fur Baby Gala to be held here at the inn." Millie's glance slid around the table again. She was waiting to see the reaction to this.

There were gasps and lots of heads shaking. Frannie spoke up first. "That sounds fantastic, but how will we pull all this off in such a short time?"

"Not easily. Actually, I really wanted to do it even sooner—the sheltie group needs money now—but I figured that was impossible."

"Okay, so if that's the plan, let's get started. What do you want from us?" Julie asked encouragingly.

Millie chewed on her lip and folded her hands on the table. "I want each of you to raise money in a way that best suits your shop. I'll give you an example. It's for Julie's business. She designs a silver charm to commemorate this event, and with every one sold, a portion of the sale goes to our charity. Now, I know I've caught you by surprise, but I'd like to know what you think."

There was lots of head-nodding, and Julie spoke up. "Millie, that's great, and I love that each person comes up with their own plan to raise money."

There was a lot of buzz in the room as everyone talked to the people they were sitting next to. Millie concluded that they were trying to come up with individual plans for their stores. She smiled as everyone seemed really excited to be doing this event. Annabel broke into her thoughts when she waved her hand in the air and announced in a smug voice, "How come you're the one to pick the charity our whole community is helping?"

Uh-oh. Millie braced herself and bit her lip to keep from shouting back at her. She knew she'd been correct to think Annabel had come to make trouble and to get under her skin. She hoped she wasn't letting her anger show when she looked Annabel squarely in the eyes and said slowly and precisely, "Annabel, I'm the one who is putting this whole project together, and so far, I have had no complaints about the charity I chose to help. If you are not onboard, you can certainly leave. This whole thing is voluntary. You can do whatever you think is best."

"You just picked this one because it involves dogs, and it will help your business," Annabel said nastily.

Millie placed her hands in her lap so no one could see her clenching them together. "I'll say it again: If you want, you are welcome to leave. No one is forcing you to stay."

Grace piped up. "Annabel, this is a good cause. I don't see why it can't help your business, too. If you donate a percentage of your sales to the charity, people will want to come to your shop as well as Millie's. For me, I'm thinking I'll make up a list of, let's say, twenty-five grocery items. If a customer buys one of the items on the list, I will donate 10 percent of the purchased price. I thought it was great when Julie suggested I put dog bones and dog food on my list."

"I like Grace's idea," Annabel said with a sneer, "and I certainly could have done something similar to that with my fancy coffees or teas before I had so much competition from Millie."

Everyone gasped. Millie raised her eyebrows. She had to try to defuse this now. "Oh, Annabel, you'll do great. You have a wonderful lunch crowd."

Enough said, she hoped. She leaned forward, keeping her eyes straightforward. "But everyone, whatever you do will be great! I'm just thrilled to have you participate in raising money for this cause." She rested her gaze on Bridget. "I have a special request for you."

"Oh?" Bridget leaned forward, smiling. A tingle of excitement ran through Millie.

"If I remember correctly, you're friends with the author who wrote a true story about a dog she rescued."

"Oh, you mean the book *Mollie's Tail*."

"Yes. I loved that book. Maybe you could ask the author to do a book signing for a few hours."

Bridget nodded. "I'll email her and ask if she's available. Knowing her, if she can, she'll come. My bookstore will also donate 10 percent for every animal book sold during the event."

"Perfect." Millie smiled. She looked at Harper. "I'm curious what you might like to do?"

Everyone turned toward Harper. "Give me some time to think about it. I'll try to come up with something if someone commissions a portrait of his or her pet. I just need to figure out the details."

"That sounds great," Millie replied. "One last thing: If any of you know of another merchant who might be interested in joining us, please ask them to come to our next meeting. Obviously, the more merchants, the more money we raise. I'll get started on printing the invitations and getting us some advertising. Samantha, can you handle getting the inn ready for the gala?"

"Sure, I can do that by myself. I know how to put on a great party."

"Okay, if no one has anything to add, that does it for today. We should plan to meet again next week. Same time, same place, if that's okay with Samantha."

"That's fine."

"Our meeting is adjourned." Millie stood up. "Annabel, can we talk before you leave?"

Annabel shrugged. "Why not?"

They walked out of the room separately. Millie led the way back to the foyer. She pointed to two wing chairs in a quiet, secluded corner. She turned the two chairs to face each other and sat waiting for Annabel to join her.

Annabel perched on the edge of the seat as if she was ready for a fight. Millie sat up straight and addressed her calmly with her hands folded in her lap. "Before we talk about what seems to be an issue between us, I want you to know one thing," she said firmly. "I refuse to allow you to try and sabotage this event. It's not about me. It's totally about the animals, so I'm willing to try and solve this problem you started with me. But if we can't work it out, you better stay out of my way. You will not ruin this."

"What are you talking about? I didn't start anything. You did!" Annabel spit out.

"Come on, Annabel, you're the one who started this feud. You put in a bid so I wouldn't get Christopher's," Millie seethed.

"You're the one who ruined everything," Annabel said. "Everything was fine until you decided to open your dog bakery. I had planned to keep that property for myself to expand my business. I was going to operate an ice cream store there just like Christopher had. It was already a known success. I could have used the extra income."

"How was I to know that? You never said anything."

"No point to saying anything when I didn't get the financing."

"That's right, so why try to ruin the bakery?"

"Are you kidding? You're the one ruining me. I am losing business to you every day."

Millie grimaced. "So that's your reason for calling the health department. You wanted to put me out of business."

"You're darn right," Annabel said furiously.

"I knew it was you. Oh, come on, Annabel. You're just being ridiculous. You're blowing this out of proportion. You've got the fancy lunchroom crowd and real food. We're only open limited hours, and we cater to dogs, so how much competition could we be for you?"

"You have no idea. I happen to know that people with dogs love your place."

Millie rolled her eyes. *Maybe it's because we're nice and accommodating,* she thought, but instead she said, "Annabel, it only stands to reason people with dogs would love our place. That's who the place is for. But honestly, there are tons of people who love your place. I used to go there all the time—your scones are the best around. And most places do not allow dogs. That's what makes us special . . . we do. There's plenty of room for both of us."

Annabel snorted. "So, what do you expect me to do?"

Millie peered at her. "Try to be civil and, in this case, help the dogs."

Not surprisingly, Annabel got up without saying another word and stormed off, leaving Millie to wonder if that was possible.

* * *

It wasn't until she was driving home that Millie realized she'd never heard from Harry. If he didn't call later, she'd try to reach him tomorrow.

The minute Millie drove into the garage and walked inside, Luke and Annie greeted her. She found Carl in his office working on his computer. She walked up behind him, draped her arms around him, and brushed her lips against his cheek. "Hi. I had an interesting day."

"How so?"

"Well, overall the meeting was interesting and productive. Harry was a no-show, but Bridget brought Annabel."

Carl turned around in his swivel chair. He raised an eyebrow. "How did that play out?"

Millie shrugged. "I think you would have been proud of me. I asked her to sit and talk to me after the meeting. We are never going to agree about our buying Christopher's, but I suggested we work together on this charity drive for the sake of the animals. Unfortunately, she stormed off, so I'm not sure what she will do. I'll just keep my fingers crossed that she'll do what I asked."

"Good for you."

"Yeah, I was happy I didn't let her get to me at the meeting. She certainly tried her best. I just hope everything is okay with Harry."

"You know him; he wouldn't have missed it unless he had an emergency."

"Yes, I know that. Anyway, I stopped at Grace's Grocery to pick up a rotisserie chicken for dinner. I'll go warm it up."

Twenty minutes later, Carl meandered into the kitchen.

"Go sit, and I'll put the food on the table." Millie took the chicken and pasta from the oven and was walking to the table when the phone rang. The caller ID showed it was Harry.

Millie picked up the phone. "Hi, Harry. How come—"

"Millie," Harry interrupted, "I know you're curious about what happened to me today, but I need to talk to you."

"Okay, but we're getting ready to eat. Can you talk fast?"

Harry paused. "I guess. There's something important I need to talk to you about."

Millie sat. "Okay, I can wait to eat. What's going on?"

"I have a problem. A big one."

"So tell me." Millie held her breath. Hopefully, it wasn't something bad.

"Well, here's the scoop. One of the first clients I acquired—who incidentally I adore—is an elderly couple that, due to unforeseen health concerns, is moving into an assisted-living facility. They eventually found a place that accepted pets. Sadly, just as they were ready to sign the contract, they found out the one they chose allows only one dog per family. Here's the punch line: They have two."

"Uh-oh! Are the dogs going to be okay?"

"I am not sure." Millie could hear the concern in Harry's voice. "My clients love their dogs and might have considered taking just one, but they are mother and son. They don't want them separated. Right now, the dogs are here with me."

Millie sighed. "I would be so sad if that happened to me. I can't imagine having to give up my dogs. But Harry, I'm not sure why you are telling me all this."

"I think you might in a second." Harry hesitated, then blurted out, "Millie, they're shelties!"

Millie froze. She didn't think Harry could surprise her, but oh boy, did he. Her mind went blank.

"Are you still there?"

Millie squirmed. "Um, I guess I am. And I guess I know where you're going with this conversation." She glanced at Carl, who had a quizzical expression on his face. Gripping the phone, she said stiffly, "This is not a good time to talk about this right now. As I said, Carl and I are getting ready to eat dinner. Do you think I can get back to you?"

"That's fine, but could you get back to me soon?"

"Yes, I'll do that." Millie reluctantly put the phone down. She hoped Harry didn't think she was being rude.

Carl sat staring at her. "You're looking at everything but me. I gather there's something you aren't eager to tell me."

Millie raised her eyes up to Carl's. She could feel tears dribbling out of the corners.

"Oh no," he groaned. "It'll be okay; just tell me what's wrong."

She whispered, afraid to say it too loudly, although she had no idea why. "Harry has two shelties. They need a home."

Carl froze. He had just about gotten a piece of chicken to his mouth when he slowly lowered the fork to his plate. "Oh, Millie, you can't be thinking Harry wants you to take them. Did he say that?"

Millie looked down at the floor. What was she thinking? Even she didn't know. Of course, she was sad and confused, and her heart felt like a hammer banging in her chest. Luke was sitting on her feet. She put her hand down under the table to pet him. That was reassuring. Instinctively, she knew Luke would not really like another dog in the house vying for attention. Even she had to admit Annie and Luke were the perfect pair.

"No, he never asked me to take them, and honestly, I'm not sure that would be right for Luke or Annie. The people specifically gave the dogs to Harry because they were hoping he'd find them a home where they can stay together. They are mother and son and have never been separated. He probably has no one else to call and just wanted to see what I thought."

Carl rubbed his neck. "Look, my guess is he's desperate and you're a softie. I do believe you are correct that taking two more dogs would not be good for Luke. Annie might not care, but Luke would never want to share you. Annie doesn't require as much attention, so Luke doesn't mind having her around."

"I know, and it is all so very sad." Millie pushed her plate away. She propped her elbows on the table and rested her hands on her chin while she quietly thought about the situation.

Her brain whirled, then her face lit up and she gave Carl a cheeky smile. "I am having an epiphany. Just so you know, I saw that word in one of my books recently, and I had to look it up in the dictionary. The definition said an *epiphany* is a moment of sudden revelation or insight. I've been dying to use it, and now it is the perfect word for what I'm thinking, because I believe I might have the perfect solution for Harry's problem."

"Does that mean I don't need to concern myself about finding two more dogs in our house?" Carl relaxed his shoulders.

"Yes, you're safe." Millie laughed. "Though you might want to let out the breath you've been holding for the past five minutes and wipe the sweat off your lip."

"I think it might be Luke who lets out a breath, not me," Carl teased. "What is this revelation you've hit on?"

"Well, it just so happens that the other day, Samantha mentioned something about getting another dog."

"Millie, need I point out that *a* dog means one dog, not two?"

"Of course, I know that, but it's worth a try." Millie leaned forward and put her hand on Carl's arm.

How lucky is this? Now it'd be easy to introduce Samantha to Harry. Her first plan that they meet at the meeting had failed, but this plan could be much better. *Wow, this could be a doubleheader. Samantha gets a dog and a boyfriend!*

She loved this matchmaking business. It made her happy to think she could pick two people who were meant for each other.

Then Millie groaned. "Harry's expecting me to call him back soon, but I need to figure how to approach Samantha." She sighed. "It seems like everything is happening at once to so many dogs. It all started with the eighty-seven, and now these two. I certainly would like to help them all."

Carl grabbed Millie's hand, and his eyes had that special twinkle he had just for her. "Millie, I have complete confidence in you."

She grinned. It was certainly nice to have a husband who was so supportive. She picked up her fork and ate her dinner.

What next?

CHAPTER TWENTY-SEVEN

Dilemma

Millie watched the numbers on the clock. First it was 1 a.m., then 2 a.m., then 5 a.m. She was never going to get any sleep with Harry's dilemma on her mind. When the alarm buzzed at six thirty and it was time to get out of bed, she was exhausted and couldn't stop yawning. That was not good. She needed her beauty rest. Now she'd need extra eye concealer to cover the bags. *Ugh!*

Poor Carl. Thanks to her bed somersaults, Millie knew he hadn't slept much either, but thankfully he remained his usual calm self, even though he did seem distracted and simply gave her a quick peck on her cheek before he left for his jobsite.

By the time Millie was ready to leave for the bakery, the only thing she was sure about was that solving Harry's problem required a face-to-face conversation with Samantha. While she dressed, Luke pawed her, letting her know he was ready to go along. "Luke, you're staying home with Annie again today. I'm not sure how my day will turn out, and you'll be better off here. I promise we'll take a long walk when I get home." She kissed him goodbye and headed to the bakery.

Some days, the four traffic lights along the route all seemed to turn red as Millie approached. Today, she must have timed her drive perfectly because all the lights were green, and she whizzed through each of them. As she pulled into the parking lot, Carolyn saw her and waved. There was an open space next to Carolyn's car and she parked there. She saw that MaryEllen's car was a few spaces farther down the line. That was good.

After locking her car, Millie walked with Carolyn to the bakery. As they made their way inside, Millie glanced at her watch. It wasn't opening time yet. She could wait to turn their door sign from Closed to Open. *Perfect.* She wanted to be able to talk to MaryEllen as soon as possible.

She draped her arm around Carolyn, and as they walked to the kitchen, she said in a hush-hush manner, "Stay with me."

"Uh-oh!" Carolyn squinted, peering into Millie's eyes. "Are you up to something? You have a silly grin on your face."

Millie stared at her friend. "Maybe! Just come on," she said as she slid open the door to the kitchen with Carolyn beside her. Seeing MaryEllen at the sink, she put her hand on her hip and blurted out, "By chance, did you talk to your brother last night?"

MaryEllen frowned. "Aren't you supposed to say hello first?"

Millie put her hand over her mouth. "Oops, I'm sorry. I hardly slept. Your brother called me last night to tell me he had two shelties that need a home. How was I supposed to sleep knowing that?"

"Oh no!" Both women said at almost the same time, and then they peppered her with questions.

"Are you taking them? I predict Luke will not be happy. And what about Carl? Doesn't he think two are enough?" MaryEllen asked, placing her hands on her hips.

Millie twisted her head from MaryEllen to Carolyn and back again, and then burst out laughing. "Hold up, you two. Yes, basically I agree with you. Two is enough, at least for right now. But I didn't spend all night awake for nothing. I have a plan, a really good one. Of course, I would like your help."

"Oh no." MaryEllen held up her hands. "The last time you came up with a plan was when you drafted me to be your baker for this place. I'm not sure I'm up for another one of your ventures."

"Don't look at me," Carolyn said emphatically. "I have more than enough to do here—especially now that you need time to prepare for your event."

"Don't worry. This plan is easy. I might not even need much help. Right now, just listen. I want to hear what you think."

"Okay, but first, take a look at these," MaryEllen said as she pointed to a tray of bones in three different sizes, ready to be baked. "I thought we could call them MaryEllen's Best Doggone Bones. Of course, I will add my signature strawberry after they're baked."

"Good idea. I love the different sizes." Millie smiled.

"Yes, me too. I was thinking of calling them Papa Bones, Mama Bones, and Baby Bones." MaryEllen picked up the tray, shoved it into the oven, and sat at the counter. "All right, I'm ready to listen." She propped her elbows on the counter with her hands under her chin.

"Papa Bones, Mama Bones, and Baby Bones—how cute is that? But you better hurry up," Carolyn said. "We should be opening our door in ten minutes."

"This won't take long." Millie sat next to MaryEllen. "The plan involves Samantha. Of course, you remember her talking about her sheltie, George."

"Are you kidding? I felt awful that day at brunch when Grant said all the wrong things." MaryEllen winced.

"So maybe we can do something wonderful for her." Millie smiled. "Here's my plan. We go to the inn. Somehow, I'll bring up Harry's name and that I was disappointed he didn't make it to our meeting." Millie tapped MaryEllen's hand. "Then you can say something like I shouldn't plan on him making our meetings since we have them at a time when he has office hours."

As MaryEllen shook her head, looking skeptical, Millie continued, "That's the perfect opening for me to suggest that since he most likely can't get to a meeting, why don't we go to his office for a quick meet and greet." She winked. "We surprise her, and she meets the two dogs with Harry being the bonus. How's that for a brilliant plan?"

MaryEllen laughed. "Oh, come on, Millie. That sounds like a stretch to me. Why would Samantha need to meet Harry when they could just email each other? Plus, what if when we get there, Harry has people waiting to see him?"

Carolyn added, "Jeez, Millie, this sounds like something only you could come up with."

"Wait." MaryEllen put her hand up. "Carolyn's right, but knowing you, this could be interesting. I'll play along. I can't wait to see how you manage this performance."

Millie smiled and said, "Just a mention here. If I remember correctly, Harry doesn't usually have appointments in the middle of the day. Only mornings and late afternoons and evenings, so if we get there, let's say between two and four, we should be okay."

Carolyn shook her head. "You two go for it. Sorry to miss it. It could be Millie at her best. Todd and I will take good care of things here."

Millie went over and hugged her friend. "Thanks, that's great." Fifteen minutes later, Millie and MaryEllen were en route.

* * *

Entering the inn, Millie looked at MaryEllen and winked. "Let's get this done."

Samantha was at the reception desk, and she waved to them. "Hi, you two. What brings you here?" she asked as they walked up to her.

"It's such a beautiful day that we thought it'd be nice to walk over and eat lunch outside on the patio. MaryEllen needed a break," Millie said casually.

MaryEllen stole a look at Millie and gleefully added, "Yes, I needed a break. We'd love for you to join us if you can."

All right, Millie thought, *MaryEllen thinks she can tease me. She should know better.* MaryEllen knew Millie's three brothers teased her all the time. She'd show MaryEllen that she was most definitely up for the challenge.

Samantha looked around. "Sure. Let me finish with Mrs. Whyte, and I'll come sit with you. I'll meet you outside in a minute."

As the maître d' led them to a table outside, Millie tapped MaryEllen's arm when they passed the dessert cart. "Look, they have those custard-filled chocolate éclairs I love."

MaryEllen smiled. "My mom used to bake ones like these. Harry loved them, too. I wonder if he knows they have them here?"

"Hmm, that might give me an idea," Millie said, chewing her lip.

It was spectacular outside. Yellow and white daffodils nodded their cheerful heads all around them, and clay pots brimmed with purple pansies. The tables and chairs appeared to have a fresh coat of black paint, and the daisy-patterned plates fit right in with a "spring has sprung" theme.

"I love this time of year," MaryEllen said, looking around at the different flowers that were in bloom. "The daffodils and pansies are so pretty." She pointed to a group of purple flowers. "Those are different. What are they?"

"They're irises," Millie said as she glanced around at all the flowers. "And they make me wish we had a patio at the bakery."

MaryEllen shrugged. "Well, for now we do have our front porch. It's a little narrow, but it will fit a few tables, and we could hang some flower boxes from the railing or put out some large clay pots filled with different blooms."

"That's a great idea." Millie nodded, placing her napkin in her lap. "Eventually, it will be nice to add a patio out back. It's shady back there, and in the hot summer months, that would be really pleasant. Our customers would love it, and so would the dogs."

"Oh, here comes Samantha," MaryEllen whispered. "Are you ready to begin your pitch? I can't wait to see how you spin this."

"Shh," Millie murmured nervously.

Samantha slid into a chair. "It sure is gorgeous out here. I'm glad you two showed up. It'll give me a chance to relax."

When the waiter came by their table a few minutes later, they gave him their orders. "So, Millie, how come Luke's not here with you?" Samantha teased.

"Believe it or not, I sometimes do things without him. He's at home. I figured Annie would enjoy having him around. I'm sure he's just as happy there, although of course he would love to be here on such a beautiful day."

"I know exactly what you're saying. George would have enjoyed sitting here, too. He loved to bask in the sun, and the stone floor would have warmed his body," Samantha said quietly.

Millie placed her hand on top of Samantha's. "Well, maybe someday you'll find another dog to sit here with you."

MaryEllen started coughing. She covered her mouth and tapped her chest.

"Are you okay?" Samantha asked.

Millie bit her lip to keep from laughing as MaryEllen said, "I'm fine. The water just went down the wrong pipe."

Millie crossed her fingers under the table. After Samantha's comment about George, it was the perfect time to make her pitch. She had come up with a small variation on her original plan after she saw the dessert cart. Hopefully, MaryEllen would catch on and play along. This could be tricky. It was a little bit silly, but it might just work.

Millie pointed to the dessert cart and said offhandedly, "I see you have one of my favorite desserts: the chocolate éclairs."

Samantha smiled. "They're our most popular dessert. We purposely display them on that three-tier cake plate so everyone notices them. We make them fresh every day."

Millie looked at MaryEllen and suggested nonchalantly, "Didn't you say that Harry loves chocolate éclairs? Let's surprise him and bring him a few. Samantha, would you like to come with us?"

MaryEllen started coughing again. "Are you sure you're okay?" Samantha jumped up to pat her on the back. "You keep coughing."

Once she regained her composure, MaryEllen took a sip of water. "I'm really fine. I don't know why I keep coughing."

Millie was afraid to look at MaryEllen. Instead she stared at Samantha and nonchalantly asked, "Is your car here? You could drive us to Harry's and then you two could meet. After all, he is your co-chair for our event, and he might have trouble getting to the meetings since we meet when he has office hours."

"I don't know. I've got to get the inn ready for the knitting club later today."

"Oh, come on, it won't take long," Millie said encouragingly.

"But what if MaryEllen wants to hang out with her brother for a while?"

MaryEllen finally came through. She laughed. "Oh, don't worry about that. He won't want me hanging around his clinic. I used to work for him, and he thinks I'm bossy. He'll be worried I'll try to tell him what he should be doing."

"Shouldn't you call first?" Samantha asked MaryEllen. "What if he's not there? He can't always be there."

Millie jumped in with a response. "Oh, I guess that could happen, but then we'll just leave the éclairs." With her fingers still crossed under the table, she thought, *This will all work out okay.*

Samantha nodded. "All right, but I need to get back here fairly soon."

Millie had to keep herself from giving MaryEllen a high five. Her plan was officially in motion. She couldn't sit still. She wanted to get on the road. She didn't want Samantha to change her mind. This was going to feel like a very long lunch.

Thankfully, they didn't have to wait long for the waiter to bring their food, and when he did, Millie asked him to pack up four éclairs. That would save some time and help them get on the road sooner.

As the group got ready to leave, Samantha said she wanted to go tell Hilary that she'd be leaving for a bit. As she walked away, MaryEllen whispered, "Jeez, Millie, what if Harry's not there? Then what will you do?"

"Honestly, I don't have a clue. I just have to hope it works out."

MaryEllen raised an eyebrow, looking skeptical. "What's your plan once you get there?"

"Oh, MaryEllen, you're making me nervous. I'm trying to remain positive. It'll be okay. We'll handle it."

"You mean you'll handle it! I'm only along for the ride, remember?"

"Oh, shush, here she comes."

CHAPTER TWENTY-EIGHT

Bailey and Berry

Samantha drove while MaryEllen sat in the front passenger seat giving directions. Millie sat in the back, holding onto the white box of éclairs. She wished she could have slipped some of MaryEllen's pupcakes inside the box for the two shelties. She laughed. That would have been a nice surprise. Most likely the dogs would love the pupcakes as much as Harry liked the éclairs.

Millie glanced at her watch. Would they ever get to Harry's? As a child, she'd bug her parents that it was taking too long to get to their destination, and they would tell her to blow on the red lights to get them to turn green. She'd be doing that now if it really worked.

Thank goodness for MaryEllen's conversational skills as she kept asking Samantha about what social events were coming up at the inn. Samantha talked about her knitting club and told MaryEllen that the class was also learning to cross-stitch, that she was planning to start a book club in the next month, and that she wanted to start a bridge group. She said she'd had numerous requests for that.

It was Millie who spotted Harry's black SUV as soon as they pulled into his parking lot. "The black SUV is Harry's," she said, leaning forward and pointing to a spot near the front door. "You can pull in right next to him." She swiped the sweat off her lip. "That means he's here. Come on, let's go."

Samantha turned around to talk to Millie. "I've been thinking about it; I need to get back to the inn. I forgot I have someone I need to call, and I won't have time to talk to Harry now. Why don't you just run the éclairs in to him? If he's not busy, maybe you can have him walk outside and just say hi, and then we can trade email addresses."

Millie's stomach dropped. She gripped the box in her hands so tightly that she hoped she hadn't squished the éclairs. What to say now? "Oh, come on, I promise we won't take long."

MaryEllen finally came to the rescue. "Samantha, come on. I hate to mention this, but if you ever get another dog, you'll be glad you know him."

Samantha shrugged. "Oh, all right. I guess that makes good sense."

Millie breathed a sigh of relief. Her hands were so sweaty that she could barely keep a grip on the box of éclairs. This "plan" wasn't falling into place so easily. Right now, it felt like running the bakery was a cinch compared to this. Again she said, "Let's go."

The threesome entered the vet practice. Alexis, Harry's cute receptionist, was behind the reception desk. "Hi!" MaryEllen chirped. "I have something for my brother." She grabbed the box from Millie and held it up. "Can you tell him I'd like to say hello?"

"Of course," Alexis said. "Do you want to wait here or go into one of the exam rooms?"

MaryEllen glanced around the waiting room. "No one's here, so we're fine here." She turned to Millie and Samantha. "Let's sit while we wait."

Millie stood rooted in place and watched as Samantha and MaryEllen sat. Her legs were shaky, and her knees felt like they might give out. She needed to sit, but she felt like turning around and bolting out the door. Never mind that an hour ago, she had thought she was brilliant. This could turn out to be a disaster. She told herself to breathe. The lunch she had just finished was making her feel sick.

Millie gingerly sat on the edge of the leather sofa next to Samantha and glanced at her watch. *Where the heck is Harry?* Her hands were shaking. She slipped them underneath her to keep them still. She was really feeling sick. Maybe they should just leave, but just as she was about to suggest that, the door behind Alexis opened.

"Hi!" MaryEllen said and waved. She got up and walked over to her brother. "I brought you a treat." She held up the small white bakery box.

Suddenly, Millie felt a sharp jab in her side. Samantha had turned and was staring at her as she whispered out of the side of her mouth, "That's Harry?"

Before Millie could answer, she felt a second jab in her side. She raised her eyebrows and glanced at Samantha, feeling the heat of her gaze. She tried not to smile when Samantha murmured softly, "Did you think you might have mentioned he is drop-dead gorgeous?" Millie found that amusing, considering how gorgeous Samantha was. This was good. Maybe everything would be okay after all. Millie bit her lip to keep from grinning and watched Harry walk over to her. "Hi, Millie."

"Hello, Harry," she said, smiling as she turned to Samantha and tapped her on her knee. "Say hello to Harry."

Samantha sat frozen. Millie almost giggled out loud. She thought Harry was cute, but Samantha was positively dumbstruck. Her pale skin couldn't hide the blush rising up her face. "Oh, hel-lo," Samantha stumbled. "Nice to meet you."

Harry flashed a quick smile, showing off his dimples. "Hi, Samantha. Millie, I only have a few minutes. Are you here because of my phone call last night?"

Feeling everyone's eyes on her, now it was Millie's turn to blush and freeze up. She gazed from Harry to Samantha, then over to MaryEllen.

MaryEllen piped up, "We're here because I brought you that little white box of goodies you just put down on your counter. Chocolate éclairs. You know, the ones that you love."

"Thanks! That's great, sis. Nice surprise. I appreciate it." He put his arm around his sister and gave her a brotherly squeeze. "So, Millie, I really do need to get back to work. Did you come up with a plan for Bailey and Berry?"

Millie choked. She couldn't look at Harry. She couldn't talk. She definitely didn't want to look at Samantha. She shifted her glance to the floor, which was looking really good about now. It was Samantha who finally spoke: "What's going on here? Can someone tell me please?" Millie once again felt the heat of Samantha's glare. "Now that I think about it, you were rather insistent that I come here."

Squirming and avoiding eye contact, Millie mumbled, "Uh, where are the dogs now?"

"They're in my office. Why?" Harry asked curiously.

"Could I see them?"

"Of course. Why not? Alexis, can you get Bailey and Berry?"

Millie refused to look at Samantha. She tried to breathe in and out. The moment of the big reveal was coming, and she couldn't stop it even if she wanted to.

A few seconds later, Alexis walked back into the reception area with two sable shelties on leashes, one on either side of her. Millie heard a gasp as she felt Samantha's body shudder against hers. When she stole a glance at Samantha, she knew she was in big trouble. Samantha had covered her eyes and mouth and was quietly sobbing. "Oh no, what have I done?" Millie muttered.

Harry stood ramrod straight and stared at Millie with his arms crossed. "Yes, Millie, would you please fill us in?" he said angrily.

"Okay, okay," Millie stuttered. "Please let me apologize first." She tried to pull Samantha in for a hug, but Samantha pushed back and just stared back at her with tears streaming down her face. Millie touched Samantha lightly on her arm. "Please listen to me. I never meant to hurt you."

"Oh, Millie." Samantha shook her head. "You should have asked me if I wanted to see these dogs. I know where your heart lies, and you were trying to do a good thing, but . . ."

Millie didn't let Samantha finish. She knew she was taking a chance of getting rebuked, but she got up and walked over to the dogs, took the leashes in her hands, and walked back to Samantha with them. She handed the leashes to Samantha and said, with tears flowing down her face, "Samantha, these two babies are without a home. Maybe you could . . ."

Millie held her breath as she watched Samantha get up. Was Samantha going back to her car? Was this going to be a total disaster?

When Samantha got down on the floor, Millie let her breath out. She wanted to watch. She didn't want to miss the tiniest thing. She had a feeling what was happening here would be something she would remember and hopefully cherish forever. She hoped Samantha would have the same thoughts. Millie hadn't known Samantha long, but she really liked her and wished this would turn out well for her.

Samantha spoke softly. "So, I'm being told you sweeties need a home." She buried her head in one of the shelties' fur. Millie could hear her whisper, "You look like another dog I once knew."

Millie tried to breathe—in and out. Could this turn out okay? Goodness, she hoped so with all her heart. As far as she was concerned, if Samantha decided to make the dogs hers, it was a win-win for all concerned. She sat next to MaryEllen and squeezed her hand. She really didn't want anyone angry with her.

MaryEllen seemed to understand. She took Millie's hand in hers and held onto it. Millie sat motionless, waiting to see what Samantha did. It was so sad to watch the expressions that flitted across her face. It was obvious she missed George. Millie wondered if she'd be able to give her love to these two. All Millie could do was wait it out and watch helplessly.

Harry put a hand on Samantha's shoulder and squeezed it gently. Samantha picked up her head. "My wonderful George is gone, but he'll always be with me in my memories. I think he might want me to adopt these two, but I'm just not sure. Will it make me sadder when I look at them and realize George is no longer here?"

Millie wanted to leave. The suspense was making her feel like she was about to lose her lunch. MaryEllen must have sensed it, and she squeezed Millie's hand again, tighter this time.

Harry's expression softened. Maybe he wasn't immune to Samantha any more than she was to him. He touched her arm. He asked, "I'd like to know: Who was George?"

Samantha stood with tears still trickling down her cheeks. "He was my sheltie. The sweetest, most loving boy ever. He died just before I moved here.

I know why Millie brought me here. Seems as though she thinks I'm ready for another dog to love. So tell me, what's the story with Bailey and Berry?"

Before Harry could fill her in, Millie couldn't help herself; she piped up. "Samantha, this was all a last-minute plan. And I see now that I didn't think it through very well. I didn't exactly intend to hijack you. Harry called me last night to tell me about these two shelties that needed a home." She hung her head and continued. "I was afraid if I said anything to you, you'd tell me you weren't ready. I persuaded MaryEllen to help me to try to get you here today. And just so you know, Harry is as surprised as you are that I brought you here. He had no idea what I was up to. I'm sure he's not so happy with me right now."

Harry didn't look at Millie, confirming her feelings that he was certainly not pleased with her. He focused on Samantha. "My clients, an elderly couple, rescued them when Berry was three years old, and Bailey was only six months. They are mother and son. Unfortunately, the couple who owns them have to move to assisted living, and the place they are moving to will only allow them to have one dog. They didn't know that when they signed the contract. They are hoping I can find them a loving home where they can stay together."

"Oh, that's so sad. I can't imagine having to give up my dogs after having them for years. George was a rescue." Samantha shook her head, the tears leaving a trail down her face.

Harry turned and whispered to Alexis, who left and came back a moment later with a box of tissues. He pulled out a few and handed them to Samantha. She bunched up the tissues in her hands and looked Millie squarely in the eyes. "I have to be honest. If you had simply asked me to come see the dogs, I would have told you I wasn't ready." She bowed her head and wiped tears from her face, leaving behind black streaks of mascara.

Millie bit her lip hard. Dare she ask whether Samantha was going to agree to adopt the dogs? Was the moment she'd planned for going to happen? Samantha had her head buried in Bailey's fur, and she murmured something Millie couldn't hear. *Now what?* She had no choice; she took a deep breath and asked Samantha to repeat herself.

Samantha picked up her head, and as she wiped a tear from her face, she said, "These two are going to stay together. Together with me."

Millie couldn't help herself. She jumped off the sofa, bent down, and threw her arms around the two dogs and Samantha, then she pulled them to her in a Carl-like squishy hug.

When Millie finally looked up, her eyes locked with Harry's. Everything that had happened was worth it when Harry mouthed the words, "Well done."

"I saw that," Samantha said. "Yes, Millie, well done. And for the record, I forgive you."

Millie stood up slowly and said, "Oh, thank goodness! Hooray!" Then she flew into Harry's open arms and hugged him with relief flooding her body. She too could feel tears pouring down her face.

"One last thing I need to say: I think George would approve." Millie went to sit on the sofa before her legs collapsed. She knew she had lucked out. This situation could have easily turned into a disaster.

"You are so right, Millie," Samantha said as her lips quivered. She glanced up at the clock over the reception desk and then she turned to Harry. "Jeez, I hate to leave *my* dogs here, but right now I have to get back to the inn. I can come back later this evening to pick them up if that works for you."

Harry nodded. "I'll be here."

MaryEllen turned and smiled at Millie. "I never thought you'd pull this off, but as it happens, in the end, as everyone said, you did good."

Millie was happy to sit silently in the backseat while Samantha drove back to the inn. She leaned back and closed her eyes. No one else spoke during the short ride. All that had transpired had probably overwhelmed Samantha, and MaryEllen was always pretty quiet.

When the car stopped, Millie opened her eyes. She sighed. She wanted to get back to the bakery, but then Samantha turned around to ask, "Hey, would you guys like to come in for a few minutes before you head back to the bakery?"

"Sure, but we can't stay long. Carolyn and Todd are covering for us. They're probably tired and would like some relief," Millie said, thinking it wouldn't be nice to turn Samantha down after what had just happened to her, even if it was all good.

The threesome sat outside at the same table where they had eaten lunch. "Would either of you like a glass of wine or something else to drink?" Samantha asked as she waved to one of the waitresses.

"A soda would be great," MaryEllen said. Millie nodded in agreement. Samantha ordered a glass of wine, and after the waitress left, she turned to Millie.

"I can't believe what just happened. In the last hour, I have agreed to adopt not one but two shelties, and I have met one very hot guy that I plan to see later when I go back to pick up Bailey and Berry."

MaryEllen put her hands up to cover her ears. "Just be careful what you say. That guy you're talking about is my brother," she giggled.

Samantha smiled. "Yeah, well, I bet when he got up today, he never anticipated what both of you had planned for him. Good thing we were there alone. Can you imagine if some patients had come in?" She winked as she said, "And let's just be real here. He is quite the hunk."

Millie leaned close to Samantha. "So, what do you expect to do tonight?"

"Millie, what are you thinking? My plan is to pick up Bailey and Berry and go get dog stuff."

"Maybe dinner with Harry, too?" Millie suggested.

"Why would he ask me out to dinner? I hardly know the guy, and he certainly doesn't know me," Samantha said sweetly.

"I don't know. Maybe he thought you were pretty special, too." Millie glanced at her watch. "Jeez, we've been gone a lot longer than I expected. Excuse me for a minute. I better call Carolyn. It's closing time."

She fished in her pocket for her cell phone, then got up and moved to an empty table to have some privacy. She hadn't planned to listen to MaryEllen and Samantha, but she heard them mention her name.

"I guess I'm lucky to have met Millie," Samantha said. "I haven't known her for long, but she reminds me of my best friend Meghan, who is one of the best people I know. She would have tried to do something like Millie did today. They both like to think they can make everyone happy. Poor Millie; I bet she wasn't so sure this fiasco of hers was going to turn out okay. At one point, she looked a little green around the edges."

MaryEllen laughed. "You have no idea how frightened she was. I think she knew she might have goofed big time. She grabbed my hand and was squeezing it so hard I thought she might break one of my fingers. In the end, though, you are so right. She just wanted you to be happy."

"I'm sure I will be." Samantha smiled broadly.

Millie interrupted them. "Come on, MaryEllen. I spoke to Carolyn, and she said Todd just left and she's locking up now. That means we don't need to go back to the bakery, but I'd like to get home. It's been a long day." She looked at Samantha. "Have fun with Harry and your new adoptees tonight—and maybe even give that hunk a kiss," she said with a huge grin on her face.

CHAPTER TWENTY-NINE

Signing Up

The next day there was a chill in the air. Millie threw on her quilted jacket, remembering to grab a pair of gloves before she loaded Luke into her car. She had tried to encourage Annie to come, but Annie let her know that she wanted to stay home when she refused to get into the car.

Millie and Luke arrived at the bakery and walked back to the kitchen, where MaryEllen was busy putting her signature strawberries on a tray of pumpkin pupcakes, the special of the day. Almost immediately Luke was at her side begging for a treat. MaryEllen just smiled and threw him a strawberry, which he caught easily. He liked playing catch if it involved food. Meanwhile, Carolyn was up to her elbows in flour and dough, and Todd was sweeping the floor.

Millie's eyes twinkled as she plopped her handbag and a shopping bag down on the counter and pulled out a small square of fabric. "Take a look at this." She unfolded a square, sage-colored kerchief. It had a pupcake on it with a strawberry on top. Strawberries had become their logo thanks to MaryEllen, who put strawberries on every treat in one form or another. She bent down, tied it around Luke's neck, and held out her hand, as if it were show-and-tell in kindergarten. "Ta-da! He looks cute, right? Now when we go out to take a walk, he can advertise for us."

"That's adorable," Carolyn said. "And we have a surprise for you, too.

We've been thinking that it'd be good to have a menu board outside. Not right outside, but at the top of the path. You know, right next to the arrow pointing this way to the bakery. We figured since we're not right on the main thoroughfare, people who park in the lot might be curious enough to walk over to read our menu board and then decide to visit us. I picked up a blackboard yesterday."

Millie smiled. "Oh, guys, what a super idea. I love it. I'll put it next to our arrow when I go out in a little bit."

"Wait a minute," Carolyn said. "You just got here. You're leaving again?"

"Yes." Millie looked sheepishly at her teammates. "I really would like to visit some other merchants to get them to do our event with us."

"Millie, if you want to keep doing that, it's okay, but maybe we should try to hire some part-time help to fill in," Carolyn said. "We've been getting really busy at certain times. I worry that people will get tired of waiting for us to serve them. You know, some of them come in before work when they're walking their dogs, and they won't have time to stand in a line."

"I know." Millie chewed her lip. "You're right, Carolyn. Let's try to find someone. I bet we can find some older teenagers who want to earn extra money."

"That could be helpful for me, too," MaryEllen added. "But look, you guys, if you want to chatter, could you move away from the counter? I'm trying to concentrate. I want to try a new recipe with carob chips. You know carobs and strawberries together could be something special."

Todd shook his head and rolled his eyes. "You love this experimenting, don't you?"

As she opened the refrigerator, MaryEllen turned and spoke over her shoulder. "Yup! It's fun, and I have the best customers on earth. They like everything I bake."

Everyone laughed. "Well, today you'll see if they like your new healthy choice," Todd said. "It's just about time to open."

"I'll get the blackboard done so we can use it today." Carolyn walked over to the back corner and carried the board to the center counter. She detached a small box of chalk taped to the back of the board and opened it, and after looking through and touching all the colors, she chose a pink piece.

Millie started giggling. "Oh, big surprise. You chose pink."

"So? I happen to like pink." Carolyn chuckled as everyone stood in a semicircle watching her write TODAY'S SPECIAL: PUMPKIN PUPCAKES. Below that she wrote OUR NEW HEALTHY CHOICE.

"All done." Carolyn washed the chalk dust off her hands and glanced at her watch. "Time to open. I'll go flip our sign."

Millie picked up a tray of pupcakes and straightened several of the strawberries that were falling off. "Come on, Todd. Let's get the display case filled up." She held the tray in her hands, waiting for Todd to slide open the kitchen door, and as she walked past him into the Collie Counter room, she happened to glance out the window.

"Oh look, Samantha's walking up our steps. She's got Bailey and Berry with her. Let's go meet her at the door. Come on, Todd. You too, Luke," Millie said.

Berry had a white kerchief with a pink ribbon design, while Bailey was sporting a denim one. In an effort to match both dogs, Samantha was wearing a denim baseball cap and a soft pink sweatshirt. Millie pointed and nudged Todd to look, too.

"Hi! You all look 'pawsitively' marvelous!" Millie giggled as she petted Bailey and Berry. Todd shook his head and rolled his eyes at her before stooping to pet them.

Luke pawed Millie almost immediately. "Oh, Luke, I'm just saying hello. Don't get your nose out of joint. You look marvelous yourself with your custom-made kerchief."

Samantha pressed her lips to Luke's nose. "You know you'll always be my special pal," she said as she straightened his kerchief.

"So tell me, how is everything?" Millie asked.

"Everything is great! I love having two dogs, and it's especially fun to take them to work with me. Where's MaryEllen? I was hoping she'd be here."

"She's here. She's in the kitchen trying out a new recipe. I keep telling her that all she needs now is one of those silly caps and oversized glasses, and she'll look like a mad scientist. We laugh at her all the time. Every word out of her mouth is about dogs and how she wants to invent a new recipe. Now that they eat anything she bakes, burnt or not, she loves them even more. Come on, walk back there with me."

Millie rambled on as they all walked back to the kitchen. "All kidding aside, she's a blast to watch. I've never seen anyone so good in the kitchen. I know people like coming here because it's fun to have a bakery that caters to their dogs, but I'm convinced our success is also because her baked stuff is unique. Her idea to put strawberries on her treats was brilliant. We love to watch the human faces when they see their dogs eat strawberries. Like me, not many people know they are good for dogs. And not to be forgotten, humans love her baking, too." She patted her stomach and slid open the kitchen door, leaving room for Samantha and the dogs to scoot by her.

"Are you sure it's okay if we come in?" Samantha stopped to ask. "You know, with the health rules and all?"

Millie hesitated and then said, "Luke's here sometimes. We won't stay long."

MaryEllen was taking a baking sheet out of the oven. Her hair was tinged with flour—her shirt, too. Samantha burst out laughing as she said, "Oh, it's not difficult to guess what you're doing."

MaryEllen shook her head. "Sad to say, but it seems I am always covered in flour. I unconsciously run my fingers through my hair when I bake, and it seems to drift down all over me. Oh, look how cute Bailey and Berry look!" She held her arms open and got down to hug them.

"I couldn't wait to show them off and at the same time tell you how attentive your brother has been."

Millie snuck a peek at MaryEllen. The shock on her face was priceless. Millie knew she'd need a minute to recover, so she pulled out a stool for Samantha and pointed, "Here, have a seat at the counter and tell us what Harry's been up to!"

Samantha got up and put her hands on the back of the stool. "That's okay; I can't stay long. But I'll just tell you that Harry's been great. He ended up going with me to get all the supplies I needed, and today he's coming to the inn for lunch."

MaryEllen recovered enough to stand up and stare at Samantha. "My brother is taking a lunch break? He's coming to see the dogs?"

"Yes, of course. Why else?" Samantha said, blushing. "Anyway, I just stopped to show off Bailey and Berry, and to tell you guys everything is good. Actually, better that good, but I better get back to the inn. He'll be there soon."

"Here, I'll walk out with you," Millie said. "Luke probably needs to go outside."

After Samantha was gone and Luke had a few minutes outside to do his business, Millie raced back to the kitchen. She couldn't wait to talk to MaryEllen. "So, what's the scoop? Do you think Harry likes Samantha?"

MaryEllen ran her fingers through her hair, leaving more flour residue everywhere. "Obviously, yes! He must like her a lot! You heard what she said. He's coming to lunch. That's amazing. He almost never leaves his practice for lunch."

Millie held her hand up to high-five MaryEllen, but then she realized that was not a good idea unless she too wanted to be covered with flour. She clapped instead. "So, my matchmaking skills are possibly alive and well?"

"Sounds like it to me, but I'll call him and try to get the scoop."

"You realize you'll have to fill me in after you talk to him."

"Of course. I'll call him later tonight."

"I have to wait that long?" Millie teased.

"Yup."

Millie narrowed her eyes, stared at MaryEllen, and tapped her fingers on the steel counter, hoping it would encourage her to call Harry now. It didn't work because MaryEllen just ignored her.

"Okay, if you're not going to call him, Luke and I are going to visit some of the shops around here. Come on, Luke. Let's go take a walk." Millie remembered to grab the menu board on the way out and stomped off. She could hear MaryEllen laughing in the background.

On her way to the front door, Millie spotted Diane and Eva sitting in the library. They had Starlight, Journey, Buddy, and Cambric with them. They were talking to Carolyn. She stopped to say hello and to tell Carolyn she'd be back soon.

As she walked up the path with Luke, Millie knew the goal ahead of her was to convince more of the neighboring shop owners to join the charity event to help the eighty-seven shelties.

The first stop on her list was Karen's Knitting Needle and Cross-Stitch Studio. Millie expected Karen to sign up, but immediately upon entering the store, she sensed something was wrong. Millie could see Karen was nervously trying to avoid talking to her. When Millie finally got her to sit and talk, Karen admitted that Annabel had been there to complain that Millie was doing the charity drive for the rescue group only because ultimately it would help the bakery get new customers.

Millie just listened and did a lot of sighing and shaking her head. She wasn't sure what she could say to combat Annabel's complaints without sounding self-serving. What saved the day was that Karen had had her own problems with Annabel in the past and didn't necessarily believe her. Thankfully, before Millie left, Karen told her that she'd participate in the event.

Because she'd spent more time with Karen than she anticipated, Millie needed to pick up her pace. As she walked to her next destination, she counted on her fingers that six merchants—Frannie, Julie, Grace, Bridget, Harper, and Karen—plus the bakery had signed up. That was pretty good, but she certainly needed more to get onboard if she hoped to raise a ton of money.

Next up was Stella's Shoes, then Tina's Toys, and lastly was Colin's Clothier the newest store in the neighborhood. When Millie walked into Stella's, her go-to place for fancy footwear, Stella acted just like Karen and ended up leaving Millie with her assistant, saying she was too busy to talk. Millie shook her head in dismay. Annabel must have stopped in there too, but for the life of her, she couldn't figure why Stella would listen to Annabel. Was Stella afraid of Annabel's influence with customers? Had Annabel threatened her and Karen in some manner? That was the only thing that made sense to Millie, because she was sure Annabel never shopped at Stella's. Stella sold only designer shoes and Annabel had no fashion sense. Still, Millie was surprised Stella wouldn't even talk to her.

Millie left there disappointed and, if she was honest with herself, a tad angry that Annabel had obviously gotten to Stella first.

Next on her list was Tina's Toys. Millie was rebuffed there also. Boy, now she was not only distraught but also worried about having the charity event be a success. She was too bummed to continue. She needed to refuel.

Millie stomped off to the park with Luke and sat on one of the benches. While she absentmindedly petted him, she wondered if there was a better way to approach everyone. She had to figure a way to get past Annabel's interference. Maybe she could send an email to the shop owners asking them to attend the next committee meeting. If she had Julie or Frannie or Grace talk to them, they might have better luck and be able to change some minds. She really needed as much participation as possible if she was to achieve the monetary goal she'd set for herself. Honestly, she had expected that everyone would want to participate. It was a good cause. She tried to cheer herself up. She had to keep going. She couldn't get discouraged over a few refusals. The shelties needed help, and she had promised herself she could do this.

It was bad enough that Annabel messed with Millie and the bakery, but if Annabel had interfered with the merchants to discourage them from doing her charity event, then she might have to confront her. She'd talk to Carl and see if he had any suggestions. If it were up to her, she'd like to ban her from her event. He would have a cooler head. But in the end, she'd do whatever was best for the dogs.

Millie marched off to her next destination, Colin's Clothier. She couldn't wait to see this store. It was brand-new, and she wasn't even sure what type of clothing it was selling. She opened the door and was surprised by a bearded collie who jumped up to greet her and then went about the business of sniffing Luke. "Are you here to help me?" she teased the dog.

"Gabriel, come here. Do not jump on the customer." Millie looked up to see a man seated at a small French desk in the middle of the small space. He was strikingly handsome with cropped gray hair. She assumed he was prematurely gray, because she estimated he was about her age. He was wearing a navy suit with a gorgeous royal blue tie that set off his deep blue eyes.

The store was small but impressively laid out. Against the walls were several racks with men's suits, and intermingled among them were skirted tables with men's ties and shirts. When Millie had time, she'd have to get Carl to come here with her.

She wandered up to the desk and introduced herself. "Hi, I'm Millie Whitfield. I own the dog bakery nearby."

"Hello! I'm Colin. I've seen your sign, but I haven't had a chance to bring Gabriel there yet."

"Well, come see us when you have a chance. Anyway, I'm here today to ask you to participate in a charity event. My goal is to raise money to help eighty-seven shelties that were taken from a backyard breeder. Our next planning committee meeting is at the Buckshead Inn on Friday if you care to attend."

"Well, I own this business with my twin brother, Spencer. I'll talk to him to see if that's possible. It's only the two of us working here for now, and one of us has to be here when the store is open, but I know we'd be interested in helping the dogs."

Millie got excited. "You're a twin? I have twin brothers. Are you new around here? I'll have to introduce you to them."

Colin laughed as he answered, "Yes, we just moved here, and yes, we'd like to meet your brothers. We don't really know anyone around here."

"Good. Maybe I'll see you at our meeting."

Millie left there feeling optimistic. Colin struck her as a nice guy and pretty easygoing. If she was correct, it should be easy to convince him to participate in the charity event.

As she walked on to her next and last stop, she couldn't help wondering if either Colin or Spencer were married. If not, they could be a twosome that she could use her matchmaking skills on.

The final stop was Luke's favorite shop, Danny's Dog Emporium. Today Millie hoped to find a plush ball. She lucked out. Danny had a big red ball that Luke and Annie could play with outside, and on the plus side, Danny wanted to participate in the charity event. Annabel most likely didn't go there. That was no surprise. Annabel didn't seem to really like any animals.

Millie did another quick tally on her fingers. Now she had seven stores including the bakery participating. Hopefully Stella, Tina, and Colin would join up. It was getting down to the wire. There were only a few weeks left before the gala, and there was still a lot to accomplish. It would have been nice and more fun if this didn't have to be put together so quickly, but the shelties needed the financial assistance immediately.

The bakery was humming when Millie and Luke returned. Millie smiled. She even observed some new dog faces mixed in with the regulars. Spotting Todd, who had just handed a pupcake to someone with a cute Pomeranian, she whispered, "Is everything okay?"

"Look around, Millie. Everything is super! We're mobbed." He had a huge grin on his face. It was after Millie walked around greeting a pug, a gorgeous goldendoodle, and a German shepherd that she saw Susie sitting on the sofa with Eloise in her lap. She laughed. *Oh, so that's why Todd is so happy.* She had thought it rather strange that he was grinning from ear to ear just because the bakery was busy.

Millie wondered whether their romance could turn into something permanent, but even more, she contemplated the existence of a ghost cupid inhabiting this old building. If so, who would be the next recipient of his arrow?

CHAPTER THIRTY

Finalizing The Plans

It was time to leave for the committee meeting. This was only the second time they were to meet, but it would be the last time. They wouldn't have time to meet again. The event would be starting in ten days. As Millie packed her yellow pad and a pen in her handbag, Carolyn whispered in her ear to watch out for Annabel. Millie knew her friend tended to be a "worst-case scenario" kind of person, but the message that Annabel would like to derail the gala was messing with her head. She sighed. Obviously, it would be good if she had a plan to combat Annabel, but who knew what stunt she might pull? It left her feeling vulnerable. She just hoped she would be able to control herself and act appropriately.

By the time Millie left for her meeting, her stomach was in knots. Walking up the path, she tried to convince herself that Annabel would be a no-show, but she knew that was wishful thinking. Annabel would never miss an opportunity to torture her.

Millie bit her lip, and by the time she got to Julie's Jewels, she was happy to stop thinking about Annabel and to concentrate on seeing some pretty jewels. She spied Julie placing a stunning necklace in her front display window. Maybe Julie would like to walk with her to the meeting. She tapped on the window and waved. Julie shook her head, not understanding her hand gyrations.

Taking a deep breath, Millie opened Julie's door and told herself to try to ignore all the beautiful baubles all around her. She was like a kid in a candy store who wanted one of each. Today was not a day for shopping. Luckily, Julie was right up front. "Want to walk over to the inn with me?" Millie asked.

Julie giggled. "Oh, so that's what you meant with the hand wave. I was about to leave anyway. Let me grab my handbag and tell Susie."

As they headed to the inn, they chatted about the changes to the area, and Julie acknowledged they had been good for her business. "I guess that means you're happy to have Susie's help?" Millie said.

"Absolutely. And with Susie, I get Eloise, too."

"Todd likes having Susie around, too."

"Yes, it seems as if the two of them have a good thing going on."

"You think?" Millie giggled. "I know it's none of my business, but what are the chances Susie will stay here in Houndsville?"

"I would love if she stayed permanently. Susie's a wonderful designer, and I'd love to have her onboard. It's great to have another person to share ideas with."

"Does Susie know you want her to stay?"

"Absolutely, but there's more to the story."

"Oh?"

"Yes. Susie's mother, Serena, who you know is my sister, is a ridiculously controlling person. She's been trying to coax Susie into attending law school. She wants Susie to work with her brothers and her dad in the family law firm. Serena is capable of doing almost anything to achieve her goal. She already cut Susie off and told her she was on her own. But lucky for Susie, Serena holds no sway over me. I actually enjoy being a thorn in her side."

"How did Susie end up here with you?"

"Susie has always shown an interest in my jewelry. Most years for her birthday or Christmas, I'd design something unique for her. She would always tell me that when she grew up, she wanted to be just like me—to the great consternation of her mother." Julie laughed. "Well, when she was getting ready to go to college, her mom wanted her to major in prelaw, but Susie wanted no part of that. I gather they had a pretty big argument. Susie contacted me and asked if she could come to work here. Of course, I said yes."

"Is she living with you?"

"Yup, which I love, and one more thing my sister hates. Gives her less power over Susie."

"I wonder if Todd knows all that?"

"Knowing Susie, she won't say much to him. She's worried her mother will eventually persuade me to send her home."

"I hope she stays here, for Todd's sake. He's a really nice guy, and get this—he's been talking about going to law school. By the way, when do I get to see the charm you designed for our event?"

"I've got it with me. You're going to love it."

When Millie and Julie entered the inn, they joined Frannie and Bridget, who were chatting with Samantha. Millie took a quick glance around, but she didn't see Annabel. Dare she think her wish could come true? That Annabel would be a no-show?

"Hi, you two," Samantha said. "I think everyone else is here already. They're wandering around. I'll go find them and meet you in the dining room. I set a large table for today's meeting. I figured there'd be more people than last time."

Millie took hold of Samantha's hand and pulled her off to the side. "Is Annabel here?" she murmured.

"I haven't seen her, although I guess she could have snuck in."

"Oh great—now I have to wonder what she might be up to."

"Millie, stop worrying. She got enough grief from everyone last time. She won't make trouble today."

"I'm not sure I believe that."

As she crossed the room to have a seat, Millie saw Grace and Tina talking to Stella. *Super!* Maybe Stella was going to do the event after all. She felt like doing a happy dance, especially when she saw Colin and his twin, Spencer. She went over to greet them. "Oh, I'm so happy you both are here."

"Yes, we just hired our first employee, so this is the first time we've been able to do something together."

"Come on, you two, and have a seat," Millie said as she pointed to the table. "I'll introduce you after we sit." She chose a seat at the head of the large rectangular table and told Colin and Spencer to sit to her left. Once everyone else was seated, she tapped her spoon against the rim of her glass, using it as a gavel to get everyone's attention.

Speaking loud enough for everyone to hear, Millie said, "It's time to get started, and I'd like to welcome you all here, especially those who are joining us for the first time. And for those people who may not know, I want to mention that we have a brand-new store in the neighborhood. The two owners of Colin's Clothier, Colin and Spencer, are seated to my left. Please visit their store when you have time."

She took a sip of water before continuing. "I'll try to make this meeting quick. I'm sure everyone would like to get back to their stores. Julie, you'll notice I put a pad and pen in front of you. Could you please take notes?"

Julie nodded. "All set."

"Good." Millie gazed around the table. "I want to remind everyone we have less than two weeks until this event starts. Today, I'd like for each one of you to share with us what you have chosen to do to raise money for the charity drive. Frannie, you start."

Frannie sat up straight. "I wanted to make this interesting, so for every yellow flower I sell all week, a dollar goes to the charity." She added, looking at Samantha, "I will also donate any flower arrangements you want for the gala."

"Wow! Frannie, that's wonderful!" Samantha said, smiling at her. "Most likely I wouldn't have used flowers that night because they'd be too expensive. Now I will. Thanks a bunch!" She giggled at the one-liner.

"Okay, Karen, your turn." Millie nodded at her.

"I'll give 10 percent of the profit from all the yarn I sell."

Next up was Grace, who said she'd made a list of two hundred items and she'd donate 10 percent if customers purchased one of those items.

Millie was feeling good about this so far. Really good!

Hearing footsteps behind her, Millie turned to see Annabel marching into the room. With those black lace-up shoes she liked to wear and a black knee-length dress, she looked like the wicked witch from *The Wizard of Oz*.

Millie closed her eyes. Maybe Glinda the Good Witch would zap Annabel, and she would go *poof*. Well, that was wishful thinking because Annabel walked up to the table, stood next to her, and started ranting.

"You people are dumb for doing this with Millie. You are giving up profits that you should be keeping for yourselves. Besides, who believes this is the best way to help the rescued dogs? You could avoid all this trouble and just send a check."

Millie bit her lip. Annabel had been a thorn in her side long enough. She pushed back her chair and started to get up — to do what, she didn't know—when Julie glared at Annabel and started ranting at her.

"Annabel, you listen to me. First off, yes, we could all send checks. Obviously, that would be easy, but I've talked to other people here, and they are thrilled to be involved in this event. What Millie has accomplished in a short time is amazing. This event will not only help the dogs that desperately need it, but it is also a huge marketing opportunity for us to garner new customers. If you weren't so intent on ruining Millie and her bakery, maybe you'd see that. Besides, I don't know about everyone else here, but any check I could send would have been small compared to what I expect to raise in my store alone."

Millie glanced around the table to see everyone's reactions. Julie whispered to Bridget, who then turned to Frannie, who piped up. "Yes, Annabel, if people want to support this charity, they know they have to buy something for money to be donated. That means more sales. Julie's right in what she said."

"Frannie, if you think I will ever buy another flower arrangement for my tables from you, you are sadly mistaken," Annabel retaliated.

"Fine by me. You are always complaining about them anyway and trying to get something for free," Frannie murmured under her breath.

Millie held her fingers over her mouth and looked down at her lap. She heard a few gasps she perceived to be from Tina, who was near her. It was a shock to hear Frannie mouth off. She was one of those meek people who was always so agreeable.

At this point, Millie felt like getting up and hugging Frannie and Julie. They had taken the focus off her, but they had also pointed out Annabel's true nature to the other merchants. She needed to get the meeting back on track, so she tapped her spoon on her glass again. "Okay, everyone, we need to get back to business. And Annabel, if you don't want to participate in our event, feel free to leave."

"Now why would I do that? You all are just going to talk about me if I leave." Annabel stomped to the opposite end of the table from Millie and plopped herself in an empty chair. "I still don't understand how come you're the one to pick the charity our whole community is helping."

Uh-oh. Annabel was bent on rehashing this to make trouble. Millie looked Annabel squarely in the eyes. "Annabel, we talked about this at the last meeting."

"Yes," Annabel said as she shook her fists in the air, "but I want the new people who are here to know you picked the group we're raising money for because it helps you and your business."

Millie clenched her hands together. "That is not true. I was asked to help eighty-seven shelties in dire straits. I did something about it. I told you before, leave if you want. I don't see anyone asking you to stay."

"Millie Whitfield, I already told you I am staying!"

Millie sighed. It would have been so much better if Annabel just left. Seems that thorn in her side was going to stay planted in place. Millie noticed Colin, Spencer, and Danny whispering among themselves, and Danny piped up, "I'm going to donate two dollars for each dog toy purchased."

Millie smiled weakly. "Thanks, Danny. I'll have to remember to come get some more toys for Luke and Annie that week." She thought it was nice of him to divert attention from Annabel and her ruckus. "Okay, Harper, your turn."

"I'm having trouble coming up with something. My business is mainly by commission only, so I don't know how to help."

"I know what you can do," Samantha said. "What if we sell raffle tickets, and the winner gets a portrait of their pet done by you?"

"I like that idea. I'll do it!" Harper said excitedly.

Millie glanced around at each person sitting at the table. She was feeling a huge wave of emotion for this small group. They were standing by her. She felt the need to say something. "You all are the best. The way you have rallied to this cause is amazing. I can't begin to thank you enough."

Annabel clapped. "Nice speech, Millie. Of course, you can't thank them enough. They are all helping your bakery."

Millie sat dumbstruck. *What an unpleasant person.* She shook her head, not knowing what to say anymore.

Bridget broke the silence. "You didn't give me a turn, Millie."

"Oh, I'm sorry. I'm so overwhelmed by everyone's support, I lost my focus." She purposely stared at Annabel before turning back to Bridget. "Of course, we want to know what you are planning to donate."

"My plan is to donate a dollar for any book in my store that has a dog in it. Of course, that means mysteries and romances and not just pet books. And as Millie requested, I contacted the author of *Mollie's Tail*, and she is coming on Saturday to sign copies of her book. She has agreed to give 50 percent of the profit from any sales of *Mollie's Tail* to your charity event."

Millie smiled. "Oh, Bridget, that's perfect. I love it."

Everyone could hear Annabel mutter under her breath. "Yes, you would love that. Another way to help you and your silly dog bakery."

Millie stared at the people around the table. Everyone was fiddling with their phones as if some important message had just come through. She sighed. There was nothing to be said, nothing that would help. All Millie could think to do was to just ignore Annabel.

"Okay, Julie, I apologize. I missed you, too."

Julie opened her handbag and took out a small jewelry pouch. She opened it slowly to reveal a gold charm in the shape of a dog bone. It had one small diamond in its upper left corner. When she held it up for everyone to see, Millie's mouth dropped open. "Julie, that's fabulous. You know I'll want to buy one."

"Me too," Harper said enthusiastically.

Julie glowed at the compliment. "I will donate twenty-five dollars to our charity for each one sold, and just so you know, for anyone who wants to have the charm engraved, I can do that."

With all the chatter about the charm, Millie had to rap her spoon on her glass a third time to get everyone's attention. "I can safely say this entire event is going to be awesome. Thanks go to all of you. I can't wait to see how much money we raise for the shelties."

Colin tapped her arm to whisper, "We're in, too. We'll donate 10 percent of our sales the week of the event."

Millie smiled and announced, "Listen up, everyone. Colin and Spencer are donating 10 percent of their sales, so remember to stop in there. They're new to our area, and we need to support them. I was only there for a few minutes, but the clothes look amazing."

Spencer mouthed "thank you" and gave Millie a thumbs-up.

Samantha raised her hand. "Millie, I'd like to tell everyone about the plans for the actual gala."

Annabel banged her hand on the table. "Hold up a minute here. You never asked me what I would contribute."

"Go ahead, Annabel. I'm sure whatever you do will be fine," Millie said politely.

Annabel looked around the table and glared at everyone. "Like I suggested to everyone here, I am going to send a check. That's it. I don't care to participate in this event. Too much trouble."

Millie would have liked to respond, but she was trying to create a good impression, so she remained silent. She wanted everyone to support this endeavor, and going forward, she wanted very much to be considered an asset to the community. That was a personal goal that was very important to her as a person. In the back of her mind, she also hoped to make this a yearly event. She was not about to ruin her chances for that.

Millie peered at Annabel. It was obvious she wanted Millie to lash back at her. What if her game was to get everyone to think she was the wronged one here? Then everyone would support her instead of Millie.

Getting back on track, Millie said, "Fine. Now if you're done interrupting, Annabel, it's your turn, Samantha."

"Thanks, Millie. So, the Fur Baby Gala will be here at the inn from five to nine," Samantha announced.

"Oh, we love the name!" a few voices interjected.

"Millie came up with the name," Samantha said. "Most importantly, I told Millie that the inn's kitchen and its staff were not fully equipped to handle this large of a gathering, so I've hired a local caterer to help. The plan is to have cocktails, lots of finger appetizers, and a buffet of yummy desserts.

"Oh," Samantha added, "just so you know, we will be starting to sell tickets now. In addition, anyone can purchase them at the door the day and evening of the gala. They are twenty-five dollars per person. That money will go entirely to our charity."

Millie jumped in to ask, "Do you think I might be able to give a short speech at the end of the evening?"

"Of course. I'll set up a microphone for you to use," Samantha said.

Millie glared at Annabel, fully expecting her to comment, but surprisingly, Annabel didn't say or do anything after her request. *Could Annabel be devious enough to do something at the gala when I speak?* She shook her head. That was certainly a horrendous thought.

Millie glanced at her watch. They'd been there for forty-five minutes. It was time to end the meeting. "I forgot to mention what the bakery will donate. My partners and I decided that we'd donate a dollar for each treat we sell. Also, the bakery charges a hundred-dollar fee for a dog to have a birthday party at the bakery. We will donate fifty dollars if someone books their dog's party within the next six months."

Millie held up her hand. "Oh, and one last thing before you leave. Now that we have settled on what everyone is donating, I'm planning to order three-by-five cards that will have all the pertinent information on them, including all the participating store names. Once I have them, I'll hand-deliver them, and you can start giving them out. I'll make sure they can be mailed out in case anyone has a mailing list and wants to do that. Also, don't forget to pick up some tickets for yourselves on the way out."

As everyone got up to leave, Millie spotted Harry. As he walked briskly into the room, she almost missed the smile he bestowed on Samantha. It was a smile with a little twinkle added in, sort of like the sexy smiles Carl saved just for her. Samantha was noticeably affected. She looked down into her lap, hiding a slight blush on her face. *Oh, this is good, really good.* Her matchmaking skills were alive and well.

Harry sidled up to Millie and tapped her on her shoulder. He spoke softly. "Sorry, Millie. I got held up. Could you ask everyone to stay? I want to make a suggestion."

Millie clapped her hands to get everyone's attention. "Could you all stay for a moment? Harry has something to tell us."

Colin, Spencer, and Danny were still chatting among themselves. They stopped talking to listen to Harry. The women were all huddled in a group, and they put their handbags back on the table and sat. The only one who paid no attention to Millie's announcement was Annabel, who bolted from the room.

"We all know Millie's goal is to help the eighty-seven shelties, but I think we can do more than that," Harry said. He put his hand on Millie's shoulder. They were friends, and hopefully soon he would become a member of Millie's extended family when Bradley married MaryEllen. She wondered if he was trying to steel her for something she might not like. "Millie's plan is great, but I have a different vision. I say we set up a foundation whose goal is not only to help this one group, but also to help others in the future."

Harry looked at Millie. She wanted to hear more, but so far this sounded good to her. He took a piece of paper from his pocket and unfolded it. "I came up with two examples of how this might work so you can understand better what I envision." He read from the paper. "First: Someone posts a photo on Facebook of a dog being dumped at a kill shelter. He is elderly and in need of extensive care. The rescue group who pulls him out of the shelter needs money. This is where we come in. They apply to us for a grant, and it's up to us to decide to what extent we want to help them. The second example is a totally different scenario. A dog needs surgery, but the owner does not have the required funds. Again, they fill out our grant application, and our committee decides whether we can help."

Harper piped up, "Isn't it expensive to set up a foundation? And once it is set up, how would someone know to contact us?"

"Good questions," Harry said. "I already contacted my friend Ted, who is a lawyer. He will donate his time to set up the foundation, and he said he can get it done fast. He is also willing to prepare the grant application for us. Then I'm sure we can find someone to help us create a website. That at least can wait till after this event. To answer your second question, I believe people who need money will be looking for help, and eventually they will find us."

Everyone's faces lit up. Millie sat up straight and grinned from ear to ear. "Harry, that's brilliant."

"Don't we need IRS approval to open a charitable foundation?" Samantha questioned him.

"Yes, we do. How did you know that?" Harry asked.

Samantha shrugged. "I just knew."

Harry raised his eyebrows, which Millie noticed, probably because she was wondering herself how Samantha knew that. She assumed Carl would know that, but she certainly didn't.

"So if everyone is onboard with this, I recommend we elect Millie to be chairman of the grant committee."

All around the table, heads bobbed and nodded. Millie blushed. She jumped up and hugged Harry. All she could think was that if his plan succeeded, she'd have a permanent way to help the rescue community. A goal she'd only dreamed about achieving was within her grasp. She couldn't wait to call Carl. He'd be proud and excited for her.

CHAPTER THIRTY-ONE

Getting Ready

Millie woke up and jumped out of bed. It was Friday. Only three more days till the kickoff of the charity drive week, with the gala itself a week from Sunday. She had to no time to lie around. The first errand for the day was to pick up the posters she had made to advertise the Fur Baby Gala. She could do that on the way to the bakery. She was sure the one she designed would garner lots of attention.

In order to make a great poster, Millie had gotten Charlotte to send her photos of some of the eighty-seven shelties. All the photos were gut-wrenching, but she settled on using eight. To get the maximum impact for the poster, she decided to divide it into eight rectangles with each one showing a different sheltie with the name of the dog underneath. It looked like the old wanted posters for fugitives, and Millie played that up with the simple slogan **Help Wanted!** at the top in bold black letters. And then, underneath the photos, was the bold statement **EVENT TO RAISE MONEY FOR US AND MANY OTHERS**. Lastly, in small print it listed whom to contact for more information. Millie had ordered fifty, hoping to hang them all around town.

Once she got to the bakery, Millie found a small ladder and set it up on the porch. She carefully climbed up to the top rung and was attempting to secure a poster outside on the front wall of the bakery's siding when Todd called out, "Would you like some help?"

"Yikes!" Millie glared at him as she swayed from side to side, dropping the poster and pressing her hands against the wall. "Jeez, I almost fell. Nothing like coming up on someone from behind and shouting at them." She perched on the top rung of the ladder. "Yes, I can use help. Just let me catch my breath."

Millie had her hand on her chest for a moment. "Now, if you hand me back the poster, you can help me find the best spot to hang it."

Todd handed Millie the poster and stood close by in case she needed help, and he didn't open his mouth when he thought she had the perfect location—he simply gave her the thumbs-up signal.

MaryEllen and Carolyn had walked up, so they stood back to watch. MaryEllen wiped a tear from her face. "What a great poster. Who could look at those faces and not help? I feel like I should be baking something special just for them."

"Gosh, MaryEllen, you really have become this crazy dog baker," Todd said teasingly, holding the ladder for Millie as she lowered herself back down to the porch.

Millie dusted herself off. "Wait till you see the postcards. They're in the bag next to the door."

The threesome raced up the steps together and leaned over MaryEllen's shoulder as she opened Millie's tote and carefully pulled one postcard from the stack, which had a rubber band around it. "They look like an invitation," MaryEllen said hesitantly.

Millie nodded. "Well, they are an invitation. We're inviting them to the gala. Plus, I guess you could say we're inviting them to spend money so that we can raise money for our charity."

"Well, I like them, and the paw-print cutouts were a clever idea," Todd added.

"The printer suggested that. It was also his idea to make them five-by-seven and put a border on them. He was right. They came out really nice," Millie said as she stood reviewing them with her partners.

Todd looked at Millie. "I know you're pressed for time. If you want, I'm sure I can get Susie to go around to the stores with me to hand out the posters and the postcards. We could even offer to help hang them, and that way we make sure they're displayed ASAP."

Millie laughed. "It seems to me that you'd do anything to spend time with Susie. But seriously, that'd be great. Then I can stay here and work. I'm sure you all are tired of me not helping around here."

"No, we all made a pact not to get uptight about that. You would do the same for us if the situation were reversed. That's what friends are for," Carolyn said, smiling.

"Hello!" They all turned to see Bridget as she waved and came into view meandering up their path.

Millie waved back and whispered, "Strange. I wonder what she's doing here? I had expected her to stop by when we first opened, but why now?" She frowned. "Oh no, I hope she's not here because Annabel is causing a problem. They are friends, you know."

"Crap, I hope that's not why she's here. She was probably just boycotting us because she's a cat person," Carolyn teased.

"Ha ha. Good attempt at trying to divert me from thinking about Annabel," Millie said. "But I happen to know her cat, Felix, likes dogs. I'm always taking Luke and Annie into the bookstore, and Felix is fine. He keeps his eyes on them from the top of the bookshelves, but he doesn't hiss at them for being in his space."

The foursome waited for Bridget to walk up the steps. Millie held the door open. "Hi, Bridget. You're out and about early. Come in."

As Bridget walked into the foyer, she stuck her nose in the air and sniffed. "Ah, vanilla. It smells good in here," she said, smiling. Almost immediately her demeanor changed, and as she stared at Millie, she wrung her hands. "I came here because I have some serious gossip that I thought you needed to know ASAP if you don't already."

Millie got a knot in the center of her stomach. *Now what?* "Okay, spit it out. Is your friend Annabel up to something again?"

Bridget shook her head. "No, nothing to do with her. I'm worried about the gala."

"Why? What's up?" Millie asked innocently.

"Brenda is selling the inn. I came here as soon as I could to tell you."

Millie stepped back, her mouth open. "What in the world are you talking about?"

The rest of the crew stood nearby, although after hearing the news, they formed a circle around Millie, as if to protect her.

Bridget went on to tell her story. Millie tried to concentrate. Yesterday, Bridget told them, Brenda had come to her shop wanting books about Australia and had talked about wanting to visit there. Then she had blurted out that she was selling the inn. Apparently, it was Samantha who'd made her realize she didn't want to be there any longer.

Millie was having trouble breathing. She did process most of what Bridget was telling her.

"Come on, Millie. Let's sit," Carolyn suggested as she put her arm around Millie and walked her over to the steps leading upstairs. "Together, all of us will help you sort this out."

"You got that right," Todd and MaryEllen chimed in as they also found spots on the steps. Millie put her hand in Carolyn's and squeezed. It was good to know her partners were there to support her. They all listened as Bridget continued.

"Brenda told me Samantha had changed a lot of things, and it made her realize how she'd allowed the inn to get run down. She loves that old place and doesn't want to see it go to pot, so she's hoping to find someone to buy it."

Millie bit her lip. She needed to focus. The gala was only days away. What now? And what would this mean for Samantha? Right then, she promised herself she'd keep it together for the sake of the eighty-seven shelties who were counting on her to pull off the best gala in the history of Houndsville. She was going to do it, too! And she couldn't forget that Carl was there for her, along with the threesome watching her back right now.

Millie looked at her partners and told them, "I refuse to get crazed about this. So Brenda is hoping to sell the inn. That doesn't mean she has had any offers. Plus, look how long it took us to buy this building. We'll be fine for the gala. I think the bigger problem is that I bet Samantha has no idea. She would have told me if she knew."

"You're right, Mil," Carolyn said. "Samantha seems so happy here in Houndsville, and what she's accomplished at the inn is remarkable. Do you think you should say anything to her?"

"I'm not sure. I have to think about it, but I'm inclined to wait and see if Samantha mentions anything first."

"I hope I didn't do anything wrong by telling you." Bridget cringed. "Brenda didn't say I couldn't tell anyone."

"Bridget, we won't say anything," Millie said. "The only person I'd even want to tell is Samantha, and I'm not even sure I should."

"Maybe she knows and didn't want you to worry about the gala being held there while Brenda is in the midst of trying to sell the old place," Todd suggested.

"That's certainly a possibility." Millie shrugged. "Besides, she might have no idea how long it takes to buy and settle on something. I still feel bad. She's worked hard to redo the inn into a place we all want to go to again. And now she just adopted those two shelties. She seems so at home here."

Bridget turned toward the door. "Well, I'm done wondering what might happen. I did what I thought was right, but now I need to get back to the bookstore. MaryEllen, I've heard your biscotti are delicious. I'd like to take some back with me, and I just have to ask: Is there a cookie Felix can have?"

"Can he have peanut butter?" MaryEllen asked.

"Sure."

"Then yes, I have something for him. I'll get you some biscotti and a peanut butter pupcake for Felix. Our pupcakes have a strawberry on top. The dogs love them, and they are very nutritional for them. I would imagine they're okay for cats, too. He can nibble it." MaryEllen got up. "Give me a minute."

"Oh, let me give you some of the postcards for our event," Millie said as she got up and took some out of her tote. "I have a poster for you, too. Can you hang it yourself?"

"Sure, I hang book posters all the time," Bridget answered quickly.

MaryEllen came back and handed a bag to Bridget, who sniffed the contents and peeked inside. "Wow, looks like you gave me a lot."

"Enjoy. Let me know if Felix enjoys his treat." MaryEllen smiled.

Once Bridget was gone, the foursome stayed huddled together on the steps. Millie thought they looked shell-shocked from Bridget's revelations. She probably didn't look any better.

"I can't imagine what's going to happen to Samantha if Brenda sells the inn," MaryEllen said, frowning. "What's worse is I wonder what will happen between her and my brother. Here we plotted to get them together thinking Samantha was here forever."

Millie shook her head and sighed. "MaryEllen, to be honest, so many things are going through my head." She pushed herself up from her spot on the steps and started pacing the foyer. "I'm thinking about Samantha. What do we really know about her? Will she be able to survive without a job? Then there is her budding relationship with Harry. Will it survive if she moves away?"

"Millie, shouldn't you be more worried about the gala?" Carolyn said.

"Of course, I'm concerned. But I'm going with the thought that Brenda won't mess that up for us, that selling the inn won't interfere with our plans."

Carolyn scowled. "Maybe you should start by going to Brenda. What if she already sold the inn and the new owners are some corporate bigwigs who don't care about the locals? Maybe they want to use it as a weekend getaway for themselves and the gala is an annoying intrusion? You have no contract with Brenda, so they could cancel you at the last minute."

"Carolyn, I could do without your doomsday scenarios. The gala is coming up fast. I have no way to reschedule all the details at this late date.

I'm sufficiently worried enough already, and for once, I'm trying not to be impulsive and rush into doing anything. This is all too important for me to mess up now. I honestly think we'll be fine."

Todd peered at his watch. "Guys, I hate to tell you this, but Woody and Peter are standing outside. We'll have to talk about this later."

CHAPTER THIRTY-TWO

Time is Running Out

"Hi!" Peter said. "Poor Woody has been whining for what seems like forever. I'm surprised you didn't hear him."

"Sorry, we were preoccupied, " Millie said apologetically.

"I hope everything is okay. I know the charity drive starts on Monday, but I have a really busy week coming up. I'm worried that I will be stuck in the office. I thought if I got here today I could give you an order for some of Woody's favorite Woof-a-Roos and have someone come and pick them up for me. I figured that would help your charity drive. Are you almost ready? How are you all doing?"

"We're doing great!" Todd held the door open. "MaryEllen is baking constantly."

"Super, I guess that means you have cookies for Woody. He was in such a hurry to get here that my slowpoke turned into a speed hound."

Millie leaned over and took Woody's head in her hands. She couldn't see his eyes for all the hair covering them. "Ah, Woody, of course we have cookies for you. Let's get you some Woof-a-Roos. Those are your favorite, right?"

Peter and the foursome walked back to the Collie Counter room. "Oh, by the way, Woody's birthday is next month. I'd like to celebrate his birthday here. Carolyn told me that if I book it during the charity drive, you will donate fifty bucks to your charity."

Millie laughed. "Are you doing this because Woody had so much fun at Luke's party?"

"I think you're confused. It was me who had fun. And dressing him up was a blast."

"Please remember to invite Hickory," MaryEllen said. Then she burst out laughing. "I can't believe I just said that."

"See? I'm just full of good ideas," Millie said. "Are you coming to the gala? That should be fun, too."

"Yes, as a matter of fact, I'm going with Harper. She called to invite me," Peter answered.

Millie stopped in her tracks. She was tempted to clap her hands. "So, this is news! Are you and Harper seeing each other?"

"Millie, stop asking personal questions," Carolyn piped up. "Assume the obvious."

"Fine. I need to make a phone call anyway. See you at the gala with Harper." Millie smiled. She slid open the kitchen door, but of course, she left it open a smidgen. She wasn't about to miss out on any juicy conversations.

"Ah, so you're going out with Harper. I'd say the plot thickens." Todd handed Peter a Woof-a-Roo.

"Yeah, I'm looking forward to it. I don't know her all that well." He paused and smiled. "But I'm hoping to change that."

"Millie calls this place a recipe for romance." Todd chuckled. "Whenever she says that, I laugh at her, but lately I'm starting to think she just might be right. You and Harper met here, I met Susie here, and if Millie has her way, she'll have Samantha hooked up with Harry."

"Wow! I didn't know there was a matchmaker in our midst." Peter laughed. "But who's Susie?"

"She's Julie Starr's niece, the owner of Julie's Jewels. I met her here. And what's perfect is she works nearby with her aunt."

Peter looked down at Woody. "Okay, I hear you. Stop whining. You'll get your Woof-a-Roo in a minute." He took the bag off the counter. "Todd, I'm going to go sit down and give Woody this cookie. Otherwise, he'll never leave me alone. I'll see you later."

Millie tiptoed away from the door. It wouldn't be good if Todd slid the door open only to find her pinned to it. He and Peter were done anyway. Now she needed to call Samantha. She just wasn't sure what to say. She'd buy herself some time by asking if it was okay if she stopped by the inn to review the logistics for the gala.

After she contacted Samantha and said she'd be walking over, Millie had to tell her partners she was leaving once again. *Thank goodness for them.* They were the best. Carolyn, for once, didn't even tell her what could go wrong when she talked to Samantha.

As Millie walked to the inn, she tried to keep her mind on anything but the Brenda issue. She could think about her matchmaking efforts. She loved being called a matchmaker and seeing people coupled up. She giggled when she thought about Harry. He'd played right into her hands when he called looking for a home for Bailey and Berry.

She recalled her first attempt at matchmaking. Years ago, MaryEllen was Harry's receptionist, and the two women met when Millie first starting using Harry as her vet. Millie was convinced MaryEllen would be perfect for her brother Bradley. Accordingly, she came up with a plan. Millie called Harry to say that Annie was scratching and that he needed to see her. On the evening of the appointment, Millie's dreamed-up excuse was that she'd forgotten she and Carl had symphony tickets, and since she didn't want to cancel the vet appointment at the last minute, she sent Bradley in her place. Bradley met MaryEllen that night. And now they were living together

When Millie knocked on Samantha's open office door, Samantha had the phone up to her ear. Millie tiptoed in, and that's when she saw Bailey and Berry underneath the desk. She got down on the floor and sat cross-legged to pet the twosome and waited for Samantha to finish the phone call.

A minute later, when Samantha hung up, Millie couldn't wait to ask, "How are they doing? They certainly look wonderful."

"They've been perfect angels. They're even sleeping on my bed. I've missed having a dog in my bed, and now I have two."

Millie noticed that Samantha seemed distracted and watched her drumming her fingers on her desk, as if debating with herself about something. Just as Millie was about to question her, Samantha blurted out, "Listen, I have bad news. I need to spit it out."

Millie didn't say anything and tried to keep her face noncommittal. Did Samantha already know about Brenda selling the inn? She held her breath and kept her hands tightly clasped together.

Thankfully, Samantha didn't appear to notice how nervous Millie was and continued speaking. "The caterer for the gala is having a ginormous panic attack because I originally told him fifty people, and now I told him there'd be more likely around eighty to ninety people coming. He's threatening to cancel."

At first Millie was relieved, but then she realized this was serious. She jumped up, hoping she didn't spook Bailey and Berry. "Oh, come on, that's ridiculous . . . can't he work out something?"

"He says he can't. I already begged. It's all my fault. I hired this small outfit that's new in town. I thought it'd be nice to give them some good exposure. It's only the owner and seven other people, and now he says he's in way over his head. He'd rather quit than do a crummy job. He says that will ruin him."

"First of all, this is not your fault. You were trying to do a good thing. We will work this out," Millie said as she clenched the back of the chair she was leaning against. "We just might need some help with this."

Millie walked around and sank into the chair. "You're new around here. Carolyn is great at solving problems. Give me a few hours, and I'll get back to you." She got up back up and walked around the desk to hug Samantha. "I do not want you to worry about this. Someone will want to do this job for us. It's a good cause and great exposure."

Running back to the bakery wasn't an option even if Millie had wanted to. Her new booties weren't made for that. She did walk really fast, though, and when she burst through the door, she hollered, "Where's Carolyn? I could use help ASAP."

Millie was so lost in her own problem that she forgot people would be in the bakery. *What a dope I am.* The bakery was mobbed, and she had just come running in like an idiot. She slid to a sudden stop. She saw blood on the floor. "Oh no, what happened here?"

242

Carolyn was sitting on the floor with a towel wrapped around a basset hound's ear. Woody was nearby looking guilty. Carolyn glanced up. "No worries, Mil, we have everything under control now. Good thing you weren't here fifteen minutes ago. It was pandemonium in here."

Todd sank onto the chair nearby. "Yeah, it was crazy. We had a group of new dogs and their owners who didn't quite know how to make their dogs behave. There was a very cute Jack Russell terrier named Howard that only wanted to run and jump from the sofa to the chairs and back again. It was like he wanted to say hi to all the other dogs. Next, he put on a show and did somersaults, which I think everyone found hilarious, except two little Yorkshire terriers who snapped whenever he got near them. All of that wasn't too bad until Angela came in with her basset hound, Dante. Peter knew her and went to say hello. That's when the trouble started, according to Peter." Todd laughed and shook his head. "Woody grabbed Dante's cookie. At least, Dante thought it was his cookie. And as you can imagine, he didn't like that. He barked at Woody, and Woody barked back at him."

Todd put his hands over his ears. "Do you have any idea how loud a basset hound sounds? Add in an Old English sheepdog at the same time— deafening. Peter was able to get Woody to quiet down, but Dante's owner couldn't convince him to stop."

Carolyn sighed. "It really was wild in here. Finally, Angela went to leave, and Dante's ear somehow got caught on the table edge and ripped. It was awful. Blood everywhere. We're just in a holding pattern waiting for Angela. She left to get her car and bring it as close as she can to us. Luckily, Harry's her vet. We called, and he's waiting for her."

"Oh, I can't believe I left you to handle this alone." Millie grabbed Carolyn to give her a hug and mouthed to Todd, "Thank you."

Carolyn hugged back and mumbled, "I wasn't alone. I had MaryEllen and Todd to help, and it's fine now. We told all the customers when they come back—that is, hoping they do—their first dog treat would be on us. Now, tell us why you came in screaming for me."

"It's the gala. The caterer wants to bail. It's really our fault. We were so busy we forgot to tell him the number of guests has about doubled from what we contracted for. I have to come up with something, and I don't even have days left, I only have hours."

"Do you think they would know if we gave them some of MaryEllen's pupcakes? She's great at making them," Todd suggested as he smirked at Millie. She glared right back at him, but before she could strangle him, he added as he smiled, "Just trying to lighten the mood here."

Millie burst out laughing. "Thanks! I needed that. But you know, you might have inadvertently solved my problem. The other day at our meeting, Colin, one of the co-owners of that new shop, Colin's Clothier, was talking about some person who bakes phenomenal cupcakes. He and his brother just opened their store, and for opening day they served cupcakes. He went on to tell us the cupcake person had all sorts of wonderful selections, like chocolate espresso, corn cupcakes, and even gluten-free ones. I'll call Colin and get her number. This might be the perfect solution. I can tell our caterer he only needs to do the finger foods, and the desserts will be provided by someone else."

* * *

When Millie got home and saw Carl's car in the garage, she ran inside to talk to him. Luke and Annie came to greet her. She gave them each a fast hug and a pat on the head, and then she headed into the den. Carl looked up at her, as if he were surprised to see her, and then appeared to slide some small papers under the cushion of the chair. She wondered what that was about, but she didn't have time for that now.

She plopped down on the ottoman in front of his chair. "You won't believe what happened today. First, Bridget walked over to tell us that Brenda is selling the inn, and then I find out the caterer for the gala wants to quit. Then there was this incident at the bakery . . ."

Carl put his hand on her knee and patted her like she was Luke. "Millie, slow down."

"Okay, I'll try, but I'm so wound up. Anyway, if you caught what I was saying, the caterer wants to quit, but I believe I have that problem solved. I called a person who knows a person who does cupcakes and—"

"Millie, there is no way I can follow what you are saying." Carl shook his head and chuckled.

Millie patted his hand. She was probably making him dizzy. She tried again to explain, more slowly this time. "Samantha got a call from the caterer. They wanted to bail. We have more people coming than we originally told them, and they didn't think they could do a good job, so they didn't want to do it at all."

"Well, sounds like they are right in what they said. You wouldn't want them to do a lousy job."

"I know we goofed, but I think I've solved the problem. Inspiration hit, and I called a cupcake person and she's happy to provide all our desserts. Samantha called the caterer and she's waiting for him to get back to her with the new plan that calls for him to only do the finger foods. Hopefully, he'll be fine with that, and that problem is solved. It's the next dilemma I am not sure how to solve. It's big. Brenda is supposedly selling the inn. So do I tell Samantha?"

"Depends. If you consider her a friend, I would say it is only fair to tell her."

Millie sighed. "I figured you'd say that. Okay, I'll tell her tomorrow. Now, can I have a squishy hug? It's been one crazy day."

CHAPTER THIRTY-THREE

More Trouble

Millie was so pre-occupied that she totally forgot to check what was under the chair cushion in the den. It wasn't until days later that she remembered, and she had to wait for Carl to leave for work so she could check it out. The second she saw the two small squares of paper, she giggled. She knew right away what Carl was up to.

When the twins had been in college for only a few months, Carl invented a way to solve the problem of who received the first phone call from either him or Millie. He would take two squares of paper, write one name on each piece, and fold them up. He'd shake them up in his hand and throw them like dice, and then pick one of them. The name revealed on the paper he picked would be the first twin called. It became a running joke, and every time Millie and Carl called, the twins questioned them on which one they had called first. This solution meant one twin was not favored over the other. It had worked for years now. Millie wondered if Carl had the papers out because he was trying to get them to surprise her and attend the gala. She really wanted them to come, but she'd be sure not to let anyone know she'd seen the papers and ruined her own surprise.

Millie got to the bakery extra early, saw that everything was in order, and decided to walk to the inn. She left a note for her partners that she hoped to be back right around opening time.

As she strolled to the inn, Millie bumped into a few customers walking their dogs, but the streets were mostly empty. The silence gave her time to think about how she'd tell Samantha about Brenda and the inn. She ended up realizing there was no particularly good way to present it, so she'd tell it in the way she had heard it from Bridget.

When Millie walked into the inn, Samantha and Hilary were standing at the reception desk. Millie walked over to them and asked Samantha to sit with her, and as they walked off together, Samantha said, "I was going to call you. I just got off the phone with the caterer. He's thrilled with the new plan, and thank goodness he's back onboard. He was relieved, and I was happy for him. He does seem to be a good person. Never mind that I almost lost my breakfast after he wanted to bail on us."

"Oh, thank goodness," Millie said. "That problem is solved. Let's hope no more crop up." She touched Samantha on her forearm. "Now I have something else to tell you. Can we go sit in your office?"

"This sounds ominous. I thought everything was good."

Millie didn't answer. She walked into Samantha's office and took the chair across from the desk. Samantha perched herself on the edge of the desk. "Well, what's up?"

Millie related the story as Bridget had told her the day before. "Wow," Samantha said. "You really caught me off guard. It would have been nice if Brenda had told me before it got around town."

Millie nodded. "This was a crappy time to tell you, but I consider you a friend. It wouldn't be fair to keep it from you."

Samantha got up and paced around the room before sitting down in her desk chair. She leaned forward. "Look, Millie, now that you've told me this, I've got to tell you something important. I had planned to tell you after the gala and after I told Harry, but I'm going to tell you now. It's something personal, so I have a favor. I need to tell Harry before he hears it from someone else."

"Okay, now *you* are sounding ominous." Millie frowned.

Millie sat still with her hands folded in her lap. She felt like she'd been doing that a lot lately. She bit her lip as she watched Samantha carefully, noticing that Samantha wouldn't look directly at her and was tapping her feet on the floor. She waited. Samantha briefly closed her eyes, and when she opened them, she blurted out, "My name is not Samantha Golden. It's Samantha Gold. My father is Allan Gold."

Millie froze. Her brain couldn't absorb this astonishing statement. "What?" she eventually exclaimed, jumping up and almost hitting her hip on the desk. "Are you saying the billionaire hotelier is your father?" She smacked her hand against her forehead. "That's why MaryEllen thought you looked familiar. Your photos sometimes appeared in the tabloids."

"Yes, especially when I was younger."

"Wait a minute. This is just sinking in. It's the best news possible. It's totally fantastic! Your dad can buy the inn! How cool is that? Then you can stay in Houndsville and marry Harry." Millie giggled. "Oops, I guess I shouldn't have said that last part."

"Millie, you are such a good person. You are only seeing the positive side to this. If my dad buys the inn for me, which I am not sure he would, everyone will just think of me as a spoiled rich girl. I don't want that. I came here to make it on my own."

Samantha started chewing her lip. Millie thought that was kind of funny, Samantha picking up her bad habit.

"Anyway," Samantha said, "I had already planned to tell Harry tonight since things have been heating up between us. I wish I could tell him now. Tonight seems like eons away."

Millie got up and walked around the desk. She bent down and hugged Samantha. "This is all going to be great! You'll be able to do whatever you want with the inn. I see happily ever after in your future. Here, I'll give you one last hug, and then I'll leave you alone. I need to get to the bakery anyway. Call me if you need me."

* * *

Three hours later, Millie got a frantic call from Samantha, asking her to please come back to the inn. *Oh no, what could be wrong now?*

Hilary was sitting at the reception desk talking to an elderly couple when Millie rushed in. She must have known why Millie was there: She held up her hand and pointed to the office. Millie walked in to find Samantha curled up in the small love seat under the window with her legs underneath her and her head laid back. She must have heard Millie come in, and she opened her eyes. Her face was blotchy, and her normally twinkling green eyes were red, flat, and lifeless. Millie took one look at her, then ran up and threw her arms around her. She sat and cradled her head against her chest.

Samantha lifted her head. She spoke so softly that Millie had difficulty hearing her. "You won't believe what happened after you left. First, Brenda showed up to tell me she was selling the inn. I told her that she should have waited until after the gala. I think she actually felt bad about her decision, but she just didn't know what she could do to reverse the course she had chosen."

Millie took a deep breath and just sat quietly.

Samantha hesitantly continued, "After she left, I came up with a plan to tell Harry my real name tonight when we were together, but in the meantime, I wanted to tell him that she was selling the inn. I really wanted some sympathy.

"He was wonderful. He told me it would be okay, that together we'd work it out and that he wanted me to stay here in Houndsville. My plan to tell him my real name tonight went out the window, and I ended up blurting it out. Right away I knew it came out all wrong. He clammed up, and he wouldn't speak to me. I tried to talk to him to explain myself, but all he said . . . I'll quote him: 'Are you telling me this because you are only here in training before you go off to work in a big hotel of your dad's?' He added before he hung up that we had made our feelings for each other pretty clear, and now he had to question my honesty."

Millie didn't know how to respond. All she knew was that she was deeply disappointed in Harry for not giving Samantha more of a chance to explain.

Samantha continued, "I'm telling you, he figures exactly what I told you this morning—that I'm a spoiled brat trying to buy my way through life. Nothing I said mattered. He's done with me."

Millie watched as Samantha burst into tears. All she could think to do was to pat Samantha on the back and murmur soothing words. Her words might have been soothing, but her thoughts were on Harry. He was the one who should have been there for Samantha. Instead, he was acting uncharacteristically like a jerk. If she was honest with herself, though, he must have been blindsided that Samantha had kept such an all-important part of her life a secret.

Millie stayed for a bit longer, trying to console Samantha, but they kept getting interrupted by either the phone or Hilary, who needed Samantha's help with something for the inn. Samantha finally shooed Millie out with a weak smile and told her she'd be in touch.

Millie desperately wanted to get back to the bakery to talk with MaryEllen and Carolyn. They might be able to help, although she wasn't sure how. She found herself rushing back to the bakery, and by the time she got there, her feet were sore, and it felt like she was getting a blister on her big toe. She limped through the door and found Carolyn plumping up the sofa cushions in Lassie's Library. She tapped Carolyn's shoulder and said, "I need to talk to you and MaryEllen right now."

Carolyn stopped in her tracks. "Jeez, Millie, is everything okay for the gala? You don't have enough time to fix any more problems."

"Different problem. I've got some shocking, really shocking, information to share."

Millie took the cushion out of Carolyn's hand, placed it on the sofa, and dragged her back to the kitchen, where they found MaryEllen in the process of decorating some of her pupcakes.

MaryEllen glanced up. "Oh good, Mil, are you here to help? We still need treats for tomorrow."

Millie couldn't help but giggle when she saw that MaryEllen's face was smeared with red frosting. She walked up to her and wiped her face. "Seems you were hungry. I'll gladly help you in just a minute. I need to tell you something first. Come sit."

MaryEllen and Carolyn sat across from Millie. She shared her entire conversation with Samantha. She mentioned that she hoped Samantha would buy the inn and stay in Houndsville, but now the problem was that Harry was not speaking to her. Millie wanted MaryEllen to call her brother.

"Millie, I don't know. He hates when I interfere in his personal life."

"This is too important. They're supposed to go to the gala together, and as of now they're not talking. They're bound to see each other. Yikes, how will that play out? And if Samantha decides to invite her dad, which I personally think she should, that might make things even more awkward."

"Okay, I get it, I'll call him. The worst he can do is to tell me to mind my own business."

MaryEllen rapped her spoon on the counter like a drill sergeant. "Now I've promised to help you, so you need to help me. We need to get these pupcakes frosted. You can put the strawberries on top. There's plenty of them in the fridge."

* * *

Millie placed dinner on the table, and while she and Carl were eating, she calmly started to fill him in on all the latest news. His fork clattered onto his plate when she revealed Samantha's true identity. And when she told him she hoped MaryEllen might call with an update, he wanted to know when that might happen. She looked at him in utter shock and then burst out giggling. Her stomach hurt by the time she stopped. Since when had Carl become interested in gossip, even if it was true?

Truthfully, Millie hoped MaryEllen would call, but she had other things on her mind, like the speech she needed to write. She lost her appetite because she was having trouble thinking about what she wanted to say. Actually, she had no problem giving a speech, but writing it was like doing homework. She promised herself she'd start right after she cleaned up the kitchen, but as she was putting the dishes in the dishwasher, Luke pawed her to go outside.

So it wasn't until a half hour later, after she was done in the kitchen, that Millie went to sit on her bed to begin writing the speech. As she made notes, Luke jumped up to sit with her. Actually, sitting with her usually meant sitting between her legs. She hugged him; he really was such a special dog.

She absentmindedly petted him while she thought about her speech and what she should say. She jumped when her cell phone rang.

It was MaryEllen. "It's me, and the news is not good." Millie waited to hear the rest. "I talked to Harry. I told him exactly what you told me to say. He told me to stick to my baking. And he had a message for you too, since he figured you had a hand in having me call him. To say it nicely, he said to stay out of this."

"Uh-oh. Thanks. Guess I'll see you tomorrow."

Millie dropped the phone on the bed, slid under the covers, and pulled the blanket over her head. She was kind of glad Carl was still in his office working. Reporting to him that she had made a huge tactical error was not something she wanted to do. Now what?

CHAPTER THIRTY-FOUR

The Day Before the Fur Baby Gala

Millie slid out of bed. Thirty-two hours and counting till the gala. When she finally made her way to the kitchen, Carl was sitting at the table having a cup of coffee and reading the *Houndsville Times*. She went to join him after retrieving her speech from the bedroom, but before she could ask if he'd help her finalize it, he proceeded to reiterate the same advice he'd given her before—she needed to stay out of Harry's personal business.

Millie smiled and gave him a small nod, trying to convey that she agreed—just not wholeheartedly. Personally, she didn't think she had done anything wrong. Harry had acted uncharacteristically like a total jerk. He hadn't given Samantha a chance to defend her actions, and Millie was simply hoping his sister's phone call would make him think twice about his reaction. And not to be denied, there was the fact that she wanted so badly for them to end up together. They were perfect for each other. At least she thought so.

"How's the speech coming?" Carl asked, changing the topic. "I'll help you if you want me to."

"I know, but after making notes, I think it's getting there. Maybe you can help me later."

"Just write what's in your heart."

Millie nodded, thinking that was good advice.

"I guess you'll be at the bakery all day today?" Carl asked as he sipped his coffee.

"Yes. Today is the last day for everyone to raise money. The weather is promising to be good, so hopefully lots of people will be visiting the shops." Millie wiggled her foot. "Luke, I know you just got comfortable, but you need to move. I want to get some coffee."

Millie filled a mug and sat, but not for long. Even though she wanted to finish her speech, she also wanted to be at the bakery before it opened. She'd just have to finish her speech later. Carl had given her good advice. She'd think it about it while she walked Luke and Annie. They'd been ignored this past week, so she'd take them for a long, leisurely walk. Well, maybe not too long—she really needed to spend time at the bakery. A better idea would be to take them on a short walk and then take them with her to the bakery. Gosh, it was difficult to have enough time for everything that mattered to her.

Thank goodness for her partners. If not for them, she could never have pulled off this gala, and when it was over, she needed to come up with some way to thank them. Maybe they could have a special dinner out one night, just the four of them. The more she thought about it, the more she thought that was a good idea.

MaryEllen and Carolyn were getting out of their cars when Millie arrived at the bakery with Luke.

"Oh look, Luke, your buddy Hickory is here. Come on. Let's go say hi."

Millie gave MaryEllen a hug. "Hey, what's up with you bringing Hickory? You never bring him."

"Bradley told me to bring him. He said he'll stop by later and pick him up, so Hickory will only be here part of the day."

"Well, Luke will be glad to have a buddy, especially since Annie, as usual, wouldn't get in the car. Let's go inside. I expect we'll be busy today. Where's Todd?"

"He should be here any minute now," Carolyn said.

They had just finished filling the bakery case when Todd arrived with Artie. "Sorry I'm late, and don't say anything, but I just saw Angela getting out of her car with Dante. They're heading this way."

Carolyn made a face. "Oh no, we don't need another incident like before."

Millie put a finger to her lips. "Shh, we don't want them to think they can't come back because Dante is a barker."

"I know that," Carolyn admitted. "Hopefully, he'll be fine. Woody was the instigator anyway."

Angela walked in with Dante, and everyone ran up to ask, "How's Dante? Is his ear okay?"

"Yes, he's fine. A few stitches, and now he's as good as new. I just wanted to stop by and say thanks. Plus, I want Dante to get a chance to try one of your cookies. He never got one because Woody grabbed his."

"Oh, my poor baby." Carolyn got down on the floor to talk to Dante. "All you got out of your visit here was stitches. So, let's get you a Luke's Hideaway. They're one of our best sellers and the special of the day. I think the treasure inside today is bacon. You'll love that."

Luke heard his name and started tapping Millie's leg. "Oh, Luke, you just ate at home. You're going to have to wait until later for a cookie. You cannot have a treat every time someone says your name."

From that moment on, the bakery was a beehive of activity. An elderly man came in with his golden retriever named Bubba, the white around his muzzle showing his age. He was gorgeous and sweet, and Millie could have petted him forever, if not for Luke complaining by pawing her constantly. A corgi strolled in next, and then a Great Pyrenees bounced in. Millie glanced around and couldn't believe every chair was filled; even the floor was crowded. Dogs were lying everywhere, and it was difficult to maneuver around them. *Wow.* She shook her head. The smiling and laughing faces all around her were a testament to how much everyone was enjoying their time here. The bakery was obviously a big hit. *This was just like I envisioned it when the bakery was just a dream.*

* * *

After they shut the door for the day, the foursome gathered together in Lassie's Library. They stood together as grins passed between them and they high-fived each other.

"Millie, what a great success this week was for us and your charity," Todd said as he took off his apron.

"Yup, I've never baked so much, but it was fun," MaryEllen added.

"Yes, I'm thrilled. It really is a good feeling to know we will be able to help those poor shelties. Now, the next step—the gala!" Millie said excitedly.

As the partners closed and locked the door and started to walk down the steps, Millie turned back. "Hey, we should put a sign on the door telling customers we're only open from nine to twelve tomorrow because of the gala. I know we tried to tell everyone, but chances are somebody will show up in the afternoon and wonder why we're closed."

"I'll take care of it," Todd said gladly. "You all can leave. I'd like to go see Susie anyway."

"Thanks. See you tomorrow," they all said.

MaryEllen, Carolyn, and Millie walked to their cars, and just as Millie waved goodbye and turned on her engine, her phone rang. It was Samantha calling to report that her dad was flying in later that evening and was staying overnight in order to attend the gala. Samantha asked if Millie would stop by the inn to meet him. It was good to hear the excitement in her voice. Millie wanted Samantha to have fun and enjoy the event. She had put a lot of time and effort into making it special, and having her dad by her side would give her something to focus on besides Harry.

Darn Harry. He had messed up Millie's plans. She couldn't get over what she considered to be his bad behavior. He had always struck her as a good guy, but right now that was not how she saw him. Besides, if Samantha and Harry were still together, Samantha would have been introducing Harry to her father and not worried about seeing Millie.

* * *

Later, when Millie showed up at the inn with Carl, Samantha was on the top step of a stepladder, trying to hang Harper's dog portraits.

"Jeez, Samantha, stop!" Millie hollered as she went to grab her. "You're going to tip over. The last thing we need is for you to fall off that ladder right before the gala. Tell us where there's a real ladder rather than that small one you're using, and Carl will help you hang those."

After rummaging around in a back room, they found an eight-foot ladder and went to hang several portraits in the Crystal Room. Carl was in the midst of hanging the last one, a collie portrait, when they heard a booming voice calling out, "Samantha!"

Samantha turned. "Daddy, you're here!" she hollered as she ran over to give him a big bear hug, and he in turn hugged her tight to his chest. Finally holding her away from him, he stared at her. "Well, I must say you're looking good. Something agrees with you around here." He smiled broadly.

"Oh, Daddy, I'm so happy you're here." Samantha grabbed her father's hand and pulled him toward her new friend. "Dad, meet Millie, one of my favorite people in Houndsville. Her husband, Carl, is on the ladder."

Allan Gold reached out to shake Millie's hand, and she was surprised when he covered her hand with both of his. "Thanks for making Samantha feel at home in your town." He smiled and waved up at Carl. "You too."

Millie was surprised. Allan was not at all what she'd expected. She had steeled herself to meet some imposing gray-haired billionaire with a cool demeanor. Instead, Allan was tall but portly and reminded her of a big old teddy bear, a warm and fuzzy one. She sighed. She missed the hugs from her own dad.

Allan put his arm around Samantha. "If you have time, I'd like a quick ten-minute tour of this place." He looked at Millie and Carl. "How about you joining us? I bet you might be able to fill me in on the history of this place."

"I do know a little," Millie piped up. "I'll tell you as we walk around."

The group started at the front door, where Allan commented on the foyer and the huge all-white flower arrangement that smelled of roses. He said they reminded him of his own hotels. Samantha beamed. Millie grabbed Carl's hand and pointed to Samantha's smiling face. He squeezed her hand.

Millie related the bits of history that she knew. "It's been in the same family since it was built at the end of the eighteenth century as a family residence. When the family fell on hard times, they started bottling bay rum in the basement during Prohibition. At some point—I'm not sure when—it was converted from the family mansion to an inn to serve travelers on their route to Canada to cover up their illegal bottling activities."

"Do you think that is truth or rumor?" Samantha asked.

"Pretty sure it's true. I have a friend whose grandfather used to tell his grandson stories about rum runners."

As the group walked around, Samantha pointed out what she had changed and what she planned to do in the future. They ended up back in the Crystal Room gazing at the patio.

"This is your best asset," Allan said. "I haven't seen stones dry-laid like that in a long time. If I owned this place, I'd make the most of this patio."

"I agree, and it took me a while, but I convinced Brenda to buy patio heaters. They'll help extend the patio season. Come on, Daddy. Time to have a drink."

Samantha led her father and her friends to a seating arrangement in the small lobby, where she had re-covered the sofa and chairs with a mixture of textures all in a warm blue-gray tone. Samantha and her dad sat on the sofa, with Carl and Millie in the barrel chairs.

Allan started right in with questions. "So tell me, Millie, how did you meet my daughter?"

Millie smiled at Samantha. "Let's just say we met over our love of shelties."

"Ah, so you're the person Samantha mentioned in one of our phone calls. And the one who convinced her to get Bailey and Berry."

"Yup, that was me." Millie wasn't sure what to say. She wondered if Allan approved. She didn't have long to find out.

"You did a good thing," Allan said. "After George died, I thought Samantha would never get another dog. I wasn't sure she'd ever find a place in her heart for another one."

Again, Allan surprised Millie. He obviously was in tune with his daughter's thoughts. Now if only Harry was here, then the story could really be a good one. She could have implied that Samantha had met a great guy at the same time she had met her dogs. That story would have a happy ending—the kind Millie liked.

Millie shook her head. *Am I seeing a mirage?* Because if thinking something made it come true, then that was exactly what happened. Harry was strolling into the room. Had MaryEllen unknowingly gotten through to him? Millie didn't care at this point. He was here. *Oh, this is good—better than good. It is great!* She was right in the thick of the action. She'd have a front row seat and get to see how this played out. She crossed her fingers. When Carl winked at her, she knew he had seen Harry too.

Samantha's back was to Harry, so she couldn't see him. He circled around to the front of the sofa, right up to her, and said hello. Millie felt like her own eyes were going to pop out of her head; she was watching a real drama play out in front of her. Samantha, to her credit, didn't appear to bat an eyelash, although Millie heard her take a deep breath before she said, "Oh, hello, Harry. This is certainly a surprise visit. Did you come to meet my dad?" She introduced them, and the two men shook hands and measured up each other.

Carl put his hand on Millie's knee. "Okay, Millie, you have a big day tomorrow. Time for us to leave." She looked at him incredulously. *What the heck is wrong with him? Doesn't he know I have to see how this works out?* Darn, of course he knew—and he was determined to get her out of there. What could she say so that she could stay? "Samantha, isn't there something else you want me to do tonight?"

Samantha looked like a deer caught in the glare of headlights. She wasn't going to say anything. *Phooey.* Carl grasped Millie's hand. "Come on, Millie. Whatever it is, it can be done tomorrow. We're going." He put his arm around her, pulled her in close to his side, and walked with her to the front door. She loved him, but right now, she wanted to strangle him.

CHAPTER THIRTY-FIVE

The Morning of the Gala

Millie bounced out of bed. She hugged Carl. She hugged Luke and Annie. Today was the big day. Only hours till the gala. She brushed her teeth, did a quick makeup and hair job, and threw on black sweatpants and a gray sweatshirt. The smell of coffee brewing drew her into the kitchen, where she grabbed a mug, filled it halfway, stood at the kitchen sink, and took a few sips. There was no way she could sit still.

"You know, you should eat something," Carl suggested as he watched Millie drinking her coffee.

"I know. I'll grab some biscotti at the bakery before I head over to the inn."

"Well, if you need me I'll be hanging around here today catching up on some paperwork."

As Millie walked out the door, she asked Carl to take Luke and Annie for a walk because she probably wouldn't have time today.

Millie drove to the bakery to make sure everything was prepared for the day's business. She grabbed a couple of biscotti, and she left before anyone else showed up. She had to get to the inn to help Samantha and to make sure they were ready for tonight, but of course she just had to know what had happened with Harry, too.

Millie shook her head, thinking about last night after she and Carl had left the inn. It was ridiculous. On the ride home, Carl had tortured her some more when he insisted he had a sweet tooth and wanted ice cream. Of course, they couldn't go to Christopher's, but there was one other place—it was just in the opposite direction from their house. It was all done on purpose, she was sure. Carl wanted to keep her occupied and out of trouble. She tried to tell him that she needed to get home to finish writing her speech, but he wasn't buying it. Well, to be honest, she would have tried to sneak in a call to MaryEllen, but by the time they got home and she'd taken Luke and Annie outside, it was too late. She did somehow manage to finish her speech before she fell asleep.

Millie shook all those thoughts out of her head when she walked up to the inn. Right away she spotted Samantha at the front door observing two men roll out a red carpet. She got goose bumps while, at the same time, her heart started thumping a mile a minute. The gala was actually going to happen in a few hours. They had pulled this off. *Wow!*

Millie ran up and put her hands on Samantha's shoulders, peering at her face. Her expression was unreadable. Millie hugged her. "Is everything okay? I'm so excited about tonight! Are you picturing Harry walking up the red carpet?"

"Are you kidding? Harry's not coming."

Millie drew back as if she'd been slapped. "What are you talking about? Didn't you two kiss and make up?"

"Not even close. He left a few minutes after you and Carl."

"Why did he come then?"

"I guess he wanted to talk. He tried to get me to take a walk with him, but I told him I was busy. Probably a good thing, because I'm not sure I can forgive him for his behavior."

Millie was at a loss for words, which was not something that happened to her often. She had been so sure that Samantha and Harry would kiss and make up and all would be good. Sometimes the happy ending was not within reach. She hugged Samantha again.

"Jeez, Samantha, maybe you should call him. I can get the stuff together here if you want to leave and go to his clinic."

"Nope. Not right now." Samantha held the door open for Millie. "Come on. I could use some help with a few last-minute details."

As she walked inside and through the foyer, Millie stopped in her tracks. She stood rooted in place and took a deep breath. In front of her was a stand-alone easel with a portrait of Luke and Annie displayed on it. It was the centerpiece in the foyer. She was overwhelmed. She turned to Samantha with a question in her eyes.

"Carl wanted to surprise you. He thought you might like to have it here for the night of the gala before you take it home."

Millie walked up to it and stared at it. The finished portrait by Harper was beyond amazing. It was her birthday present. She hadn't known it was done—or rather, she hadn't thought about it with getting ready for this event. Tears filled her eyes. Carl never ceased to amaze her.

"He really is one super special guy. I hope the same for you someday." Millie lightly ran her fingers over the portrait. It was gorgeous, and yet it brought tears to her eyes. Someday, Luke and Annie would not be around; she hoped that day was far, far away, but she would always have this prized possession that showcased them perfectly. "Before I decide to leave you to run home and give him a humongous kiss, tell me what needs to be done."

Millie and Samantha walked into the Crystal Room. Workers were still setting up the tables while another team was setting up the bar, and a third group was setting up twinkle lights out on the patio.

Samantha gazed around, looking puzzled. "I know Frannie's flower arrangements are here somewhere. Let's find them, then maybe you can help me put them on the tables."

"Sure, I can help." Millie looked around the room. "Maybe they're behind the bar."

As they walked toward the bar, Millie put her arm around Samantha and said, "I can't thank you enough for doing this. We're going to have a great evening."

"Yes, you are, and I'm going to be right by your side."

Both Millie and Samantha came to a dead stop. With her arm still around Samantha, Millie turned around to listen to the words coming from a tall, handsome guy staring solely at Samantha with a twinkle in his eyes.

Millie gasped. Samantha stood still, but then, as if she couldn't help herself, she ran into Harry's open arms.

Millie smiled and quickly realized whatever assistance Samantha needed with the flowers wasn't going to happen with her help. She needed to disappear. Not that Samantha and Harry would notice she was gone.

Millie giggled to herself as she ran back to the bakery. She'd better be careful. It would be awful if she fell: She had very high heels to wear tonight. *This is getting ridiculous.* She needed a different means of transportation, maybe a moped. It certainly would have gotten her back to the bakery faster if she didn't fall off and kill herself. She laughed.

Millie ran through the bakery door, zoomed back to the kitchen, and slid back the kitchen door with a bang. "It's going to work out!" she yelled. "Harry did it!"

"What in the world are you shouting about?" MaryEllen asked.

"Harry showed up at the inn with his heart on his sleeve. I left him and Samantha kissing in the foyer." She added that embellishment. After all, they probably kissed after she left them.

Todd and Carolyn came through the open door and rushed up to Millie. "What's happened now? Did something else go wrong?" Carolyn asked, rolling her eyes.

"No, everything is fine, better than fine. I left Harry and Samantha kissing."

"Hooray! Best news of the day!" Carolyn held up her hand, and high fives were passed around.

CHAPTER THIRTY-SIX

The Gala

Millie fiddled with her hair. She'd spent twenty minutes using her blow-dryer, but she still wasn't 100 percent satisfied. She pulled her straightening iron out of the bottom drawer of the bathroom vanity and used it to further work on her bangs. *Better.* She added another layer of mascara, more lipstick. Last step: She put on the strappy, open-toed, rhinestone-and-velvet shoes she had purchased from Stella's just for tonight. Usually she didn't go for four-inch heels, but she loved feeling tall, and these shoes were dazzling.

Millie checked her watch. She needed to be at the inn before the guests started arriving. She went back into the bathroom for one last glimpse and to apply one last dab of lip gloss. Carl came in and stood behind her. She loved the way he looked in his navy suit with the starched white spread-collar shirt she had convinced him to buy and an emerald green silk tie.

"I have something for you." His body touching hers, he held up a necklace that he carefully placed around her neck. It looked like an old antique cameo, only this one had a painted likeness of Luke and Annie in its center.

Millie fingered it and stared at it, speechless. This man in front of her had surprised her yet again. It was spectacular, and it fit perfectly in the neckline of the V-necked black chiffon dress she had chosen to wear. Plus, the gold in Luke's fur and the amber in Annie's eyes set off the gold threads interlaced throughout the dress.

She blinked her eyes fast—really fast. She didn't have time to redo her makeup if her mascara ran.

"Well, do you like it?"

Millie turned to Carl and pressed her lips to his. "It's perfectly wonderful, and so are you." She kissed him again. "Who designed this?"

"Oh, I had help from Julie and Susie. It turns out Susie is an accomplished artist, so she was able to paint a likeness of Luke and Annie."

"You are simply incredible." She held his head between her hands and kissed him lightly. "I love you."

Carl smiled his special grin that Millie considered just for her. "Are you ready?" he asked.

"Yup, I just need my handbag."

Millie grabbed a tube of lipstick off the counter and went to her closet to get her handbag. She checked to make sure she had her speech inside. She was so excited about tonight, although it was a disappointment that Nicholas and Grant wouldn't be there to celebrate with her. She was so sure that they had planned to come, but then Nicholas called to tell her that Carl had begged him to come with Grant, and they had both turned him down. They couldn't leave school. And then Grant called to wish her good luck. *Oh well.* She wouldn't think about that with everything else so perfect. She touched her new necklace. She couldn't wait to show it off.

Now that Millie was ready, she teasingly pushed Carl down the hallway and tapped her foot while he went to his office to find his car fob. It was hard to believe that, after weeks of planning, this night was finally here.

It felt like Carl drove so slowly. Would they ever get to the inn? Once they arrived, the scene before their eyes was magical. Millie could feel her heart racing. The winding driveway that led to the circle in front of the inn shone with hundreds of torch lights. Interspersed between the lights were large banners with photos of rescued dogs. The boxwoods on either side of the entrance twinkled with hundreds of tiny lights. The red velvet runner was now covered with white iridescent glow-in-the dark paw prints. *Nice!* That was a surprise. Samantha hadn't told her about that.

Even though Millie had been there in the morning, everything looked so very different with the sun going down and all the lights lit. She could feel the goose bumps all up and down her arms. She'd been waiting for this moment, and after all the planning, the party was about to begin.

Two valets dressed all in black and wearing black baseball caps with the words "Fur Baby Gala" trotted up to open Carl's door and then Millie's. Carl came around the front of the car and hooked Millie's arm in his, and together they walked up the steps to the entrance. Right before they walked through the door, he smiled at her and whispered in her ear, "You look beautiful. Now let's go have fun." She squeezed his hand.

Millie could see Samantha standing off to one side of the foyer right next to the portrait of Luke and Annie. Walking over with her hand in Carl's, she let go to hug her friend.

"Oh, Samantha, it looks amazing. The driveway, the entrance, the torch lights, the twinkle lights, and then the glow-in-the-dark paw prints. It's all just perfect!" Millie looked over Samantha's shoulder. "Where's Harry? Where's your dad?"

"My dad is up in his room. Harry left to make sure everything was okay at the clinic, and then he went home to change clothes. They both should be here any time now. You two walk around. I'll call up to my dad's room and tell him to hurry."

"I can't wait to see the Crystal Room," Millie said as she steered Carl in that direction.

As they walked into the beautiful room, Carl said, "Wow! Sure makes a difference when the chandelier is clean. It really is gorgeous."

"It makes the entire room glow," Millie added. "Let's go peek at the patio."

Carl partially opened one of the French doors for Millie. All around them were hundreds of twinkle lights on every bush and shrub. The outside tables were covered with floor-length, forest green damask cloths with gold square toppers. Hurricane lamps served as the table centerpieces, and to keep everyone comfortable, all the patio heaters were running.

"Hard to believe this is the Buckshead Inn," Carl said as he closed the door.

"And look around in here. She's performed a miracle in this old Crystal Room," Millie said.

The tables were covered with gold-threaded damask cloths and pristine white squares. On each white square were glued edible dog bones spray-painted gold. The centerpieces were simple flower arrangements placed inside large spray-painted dog bowls filled with red- and gold-sprayed carnations and sparkly gold candles glowing in the center. Surrounding them were gold lacquered chairs.

In the four corners of the room, Frannie's Flowers had placed large ornamental trees that Samantha had covered with twinkle lights. Millie recognized some as magnolias. The sweet, enchanting fragrance they gave off filled the room.

Adding to all this were the many wall sconces that bathed the pale gold walls in a shimmery glow. Even though Millie and Samantha had gone over the setup together, seeing it for real was so much better.

And yet there was more. Millie's favorite accoutrements were the dog portraits done by Harper that were displayed prominently around the perimeter of the room and lit by the low-voltage lights focused on them. Hopefully guests would love them as much as she did, and Harper would gain some new customers. Maybe next year they could have a silent auction, and guests could bid on having one done of their own pet with part of the proceeds going to the foundation. Of course, that decision would be up to Harper.

Millie tilted her head. Someone must have turned on the music. She heard strains of smooth jazz in the background. She put her arms around Carl and started swaying to the music. She whispered in his ear, "So far, so good. Now if only I don't flub my speech."

He laughed and whispered right back, "I know you'll do a great job."

They broke apart when Millie saw what she thought was a familiar face in the distance. "That's weird; I thought I just saw Nicholas," she remarked. She stared at Carl, trying to gauge his reaction, but he was stonewalling her by not looking at her but rather at an imagined stray dog hair on his suit that he was swiping away.

Millie grabbed Carl's hand and pulled him with her. She couldn't run in spiky four-inch heels, but she did manage to walk really fast, and as she did, she saw two identical people walking just as fast toward her. They crashed into each other, laughing and smiling and hugging.

And then Millie heard, "Hey, wait for us!" It was Bradley shouting as he and MaryEllen rushed up. "Couldn't you have waited for us? We wanted to be in on the surprise, but I had to settle up with the valets."

"Sorry, but our sister spotted us while we were waiting for you," Grant said.

Millie was dumbfounded. She had totally expected the twins to surprise her after she spied Carl with those little white slips of paper. That was until they had called her to tell her they weren't coming. She'd been tricked again. Good old Carl had figured out that she'd seen him with the slips of paper. He figured she knew what he was planning. To throw her off track, he'd had the brothers call and tell their little white lies, saying they'd been "asked" to surprise her but couldn't come.

Millie stared at Carl, and the silly smile on his face confirmed her suspicions. She burst out laughing. When she finally was able to catch her breath, she asked the stupidest question. "Why are you here?"

Nicholas and Grant both shook their heads at her. "Do you honestly think we'd miss your first gala?"

Carl smiled. "So now that we're all here, let's get a drink before the bar gets too crowded."

As the group weaved through the crowd, Millie gazed around the room and spotted Brenda talking with a bunch of partygoers. She really did have silver pumps, and they did match her silver evening gown. Millie could see the shoes sparkling from where she was standing. The best part was seeing Brenda having fun. She was laughing, and some man had his arm draped around her shoulders. *Huh! Could there be more to Brenda's story than her wanting to sell the inn?* Maybe that was why she'd trimmed her hair and changed her fashion choices. Millie would check that out later.

The group zigzagged up to the bar. Just as Carl waved to get a bartender's attention, Millie grabbed his arm and pointed to the right of the bar: "It's Annabel." She grabbed his hand to tug him behind her while ducking to the left and heading back toward the entrance, away from Annabel. As clumsy as she sometimes could be, it was a lucky break for the second time in a few minutes that she didn't trip in her four-inch heels. She could just imagine herself creating a huge, unforgettable scene as she slipped and fell onto the floor.

Millie stopped to catch her breath. "Did you see Annabel? She looked like she was heading our way. Can you imagine if she wanted to confront me?" She shook her head. "Nope. Not happening. I can't deal with her hostility tonight. She'd spoil the evening not just for me, but for everyone."

"You know, if she's looking for you, this place is not that large," Carl said.

"Yes, but maybe I'll have had a drink and be better able to deal with her. Oh look, there's Harry," Millie said as she pointed to Samantha, who obviously had also spotted Harry and was running up to him. She and Carl watched as Samantha threw her arms around Harry's neck and gave him a scorching kiss. Several other couples walking in the door stopped and gawked.

Millie looked at Carl. He looked at her, laughed, and lifted an eyebrow. "You're proud of yourself?"

"Yup," she answered, and she gave him a goofy smile.

Millie tried to move in Samantha's direction, but a group of people surrounded her, including Charlotte Giery, looking marvelous in a pale blue organza dress. She grabbed and hugged Millie and patted her on the back. "What you've done here is amazing! Thank you so much. The shelties will forever be grateful."

Before Millie could respond, another person pushed past Carl and tapped her on the shoulder. She had no idea who this person was or how they knew who she was, but they were intent on complimenting her. She accepted the lavish praise and extricated herself to get back to Carl, who had moved off to the side.

"Whew! It's really nice to get all the compliments, but let's find Samantha and Harry and get them to go to the bar with us. I'd love to finally get a glass of wine. I'll bet the twins are still there wondering what happened to us. They're not ones to miss a pretty face, and one of the bartenders was definitely cute."

As she and Carl headed toward the bar again, Millie enjoyed observing the elegant styles of dresses, updos, and jewelry on all the women, but what gave her goose bumps again was that she had helped put this night together. If all the chatting and smiles and handshakes and hugs that she was seeing all around her were any indication, the evening would be considered a major success.

Millie tried to spot Samantha and Harry, but she couldn't see them with what she estimated to be about seventy-five people milling about. Finally she knew she was heading in the right direction when she overheard whispering nearby.

"That man who just passed us looked like Allan Gold."

"You are most likely right; I just heard some gossip about his daughter working here."

Sure enough, when they maneuvered near the bar, Millie's brothers were there, along with MaryEllen, Samantha, Harry, and Allan.

Allan and Carl exchanged greetings, and then Allan turned to Millie. "Ah, so I was just informed my daughter met this character, Harry, on the same day she met Bailey and Berry."

"That's correct. One of my better moves," Millie said, beaming.

Allan laughed. "I might just have to agree with you. Seems like a decent fellow."

Harry laughed. "I think it was all a fine-tuned setup, but then Millie has done this before." He looked at Bradley and MaryEllen, who joined in the laughter.

"Yes, my sister has a love of matchmaking, so consider yourself warned," Bradley added.

"This seems like a good time for us to get a drink," Carl said, smiling broadly.

The group snickered. Carl took Millie's hand and moved her closer to the bar. "I hope I can finally get something to drink before Annabel appears again and you whisk me away."

Millie rolled her eyes. That comment was Carl's attempt to change the subject. She was just not sure going from matchmaking to Annabel was a very good choice. "You might enjoy being whisked away by a beautiful wife who would like nothing better than to kiss you."

Carl looked into her eyes. "How was I so lucky to get matched up with you?"

Millie leaned into him and gently kissed his cheek, careful to use her fingers to wipe off the lingering lipstick print she left. When she glanced up, she saw Carolyn furiously waving. "Look, my partners are here."

Carolyn's dress, shoes, and handbag were hot pink, and even her lips were painted a hot fuchsia pink. Millie giggled and grabbed Carl's hand. "Look, Richard has on a hot pink tie. I wonder who picked that out for him?"

Harper trailed behind Carolyn. She looked gorgeous in a scandalously revealing forest green dress with Peter holding her hand in his. He looked marvelous, too—all spiffy in a dark suit with a burgundy tie. He had even shaved and combed his hair. Pulling up the rear was Todd with his arms around both Susie and Julie, guiding them through the crush of people.

"Hi!" Carolyn said. "This event is awesome. We're having a blast. Did you get any of the mini bone-shaped grilled cheese sandwiches they're passing around? They're delicious."

"No." Millie pointed to the bar. "But did you see Nicholas and Grant are here? They surprised me—*really* surprised me. We were talking to them until I spotted Annabel and dragged Carl away. We just got back here."

"Oh no, Millie, I hope she's not planning to start up with you here. That would be awful."

"Millie, I hate to keep reminding you, but I warned you about her. She's a menace." Todd waved to the bartender. "I need a drink because if she confronts you, I'll need one to keep me from dragging her out the door. By the way, did you see how great the bar glasses look? Especially since it was me who decorated most of them."

"Yes, Todd." Millie patted him on his back. "They look fabulous. Putting beads around the stems and dog stickers on them was really a good idea. I'm betting people take them home as a memento."

"I have to give credit to Susie." Todd put his arm around Susie's shoulders. "It was her suggestion, and she is the one who painted 'Fur Baby Gala 2017' on them."

Millie smiled at Susie. "Then thanks go to you, too. Hey, you guys, hang around. I want to find Samantha so she can introduce her dad to all of you. They were just here. Maybe someone needed Samantha for something."

A minute later Millie spotted Samantha with Harry and her dad among the guests, and she waved for them to come join her. They joined the group, and Millie pulled Samantha's dad close to her. "Everyone meet Samantha's dad, Allan Gold." She smiled.

There were some furtive glances, but everyone maintained their composure. Millie had to give everyone credit. She knew her partners would pepper her with questions later, but that was fine. Samantha went on to make sure her dad knew everyone's name and the relationships between the people. The last person to be introduced was Julie. "Dad, Julie owns Julie's Jewels, a store near the bakery."

Allan leaned in close to Julie and questioned her about her store. Millie's antenna went up. *Maybe he has an eye for a beautiful woman.* Was there another possible matchup in Millie's future?

At that moment Millie's attention was diverted to Hilary, Samantha's assistant, who walked up to murmur something to Samantha. Samantha then whispered to Millie, "I was just told JSCTV is here to talk to us about this event." Millie in turn whispered the message to Carl.

"Jeez, you guys, what's up? Do we get to know the secret, too?" Carolyn wanted to know.

Just for fun Millie whispered into Carolyn's ear, and she then let out, "Whoopee!"

"Okay, would you please include us in the secret?" MaryEllen asked nicely.

This time Millie said loud enough for everyone to hear, "JSCTV is here to interview us about our event and take some video for the local news."

"That's really great. Why do you think they're covering this event, sis?" Nicholas asked.

Millie shrugged. "My guess is they heard that Allan Gold is here. That's big local news. I'd also like to think they found out we're trying to help the eighty-seven shelties. They were seized from around here, and there was some coverage on the news when it all happened. Now that I think about it, maybe Charlotte called them."

She turned to Samantha. "Did Hilary say if there's anything we need to do?" she asked.

"The newscaster and the cameraman are in my office. You stay here, and I'll go see if they need anything," Samantha offered with a wave of her hand.

Before Samantha started walking away, someone put their hands over Millie's eyes and said, "Guess who?"

Millie removed the hands and turned around. It was Alfred. They exchanged air kisses and hugs.

"I saw you over here when I first got here, but every time I started to walk over, someone else grabbed you. This place is mobbed. You should feel marvelous."

"Good to see you," Samantha interrupted.

Millie looked at Samantha. "Do you two know each other?"

"Yes. He came to the inn, at my request, to give me some design advice."

Millie smiled. "Alfred designed the bakery. He also works with me at my home whenever I can convince Carl we need an update."

"I wondered if a professional helped you with the bakery," Samantha said. "The space works so perfectly."

"You mean you didn't think my wife did it by herself?" Carl laughed.

Samantha put her hand over her mouth. "Oops, I didn't mean to insult you, Millie." She smiled. "I guess this is a good time to go to my office."

Millie laughed then peeked at her watch. "I'll see you in a few minutes. I have just enough time to go to the ladies' room and do a last-minute lipstick and hair check before I give my speech." She turned to Alfred. "You should stop by the bakery soon. It's really hopping."

"I know. I'll get Bonnie all dolled up one day, and we'll come."

"Are you going to walk with me?" Millie asked Carl.

"No, I'll stay here and hang around with your brothers. Maybe grab something to eat. I see they have a hot dog bar—clever." He gave her a gentle squishy hug, so as not to mess her dress or makeup, and then he stood back and straightened the cameo around her neck before she walked away.

Millie stopped at the table where she'd left her handbag to pick up her lipstick. She was in a hurry now, so she rushed off to the ladies' room, lipstick in hand. She didn't have much time. Hopefully no one would stop her.

It surprised her to find both MaryEllen and Carolyn at the mirror— Carolyn reapplying her hot pink lipstick and lip pencil, and MaryEllen her blush. The threesome walked back to the table together. MaryEllen and Carolyn stood by as Millie opened her handbag to put her lipstick away and grab her speech. *It isn't here! How is that possible?*

"Hey, you two. I must have dropped the cards I wrote my speech on. Help me find them. They're pink index cards."

"Crap, Millie, did you leave them at home?" Carolyn groaned loudly.

"I'm sure I didn't. Maybe they fell on the floor when I got my lipstick. Help me look."

MaryEllen and Carolyn both looked around the table. Millie bent down and lifted the cloth to see if the cards had possibly fallen underneath. Nope. It made no sense.

That's when Carolyn tapped Millie's shoulder. Carolyn's eyes looked like they were ready to pop out of her head. When she tried to talk, no words were coming out of her mouth. Millie thought, *What now?* She stood up and turned around, and Annabel was standing there, gloating.

Millie's stomach churned as she tried to remain calm. "Hello, Annabel," she said, trying to back away from her and toward the podium. "I'd love to stay and chat, but I'm getting ready to give my speech."

"Ah, the famous speech. You know it should have been me giving a speech. Until you showed up, I was the undisputed leader of the Commons. You stole my place," Annabel hissed as spit trickled down her chin. "I don't appreciate it either, and I'm not finished with you. You may think you've won, but we'll see about that."

Both Carolyn and MaryEllen gathered around Millie while MaryEllen tried her best to defuse the situation. "Annabel, this is not the right time or place for this. You and Millie can discuss this another time."

"Fine," Annabel harrumphed. "And oh, by the way, is this what you're looking for?" She held up Millie's index cards and, in a grand gesture, ripped them in half. "Now we'll see who gives a good speech." She threw the torn cards onto the table and stomped off.

"She's *lost* it," Carolyn said. "But what are you going to do? You have to give your speech in one minute."

There was no time to think about the fact that Annabel must have seen Millie get her lipstick out of her purse and, for whatever reason, decided to see what else was in it. "Wing it. What choice do I have?" Millie said. "They just stopped the music. I'm supposed to be giving my speech right now."

Millie closed her eyes for just a moment and took a deep breath. She had no choice but to go to the podium. She could hear Samantha introduce her. As she walked toward the podium, she threw a backward glance at her friends. MaryEllen and Carolyn held their hands up with their fingers crossed.

Samantha finished speaking as Millie stepped up to the podium. She hugged Samantha, tapped the microphone to get everyone's attention, and cleared her throat.

Taking a deep breath, Millie began, "I want to welcome everyone here tonight for what I hope will become an annual event. My entire committee greatly appreciates your participation. Together we will all make a difference, and many rescued dogs will benefit." Her voice cracked. She glanced around and saw the cameraman was filming her. *Sheesh!* She had no notes, and she was being filmed.

"Some of you might have either seen on TV or read in the newspaper about the eighty-seven shelties that were seized from a backyard breeder. The poor animals need extensive care and rehabilitation, and they need it now. With the amazing help of many of our local merchants, we pulled together this charity drive in just a few short weeks."

Jeez, I really am winging it. Hopefully, I am doing okay.

"I'd like to recognize two of our local merchants: Julie's Jewels designed a dog bone charm to commemorate the Fur Baby Gala and will donate a percentage of her sales, and Harper McNeely agreed to donate a portion of the proceeds from any portrait commissioned during the charity drive week. You may have noticed many of her portraits hanging up tonight, and there is one in particular to which I'd like to draw your attention. It's centered in our entrance hall on an easel. It is a portrait of my two rescued shelties, Luke and Annie. Harper just recently completed this portrait, and I am thrilled to display it here tonight."

A smattering of applause rippled through the crowd. *Whew, I must be doing okay.* The audience had clapped, and now Millie just had to finish up.

"When we began this drive, our goal was to help the shelties, but as we met and talked, we came up with a long-range plan to establish a charitable foundation. The money we raised this past week will help provide financial assistance to families or rescue groups who cannot afford veterinary care. We sincerely believe our efforts will make a difference. Going forward, we will first try to help those families in need living in Houndsville, but we will also consider helping families and groups throughout the United States. Anyone can submit an application for our grant committee to consider. Hopefully our efforts will be truly life-changing, and with your continued support, we are sure to achieve success. To that end, we hope that this is our first Fur Baby Gala and that next year, and for many years to come, we will see you here."

"Hear! Hear!" someone shouted.

Millie finished, "Before you leave tonight, please be sure you get a complimentary baseball cap commemorating tonight's event. Someone will be at the front door handing them out. Thank you."

Wow! Millie had done it, and she hadn't stammered once. She'd shown Annabel that she didn't even need her index cards.

As the audience applauded, a waiter holding a plain white envelope waved his hand in the air. He ran up to the podium and handed it to Millie before he said, "I was told to tell you to read this now."

Millie hesitantly opened the envelope, not sure if this could be another one of Annabel's dirty tricks. She pulled out a single piece of stationery and read what was written. If Annabel had written this, it was a cruel move, but then she looked out over the guests and saw two people smiling. That's when she knew this note was no joke.

"Okay, everyone, we have received an anonymous pledge of one hundred thousand dollars." Millie's hands shook as tears filled her eyes.

At first the crowd seemed as shocked as she was, and silence filled the room, but then one person clapped, and before she knew it, the clapping turned into a loud roar. This act of kindness was unbelievable. Millie chewed her lip and tried to think of something appropriate. She decided to say, "We are certainly off to an amazing start!" She smiled and stepped away from the microphone.

The cheering continued as Millie walked back toward the table. Several people even reached out to shake her hand and ask to participate in the event next year.

Once Millie reached her table, her whole group got up and surrounded her. She couldn't get over their reaction. Carl smiled and hugged her, Nicholas and Grant gave her a high five, and Carolyn shouted out, "Hooray!" Todd clapped, and MaryEllen and Bradley both said, "Good job!" She just grinned. She guessed she had "done good."

Slightly off to the side, Allan had his arm wrapped around Samantha, and both had huge smiles on their faces. Millie simply looked from one to the other and mouthed, "Thank you." She knew what they had done, even if no one else had figured it out—although with the huge amount of money given, she had a fair idea the people who mattered knew the truth.

"Can someone get me something to eat? I'm starved."

Epilogue

Millie was alone in the bakery with Luke and Annie. She looked at the clock. It was five thirty. Her partners had already packed it in and left for the day.

She meandered around the bakery, running her hands over the furniture and all the accoutrements. She walked from one room to the next, from the Collie Counter room to Lassie's Library, where she plopped herself down on the sofa. Luke jumped up to join her and lay his head on her knee. Annie settled nearby.

The past several weeks had been a whirlwind of activity, and now exactly one week had passed since the gala. The weeklong event had been a huge success, and Millie and her committee already had plans in the works to repeat it next year.

She allowed her mind to roam. She had so much to be thankful for, and so much of her life was in a good place now. It was wonderful that the event was a hit, but even more important to Millie was that the bakery was a huge success. It had been her dream for so long, but never had she expected that along the journey to success, she'd make so many new friends. She giggled thinking of all the people who had met their match at the bakery. Who could have ever imagined that a dog bakery would become a hotbed for romantic entanglements?

It was time to leave. Millie took off her apron, laid it on the counter, took one last look around, and walked to the door. As she turned the sign to Closed and locked the door, one more breath escaped. She looked down at her dogs. "Well, you two, I wonder what life will have in store for us. Let's just hope we have many more years and shared memories together."

The End

Please hug your dog today.

Acknowledgments

I want to thank all the readers who loved *Mollie's Tail* and gave me the encouragement to continue writing. It has been fabulous hearing from so many of you who have told me how much reading *Mollie's Tail* gave you hope for your own rescues. I know Mollie must be watching from the Rainbow Bridge and smiling down on us.

I also want to thank all my Facebook friends who have shared their dogs' lives with me. Some of those special fur babies who really touched my life have their names mentioned.

Special thanks to Sherry Lee, my critique partner—I have loved every minute of working with you. Your support has been inspiring.

About the Author

Ellen Gilman is the author of *Mollie's Tail*, a true story of Ellen and her family's first rescued sheltie. Mollie was a horribly abused sheltie who became a beloved member of Ellen's family. Readers of all ages will enjoy this warm and tender tale of an extraordinary dog and her family.

Ellen lives in Maryland with her husband, Steven, her two shelties, Louie and Sadie, and her first collie, Max.

Visit her website at ellengbooks.com or her *Mollie's Tail* Facebook page.